Walk Through Darkness

Walk Through

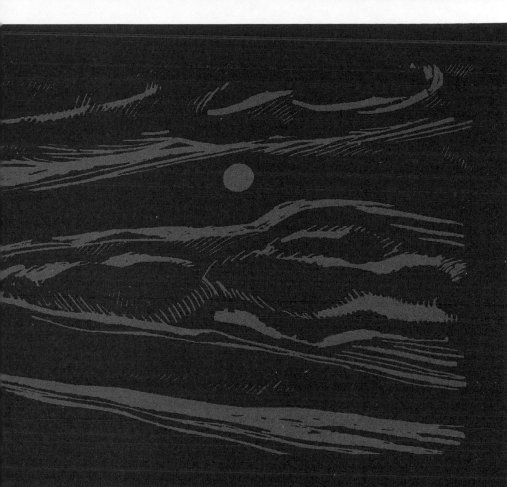

Darkness

DAVID ANTHONY DURHAM

DOUBLEDAY

NEW YORK LONDON TORONTO

SYDNEY AUCKLAND

PUBLISHED BY DOUBLEDAY
a division of Random House, Inc.
1540 Broadway, New York, New York 10036

DOUBLEDAY and the portrayal of an anchor with a dolphin
are trademarks of Doubleday, a division
of Random House, Inc.

This book is a work of fiction. Names, characters, businesses,
organizations, places, events, and incidents either are the product
of the author's imagination or are used fictitiously. Any
resemblance to actual persons, living or dead, events, or locales is
entirely coincidental.

Book design by Pei Loi Koay
Illustration by Meinrad Craighead

Library of Congress Cataloging-in-Publication Data has been
applied for.

Copyright © 2002 by David Anthony Durham
ISBN 0-385-49925-6

PRINTED IN THE UNITED STATES OF AMERICA

May 2002
First Edition

10   9   8   7   6   5   4   3   2   1

To my mother,

whom I remember daily,

and miss dearly.

Walk Through Darkness

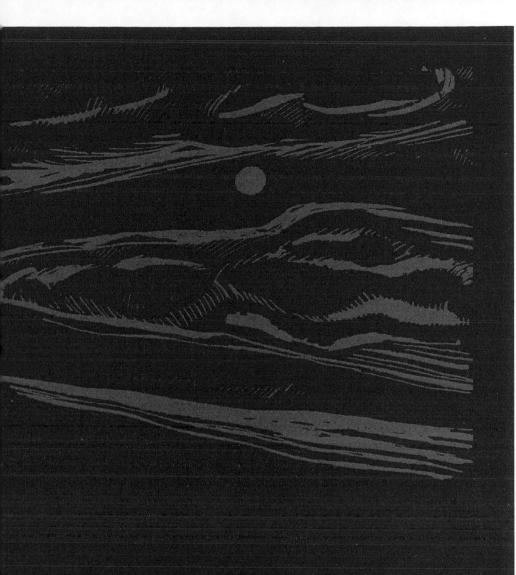

PART ONE

One

A humid July evening. Moon high in the sky and bright. A
grove of trees near a waterfront, centered around one massive
oak, a monster of a thing whose lower branches were as thick
around as a person. In the shadows beneath this, a man caught
his breath, rested, and planned. His body was mostly in shadow,
but patches of moonlight fell down through the branches and
stenciled highlights across his features. His face was handsome
even in the partial light. Clean lines of his jaw. Thin bridged
nose that flared strongly at the nostrils. Dark eyes that sat heavy
on their lower lids. His complexion was hard to classify, neither
pale nor truly dark, but some shade between. His face betrayed
commingled cultures, bits and pieces of foreign lands set beside
each other and somehow more beautiful for it.

Although he was still, his mind hummed with energy.
He had already escaped the tidewater plantation on which he
labored, but the night was only half over. He had crawled from
his straw mattress and crept around the back of the hut, past

the house in which the white man slept and out through the woods. His feet made barely a sound for the first mile, but farther on he gave up caution and splashed down the center of a thin creek. In a hollow beneath a wooden bridge he gathered the strange array of supplies he had hidden over the last week: internal organs of hogs, inflated and bound airtight; strips of leather and hemp twine; and a corn knife, stolen only the night before. He stuffed all of these things into a sack and ran. He sprinted along the edge of several tobacco fields, directly through another, and on through the forested bracken. As he felt each passing mile slip away behind him he almost began to believe in his own scheme. He ran north to begin with but soon cut to the west toward the shore of the Bay. It was on this move that his plan depended.

He had accomplished all of this in half a night, but it was the crossing yet to come that truly concerned him. He listened to the surge of the waves against the beach some fifty yards away. They called to him, but he needed a few more minutes to steady himself, to steel his mind. Just a few moments to accept the magnitude of the journey ahead and to remember why he must take it.

HE HAD BEEN BORN a slave. He emerged into the world with an ancient face, the color of wet brown sand, with black hair plastered to his skull. When offered his mother's breast, he took to it hungrily, eyes shut tight, a loop of hair entwined in a tiny fist. Looking down on him, his mother was filled with emotion she could not contain. She knew then that there were wonders yet to be found in life. There was meaning yet to be divined. There was a God and She gave birth, for no man could invent this love. She told him this many times later in life, embarrassing, blasphemous, beautiful. His mother. There was no other like her.

Their master wrote in his ledger: "Boy child, born March the fifteenth, eighteen hundred and thirty-two, Annapolis, Maryland. Valued at twenty dollars." He instructed the mother to raise him in good health so that he would live through his first dangerous years and grow to work in the man's behalf. Without consulting the mother, the master named the boy William. Simply William, and should a surname be needed the child would borrow his, less a name than a tag of identification.

Knowing what life held for her child, the mother slung him close to her body for as long as she could. She loved the weight of him, the strong pull of him in feeding. He reminded her daily of joy, a secret in a life otherwise measured in toil. At night, in the breezy shelter of their cabin, she told him of his father. "There are some good men in this world," she said. "He crossed all that water to get you inside of me. That's what he done: got into me and come out you and that's why he ain't truly dead. You're him going on forever; and your children be you and him and all the rest going on forever. That ain't no small act in this world."

She admitted to him—as she might to an adult—that it was hard mothering a slave, loving a child that someone else called his property. Some mothers tried not to love too deeply, not to connect to that which was not theirs. Some mothers tried to deal with being chattel by becoming chattel. She said other slaves might have forgotten that they were human beings and might have accepted their roles as beasts of burden, but she never would, and her son had better not either. They were much better than that. There was no shame on them. The shame was on the world of men for blurring the truth, and one day they would all pay for it.

At eight William was valued at seven hundred dollars and put out to hire. He spent the year away from his mother, as the playmate of a white child. He was with this boy always, figuring when he did, saying prayers when he did, reciting silently while the boy did so aloud. He listened when he shouldn't and thought about the things he heard. But in his joy at knowledge he forgot himself. One day he pointed out a mistake in the boy's workbook. For this he was stripped and whipped across his bare back and bottom. He clasped his hands before him, hiding his nakedness, feeling the shame of his body more acutely than he did the snap of the switch. He put away reading and never spoke of it again. He sealed away his heart's thoughts, held them close and sought to be whole unto himself.

He was hired out again and again: in the fields, in the boatyard, in the tavern kitchen. He named and fed pigs, and then slaughtered them in their season. He stepped from walkways to let whites past, mumbling the answers they wanted to hear, dropping his eyes and pretending that his back wasn't broad, his arms not corded with muscle. While he pretended to be less than a man is he grew into one. He still loved his mother, but there was a distance between them. He rarely saw her, and when he did she made him uncomfortable. She pulled him close to her and ran her fingers over his nappy hair and spoke to him of times long ago, of things he couldn't remember and didn't believe.

At twenty-two, two things happened that changed the course of his life. First, his mother died during the April rains. He didn't see her in death, for he'd been hired out away from the town. He wasn't there when she went into the earth. It wasn't until some months later that he first laid eyes on the plot of ground that swallowed her. He stared at the new grass there, unsure how to measure his emotions. There was something like remorse, something like anger, something like the hunger of a nursing child. He felt all of these things, but they were muted feelings that he tried to keep at arm's length.

In the waning heat of the same year he met a woman.

Dover. She was as black as deep water, forged in the blood of another land, named in the irony of this one. Her skin reflected the moon in blue. She was sharp, all spirit and anger, a blade that sawed at her bondage. Though her barbs cut him at times, he wrapped his arms around her and adored everything about her. The lasting memory he took from their first lovemaking was not the act itself but rather the moments after, when he felt her weight upon him, her breath exhaled onto his chest, her eyelids flickering across his skin.

At twenty-three his owner valued him at one thousand five hundred dollars. Again he was put out for a year's hire. He stood with the others in the crystalline January air, the trees like skeletons in the dawn light, sparkling in tortured rigidity. White men wandered among them, exhaling plumes of smoke, rubbing heat into their palms. They had the Negroes lift their shirts and show their backs, open their mouths and bare their teeth. They tilted their skin to the light and had them walk for-ward and back. They asked them the rote questions, the an-swers to which had been embedded early in each participant's education.

It was on this day that William first met St. John Hum-boldt. He would always remember the taste of the man's finger in his mouth, probing his teeth. The planter's face was flushed with crimson highlights, hair raven black, mouth a crevice in parched clay, nose the bulbous knob of a whiskey drinker. Compared to the girth of his torso and the square bulk of his head, his eyes were small things, two tadpoles slipped between his eyelids. The man hired him and took him across the Bay to his Eastern Shore plantation. The next day he took ribbons out of his back to prove that he could and would do so, with reason or without.

William worked through the frozen days with chapped, raw hands. He cut and hauled wood, mended fences and dug up tree stumps to clear new fields. The ground was a frozen lace-work of frost. His hands went so numb that he couldn't hold the tools. Sometimes the spade fell from his grasp, and he stood beating his palms against his thighs.

In the evenings he thawed himself beside the fire the slaves cooked their biscuits on, writhing at the pain of the life returning to his fingers. He showed the state of his hands to an old man who sat beside him. The man grasped them and turned them over, probing the worn and soft spots with his thumbs. After a moment of inspection, the old one kicked off his boots and showed him the true damage inflicted by frostbite. And so William learned to keep his ails to himself. He labored without complaint, and he counted the days of the year, praying that when it ended he would return to the mainland and to his love. He knew that such things were never certain, but he prayed with a slave's faith, a slave's hope.

In the heat of midsummer a messenger came from across the water. He stood before William and brought him this news: Dover was gone. Not dead, but gone to the North. And not just that. She carried a part of William within her, a new life.

THAT'S WHY HE WAS SITTING beneath a massive oak, with tremors rippling up his thighs, sweating though he was as still as he could be. He tried to block out the things he had to fear and listen only to the waves surging against the shore. He counted them, not with numbers, but in breaths. They had rhythm that he tried to learn. He closed his eyes and asked his doubts to float up and away from him. They didn't do so completely, but when he felt the waves within his own breathing they granted him a new calm. He rose and picked his way beneath the trees to the shore.

The water moved like a living thing, a slick, seething being blacker than the night sky. Pinpoints of light marked the far shore. He picked out one of these, a little brighter than the others, alone and like a star afloat on the sea. That one would be his. He yanked open the drawstring neck of his sack and spread the contents before him. He tied the organs together, measured and sorted out the leather strips, creating a strange encryption on the sand.

When the materials had been arranged to his liking, he lifted the lacework of leather and internals and draped it over his head. He moved gingerly, pulling the cords taut around his torso, cringing as the leather pressed against his recently scarred back. The weight of the knife settled between his shoulder blades. He yanked the drawstring of the sack tight, looped it over his head and likewise strung the boots around his neck. He rose, tested the feel of the strange garment and then waded out into the Bay.

The water was warmer than he expected, almost warmer than the air, and just saline enough to sting his wounds. As it inched up his chest, the inflated organs slipped around to his back and bunched behind his shoulders. He paused when the water reached his chin, just then beginning to feel the aid of his makeshift flotation. He kicked free of the bottom and felt his legs moving beneath him, just like when he was a child, when he had learned to swim on a dare from his companions. He pulled at the cords until the organs settled one in the crook of each armpit and the rest were tight across his back. This increased their lift. Yes, they would aid his journey. He set his eyes on that light as best he could and swam forward, kicking, arms thrusting forward. He pulled the water into him and pushed it beyond him and reached forward again. He held his head high to keep water from washing into his mouth. He was fatigued after the first few strokes but he worked best when he was tired. His body learned the movements and he repeated them again and again, losing himself in the monotony of it.

Near the midpoint of the crossing he realized he had much farther to swim than the miles from shore to shore. Each time he looked up, his target light shifted and danced. It skimmed the surface of the water, sliding away to one side so that he kept needing to adjust his course. He stopped swimming and bobbed. His arms floated around him with numb buoyancy, disconnected from his body, like driftwood bumping against him. He feared they couldn't possibly push him through the water before him. And his legs couldn't carry him beyond that, across the miles of land still ahead, through the woods and fields and over hills. He was in pursuit of a single being in the entire universe, a woman miles and miles away, and he had no real idea how to find her. He whispered her name, Dover, as if she might hear him over all that distance and provide some answer.

A moment later something brushed against the back of his legs. He knew that it was not one of the tiny fish that had been nibbling at bits of his exposed flesh. He bowed his body forward, but not before he felt the slow sensation of something heavy and slick sliding through the water just behind him. His arms lashed out to steady him. He stretched his body horizontally and searched the horizon for his light. He found it, or what he hoped was it, and he set off with renewed energy. Every wave and current and rip in the water seemed to disguise the ridged backbone of a leviathan. He could have no idea what that creature was, no understanding of its genus or species, nor could he explain the sensation away. He just had to outswim it.

He made landfall in the early light of the rising sun. He collapsed with the organs bunched about him, watching the sky through the swaying reeds. It was done now. There was no going back. By now Humboldt would've found him gone. That white man would be consumed with rage. He would be shouting and cursing. The arteries in his forehead would bulge and wrinkle like worms beneath his skin. The other slaves would run to their work, but he would find one to beat and abuse. He would vent himself by cracking black skin and watching it go red. And when all that was completed, he would send out a cry across the land. He would call the motley agents of slavery to him and invite them to a hunt.

THAT EVENING WILLIAM HUDDLED near a stream, covered again in that film of sweat, beads that neither ran nor evaporated but that simply clung to him like a part of skin. He tried to count the minutes and figure the hour, but he wasn't even sure whether or not time was passing. The drone of insects never changed. The stream was silent as it flowed, slow and cur-rentless and deceiving. One minute folded into the next and left no true sign of its passing. But he waited as he'd agreed to.

He sighed in relief when he finally heard the woman. She moved haltingly, the crackling of branches and leaves marking her progress on the far side of the water. She crossed the stream and emerged with wet ankles, brogans sloshing with each placement of her feet. He was up and questioning her before she had even reached him, but she shushed him quiet. She would get to that, she said, but first she bent and spread out the supplies that had laden her: hard flats of wheat bread, a bag of cornmeal, and a few slices of bacon wrapped in grease-soaked paper. Those were for his journey. To feed his immediate hunger she produced a clutch of five chicken eggs, hard-boiled and still warm from the cooking.

"Kate, where'd you come by this?" he asked. "I can't hardly take all this from you."

"Don't worry bout it. Ain't every day a runaway comes a-calling on your back door. Sorry this was all I could get."

William was still slow to accept the gift, but Kate motioned that there'd be no more conversation until he got some food in him. She knelt a few feet away. She was ten years older than Dover, had a different father, and looked almost nothing like her. She was tall and full-bodied, while Dover was spare and compact. There was an anxious energy at the corners of her mouth, although her body moved with the calm assurance of age and motherhood. They were similar only around the eyes and in their high foreheads, but this was enough to mark them as the sisters they were.

"Who told you?" she asked.

William paused with a half-peeled egg in his fingertips. "Couple of Humboldt's slaves come down with a fever. Nance came across to take up some slack. He told me, but I didn't know to believe him. I mean, I did believe him, but I had to see for myself."

Kate nodded and motioned for him to eat again. "Nance told you true," she said. "And I'll do the same. Dover left in the spring, headed North with Miss Sacks. Don't think she just up and run off or something. It wasn't like that. Miss Sacks gone back to her people in Philadelphia. You know the Missus come from deep money there. She never did care for down this way. She finally caught Sacks hisself up on the back of that girl Sally. That sight made up her mind. Packed her bags and left the house that very evening. Couple days after she hired a coach to Philadelphia."

Kate paused and listened to the night. It was as before and she continued. "That's all fine. Problem is she took Dover with her. Gave her that one night to gather her things. And that's what my girl did, one long night a grief and next morning she was gone. I know this gonna hurt you to hear, but it don't happen every day that a slave gets took to a free state. Think bout that. I don't know what's happened to her since, but she must be living a better life then us down here. 'Cept she ain't got no family around. And she ain't got you with her."

William bit into his fourth egg. Though the first few had been rich and strong, he didn't seem to taste them anymore. He just chewed the soft matter and swallowed it down and flicked the shells from his fingertips. It wasn't that Kate had told him anything different than what he'd imagined. Nance had given him an abbreviated version of the same story. Kate just confirmed it. But he had always hoped that Nance had made some mistake. Perhaps Miss Sacks had only left the Annapolis house for their country home. Perhaps Dover had never gotten on that coach. Perhaps the mistress had changed her mind halfway and turned back. A part of him had believed that he would find Dover here, just as he had left her. He would end the journey simply, lay his eyes and hands on her again, then return to another beating and more labor on Kent Island.

A dog barked in the distance. Three clipped notes that came and went and left the world slightly different. William's fingers touched the ground, ready to push him to his feet if need be. But no more howls followed, and the other night sounds took their places around them. The man plucked his fingers out of the soil. There was something else he had to ask and both of them awaited it.

"And the baby?"

Kate watched him before answering. "Guess Nance done told you everything. Yeah, she got a chile in her. Your chile."

William took the news with his eyes closed, face motionless, brittle.

"Look here, William," Kate said, but having said it, she faltered for the right words. She reached out and rested the palm of her hand on his shoulder. "Dover never had a choice in all this. Missus told her what she was doing. Didn't ask her inclination on it. Just told her. Even so, she almost didn't go and that's cause of you. But she had a chance to take her baby into a free state. That's why she went along with it, just thinking bout the best for that chile. Remember that before you lose hope or get angry or run out of here after her. She was thinking about what was for the best. You might want to do that too." Kate drew her hand back, not sure where to place it or whether the contact between them was helping.

"I shoulda known all along," William said. He opened his eyes but didn't look at Kate. "How'd I go all them months without knowing? Dover with a child in her . . . Don't that seem wrong? Me just getting up each morning and going on bout the day. Don't that seem wrong? Man should know something like this. Should just know it."

"Don't start worry on right and wrong just now," Kate said. "You couldn't a known nothing bout it. I know it seems like you should, but that ain't the way God put us together." She paused and watched him. He still didn't turn toward her. "Wish I had some wisdom to ease you."

William shook his head, knowing that the gesture seemed to say that he didn't need her wisdom, or that he thanked her for what she had already given. But inside he was pushing her away. She couldn't know how he felt. Yes, she had a mate that she might imagine losing. Yes, she had three children of her own. But this was *his* pain. Part of *him* had been torn away. It felt as if the fingers of a vengeful God had reached down and snatched Dover up. And it wasn't just her the physical being. Even more he had been robbed of all the ways she made life livable. He understood something that he hadn't before—that he could've spent his entire life as a slave so long as she would've borne that life with him. And as for the child . . . He didn't even know it. He had never seen its face. Never touched it. But even unborn it was part of the world. He knew that now, and he knew in all likelihood that the child would be born and live and die without ever knowing his father. How easy was that for another person to feel and understand completely?

He began to sort through his supplies, stuffing all the gifts inside his sack, including the one remaining egg. He knew this seemed abrupt, but he couldn't stand still before her, not with his emotions so close to flooding out of him. He focussed on the work of his hands. They trembled, but that just made him work faster. He hefted his bundle up to his shoulder and tested the weight of it. When he was finished he met the woman's gaze again.

"Kate," he said, "one more thing, the folks Dover's with— what name they go by?"

"Family name's Carr. That's all I know."

"Carr." He repeated the name several times. Once he heard it sounding within him, he raised a hand in thanks.

"You know what you doing?" Kate asked.

William understood the question but didn't answer immediately. Of course he didn't know what he was doing. He had no idea of the geography of the country before him. He had names of cities and notions of things Northern, but only in the vaguest terms. He had no true strategies for getting through the obstacles ahead, just motion and will and all the instinct he could muster. The question was too daunting to answer in any detail, so he answered simply.

"Going to find Dover," he said. "I just want to stand before her and that baby of mine and see if we can't make a life, the three of us. That ain't too much to ask, is it?"

The two parted with a tentative embrace. Kate moved away as she had come, the same passage through the slack stream, out on the far bank and away. William stood with his supplies draped around him, rolling his shoulders, eyes moving from shadow to shadow, solitude complete upon him as soon as the woman faded out of hearing. It wasn't that far from this very spot that he had last met Dover. But it had been a different season then. Ice cold. Silent. Brittle. Standing there, in the heat, delaying, he remembered their last evening together. It was back in January, just after Humboldt had decided the fate of the next year of his life.

He had waited for her behind the Sackses' house. He whispered his news in the crystalline evening air, and the two walked to the cabin she shared with her family. They sat on the loose straw that sufficed as her bed. A tallow candle burned on the floor before them. It was almost out, little more than a congealed puddle of fat in which the tail of the wick leaned precariously. In its sputtering light Dover was all the more beautiful. She was slim, a brevity of muscle and bone, although one forgot this when looking at her. There was pride in the width of her full lips, in the dark, majestic brown of her skin. Her cheeks curved upward in smooth, diagonal lines. Her nose had a gentle bridge, with small nostrils, spaced wide and delicate. Her eyes, recessed far back into her skull, looked out at the world with a defiant directness. She rarely faltered or looked away from the eyes of the person to whom she spoke.

"William," she had whispered, "let's just do it now."

He knew what she meant. It wasn't the first time she had proposed it.

"Dover, it's the dead of winter," he said. "We can't run now." He slid an arm around her and felt how her shoulder fit into his side. He could smell her hair, a scent of nothing in particular except of her, a fragrance he couldn't have described by comparison to anything else. He inhaled it and explained once more that it was just the wrong time of the year. They didn't have the proper clothes for the weather. They'd freeze solid before they'd left the county. And what would they do for food? In the summer they might steal right from the fields, but in the dead of winter there would be no easy forage. They'd leave tracks in the snow for any fool white man to follow. And what was the use in trying something that was bound to fail? It just didn't make sense. Patience was the key.

"Anyhow," he had said, "it's only a year. That's a painful long time, but it'll pass. I'll be back before you know it."

"A year? You think that's what this about?"

"Naw, that ain't what I'm saying. That ain't it at all, but . . ."

Dover slid away and turned her gaze on him. "How many years you think we got? These people eating up our lives, William. They eating us up and you letting them. You act like you just glad to be at the dinner table, no matter that you're the main course."

He tried to interrupt her, but her eyes cut him to silence. She went on, letting him know through pauses in her speech just how considered her words were. She told him how she felt for him, how she had wanted him beside her and inside her since the first time she saw him. There was a part of her heart that was his completely. But she wanted more, more for both of them. She wanted freedom, and sometimes it felt like she was tugging him along behind with a rope. She was pulling hard to keep him with her, but he wouldn't budge and the effort of it was wearing her down. That rope was sliding through her grip. "You hear? That rope trying to burn me, and I ain't about to get burned. You hear what I'm saying? William, one day you gonna learn the rage. You all right now, but you gonna be beautiful then."

Those words were some of the last she had spoken to him. He had pulled her to him and whispered meaningless excuses, invoked patience and said again and again that the time just needed to be right. He covered her with kisses and peeled the clothes from her body and made love to her with a painful urgency. Perhaps that was the night. Perhaps that final embrace planted a new life. Of course he couldn't know, but now it seemed so obvious. There was a part of him that was angry with her for leaving and taking his child away, but he was already forgetting this anger. It was loosening its fingers and fading away. It wasn't her fault. She had made the only choices she could. He had, after all, burdened her and pressed his reluctance on her. He had failed to recognize the resolve behind her strong words and had set the stage for the events that followed. Now he was finally beginning the journey that she had proposed. Strange that he was heading for the land of freedom without her whispering in his ear. Strange that he wasn't thinking of freedom at all, but only of her, of an unborn child, of love. He had so many things to set to rights. Freedom wasn't even foremost on his list.

Two

When Morrison appeared along the banks of the Chesapeake he had already walked a thousand miles. If he had been of a mind to talk, he would have had a thousand tales to tell. He entered Maryland through the Cumberland Gap, leaving behind the aged Appalachians and the hills and the plains and the city of St. Louis, which had been his gateway to the heart of the continent for some twenty years. He had been as far west as the Front Range of the Rockies, far enough north that he entered a marshy land of lakes and blackflies, and far enough south that he had viewed a panorama of craters, barren spaces, and skeletal protrusions that betrayed the earth's mortality. He had walked across native lands, sparred with native warriors, and slept with native women. He had watched one man scalped, seen several hanged by the neck and had spied from a distance as a group of soldiers swarmed upon a village of the old and infirm and set them all ablaze. He had made a life of killing. Thus he knew the internal structures of beavers and raccoons, deer and caribou, grizzlies, mountain lions and buffaloes. There was a space of years in that past when he had discovered he was inordinately skilled at taking human life. His body and mind found through violence a clarity denied him in quiet thought. All this he had done so that he might forget the country of his birth and leave behind the memories of his youth and fill his days with images of sublime beauty or instinctual violence. As he returned into the land of brackish water he knew he had failed on all accounts. A note had brought him back, a piece of paper, thirty-two sentences written in a tremulous hand.

He was a gaunt man, simply clothed. His trousers were thick and earth-toned and oft-patched, reinforced with leather around the shins and buttocks. His shirt had a similar construction to it, as if he made his own additions or subtractions purely as fitted function, with no concern for visual appearance. Across his back he carried a canvas pack and a bedroll, and over his shoulder he had slung a mountain rifle, a sturdy, short-barreled weapon weighing some twelve pounds. He walked with his chin lifted, body canted far forward, arms crooked at the elbow. His jawline was just as sharp as it had been during his youth, his nose just as prominent, and his eyebrows cut the same jagged lines they always had. Nothing in his visage disguised the fifty-odd years of hard life they'd seen, but neither had they been weakened by it. At least not in ways the world was likely to notice.

Beside him loped a long-legged hound of questionable parentage. She was lean around the rump and narrow when viewed from the front or rear. Her fur was a motley mix of strands at war with themselves, an undercoat of curly gray hairs and an outer of straight black ones, thick and recalcitrant like metal shavings. Her paws were large and cumbersome, and her head was so flat above the eyes that she could have balanced a plate on it. But for all this the hound was a faithful one. She watched her master with quiet eyes and set her own moods and temperament in accordance with his.

The two travelers stood for some time on the outskirts of Annapolis, staring at the ruins of what had once been a cabin. It sat crooked and eschewed, with the haphazard look of flotsam caught against a riverside tree. The most noticeable thing about it was the great oak trunk that stood in the center of it. It provided the central, living support, around which the house was built. It pierced through the ceiling and branched out above the roof like some colossal accident of architecture. The man studied it for some time, humbled by the damage wreaked upon the world by the passing of time and amazed by the clarity of his memories. Eventually, he whistled to the hound and walked on.

He stopped next at the Annapolis town home of a planter's widow. He received what information she could offer and moved on to the lumberyard of a man he had not spoken to in years and could not now for he was dead. He spent the early afternoon in a tavern and there he gained the most useful information yet. Before two he was patrolling the wharf area and by three he was aboard a sloop outward bound with a fair wind behind it. In that evening's dusky light he rapped upon the door of a plantation house on Kent Island. He asked for the man in charge, one St. John Humboldt. When he appeared Morrison posed his questions and offered his services.

Humboldt looked the man and his dog over with skeptical eyes. You got any history hunting niggers? he asked.

Morrison kept his eyes lowered. No, he said, but I've hunted nearly everything else. Don't see that a man'd be any different.

They a might bit different. Trust me on that. And you're a bit old to be entering the trade. Where you from anyway?

St. Louis.

St. Louis? Hell, you ain't from St. Louis. Where you from before that? I mean to say, where were you born?

Morrison looked from the ground to the man and to the ground again. A few moments passed and it was clear no further answer was forthcoming.

The planter chewed on this for a moment and then eyed the hound. That's one helluva dog you got there, he said. What is it, part rat and part horse? The man smiled and invited mirth, but the other would not be led.

Well, you want I should tail this lad or no?

Humboldt said that he might as well, though there were others already out after him. He told him what he could of the runaway and of the circumstances of his flight, and he provided him with a shirt still ripe with his sweat. Morrison placed this before the hound's nose and explained the situation to her. The dog seemed to understand the order of things well enough. She inhaled deeply and the muscles in her back began to quiver.

Now, Humboldt said, don't go thinking I'm hiring you on wages or anything. This here's a matter of pay on delivery or no pay at all. And I want that boy back healthy. He's no use to me as a corpse. The man ripped off a portion of the shirt for the tracker to keep and told him where he might begin his journey. When all this was concluded the planter looked him over as if seeing him anew.

Ain't you got a horse? he asked. You don't mean to walk the boy down, do you?

Aye, Morrison said, I'm afoot. Can't abide a horse.

With that the tracker turned and strode away, pack tied firm to his back and rifle swinging from one arm, horizontal to the ground and in line with his direction, like a compass point. The dog loped before him, paused and checked the man's progress, then loped on again. The two of them were soon on the tree-lined lane, down it and away into the haze of the July dusk.

Three

On William's third day of flight it began to rain. The first drops fell just after dark. Big, pebble-sized jewels that thumped against the leaves above his head. He felt them through the thin material of his shirt and on the knees of his trousers and down his shoulders, then on his hands as he pushed branches out of the way. It was pleasant at first, these cooling touches of moisture, but it was soon overdone. These first were messengers of the horde to come, and come they did, with wind and thunder. Before long every inch of him was drenched. Cold seeped into his pores and dribbled down his back and collected at the corners of his lips and in the spaces between his toes. The woods became a sleek, water-black maze of limbs and protrusions and thorns.

Later that night he slipped and fell and doubted he had the power to rise. He had been more fatigued before and that wasn't the issue. Nor was it the wounds that creased his back, for he was too numb to feel them. It was that nature seemed so intent on beating him down. He was surrounded by an enormous world in which he was entirely alone. How great an ordeal had he let himself in for? Without his being aware of it, one of his hands slipped across his abdomen and through the opening of his shirt. He sought out an object sewn into the inside of the garment and thereby hidden from view, a tiny disk of metal no larger than a coin. This he held between his fingertips, pressed tight, a comfort though he was barely aware of the action.

He hardly noticed the rising of the sun, though its light brought some faint hues back to the world. He rose and trudged on. The rain didn't let up that day nor the next evening nor on the day following. He moved through a dripping world just beyond the margins of human society, over miles of geography he had never viewed on map or chart. The Bay and its many arms thrust themselves into his path, making it into a half-terrestrial, half-marine route. Stands of reeds threw up impenetrable walls nearly twice his height. He skirted the edges of them, running a palm over the coarse shoots like a child might over fence slats.

There were more than a few mishaps in those early days. There were farms stumbled upon and dogs set to barking and landowners calling out into the night, shotguns in hand. There were passing horsemen in the woods, fields sprinted through beneath the moonlight, and country lanes that he dared to follow for short distances. There was the grunting progress of an unseen animal that kept pace with him through one entire night's travel. And there was the girl-child in a barge floating past his shoreline hiding place one afternoon. She picked him out among the undergrowth and studied him, her blond head cocked to one side, rainwater dripping from her nose and chin. She had only to whisper a word to the men that piloted the vessel to bring down upon him a hail of bullets and indignant rage. And yet she didn't. They floated on into the haze, were swallowed by it, and that was all.

Eventually, the rain abated and the heat returned. He passed within sight of a city, smoldering like a fire recently doused. He circled around it in a wide arc that put him into a landscape of an altogether different temperament: rolling hills, farmland, and ruinate stretches that had once been forest. Great swathes of woodland had been hewn for fuel or lumber and left a wasteland of stumps. Some of these were of enormous girth, flat plateaus atop which bizarre lichens grew, tiny wax statues topped with plumes of red. Between the stumps the forest tried to re-create itself. In some patches it was on its way, but in too many others the plant life was a tangle of sumac and ragweed and vines woven together like so many thorny snakes. It took him two nights of travel to circumnavigate that city and three days on he still fancied he could see its glow tainting the night sky.

He spent one evening in the hollowed-out corpse of an ancient oak. He stepped inside the thing, followed by a swarm of mosquitoes so numerous he gave up on swatting them. He stood surrounded by the shell of the tree; the sky above him framed in a single circlet. The smell of decay was thick in the cramped space. Its essence seeped out of the wood like oil, tainting every sweaty quadrant of his body. Strangely, he found these sensations comforting. They reminded him of Dover. Something about the place made him imagine running his fingertip down her bare back, drawing a line in her flesh, a track left in the wake of his touch that the skin forgave in passing. Their intimate moments had been that much more fragile for the proximity of others. They had whispered, murmured and moaned only for each other. He used to speak with his mouth brushing against her ear, the scent of her hair filling him. She would taste him with the tip of her tongue. She said she loved the sweat of him, that she wanted him most when he was ripest, for then he seemed that much more a man. Sometimes she would run her hands across his sweaty shoulders. She did this as if she were cleaning him, but he knew that she wanted his scent on her, a reminder of him that she could carry with her.

ONE MORNING NEAR THE END of his second week of flight, William halted near a narrow lane in the woods. Some fifty yards from it, he paused and squatted in the bushes, waiting to see what type of traffic the road might carry, if any. The path meandered off to the east, vanishing into the trees; to the west it rose up a gentle hill and dropped out of sight. He sat for twenty minutes without anyone passing. He had just decided to cross the road and carry on when a motion stopped him. A man, marked first by his prominent headdress, crested the western rise and came down the trail at a brisk pace. It was a white man, and though he propelled himself by the power of his own two feet, he was clothed in the garb of the gentry. William froze. His first thought was how tenuous his situation was. Here, yet again, was a moment of providence. If he had stepped forward a few moments earlier . . . If, at any time, for any reason, God and circumstance conspired against him . . . He had to be more careful still. He pressed himself low to the ground. It was from there, with his nose touching the leaves of the forest floor, that he noticed the man wasn't alone.

A Negro boy trailed behind the man. He was tiny, barefoot, and dressed only in the rough shirt of childhood, his legs and feet bare. His steps doubled to keep time with the man's. He was anxious in this work, his full attention focused on the back of the man's thighs, on timing his own steps and not letting himself fall behind. William saw something frantic in the child's motions and he wondered what particular variation of the slave's curse this child was living. Had he been sold away from his mother? Was this his first day with a new master? Or did he even remember his mother? Was this man and his whims all the child had to anchor him to the world? He was too young to do much work, but one never knew what type of service a white man might require.

William felt his insides knot. This one image filled him with the fear of fatherhood. It was one thing to suffer a life of slavery oneself, but to bring a child into this world, into all of its dangers and indignities . . . The thought of it was enough to keep him still long after the man and boy had disappeared down the path. The image of the two lingered long in his mind, bringing back memories of his own childhood, his old owner, dead some years now but not forgotten.

Howard Mason had generally been considered a good master. He didn't push his slaves beyond the limits of their endurance. He didn't beat them overly, break up families permanently, or take liberties with the female servants. He was a much-avowed man of learning and of God, who tried hard to live by Christian principles. He sustained his family's finances upon the lifeblood of some fifty to sixty slaves, but he did so with the permission of his God. Or so he believed. He found this consent within his religion's text, as he explained to William two days after his eighth birthday.

Mason had ridden up to William and greeted him cordially, an act which set the boy trembling from his knees right down to his bare feet. He had heard it was the boy's birthday, and he offered him a present, a large, golden apple. It was no small feat for a Negro to make it through to a good working age, he said. William was a fine boy for doing so. He dismounted, left his horse to graze and directed the boy to sit down at the base of a boysenberry tree. He bade him to eat his apple.

William fumbled with the fruit. He went so far as to bring it up to his mouth and to test the skin against his teeth, but he didn't bite into it. He could barely keep his hands from shaking, and he feared that any action, even chewing, would somehow betray him. He sat on the verge of flinching every time the man moved, however innocent his gesture: raising a hand to shoo away the flies, pulling a handkerchief from his breast pocket, a phlegmy clearing of his throat. He had never experienced his owner in such proximity. Mason's odor was almost overpowering. A fragrant powder wafted up out of his clothing, an irritating substance like pollen. It was all William could do to hold the apple near his face and keep from coughing.

Mason cracked open a book and read of the world's creation, of the darkness that had been upon the lifeless void and how God filled it with light and life and water and all the creatures that roamed the earth. He read some of the story of the first human couple. Then he skipped forward and told of the evil that so soon came to rule the land and the flood that God sent to cleanse it away. He told of Noah and his sons, Shem, Ham, and Japheth, from whom all the people of the world were descended. He paused and studied the boy for a moment. He dabbed his brow with his handkerchief and asked if he recognized the Truth contained within this book? Did he know that it had been written at the command of the one and only God of all creation? Did he understand that its doctrines were the Word of the Lord and that they could never be doubted, for in doubting was sin and in sin was eternal damnation?

William mumbled, "Yessuh."

"Is that 'yes, sir' meant to encompass everything I have read thus far? *Everything*?"

William hesitated. He wasn't sure how to answer. The man wanted to hear that he understood, didn't he? Or did he want to hear that he didn't understand? He wasn't sure which way to respond, and it didn't occur to him for a second to answer truthfully. "Suh?" he said, casting the word somewhere between a statement and a question.

"Do you . . . Well, I mean to say, do you . . ." Mason exhaled in an exasperated way that set the boy's heart beating even more rapidly. "It is a lot I ask of you, I know. Just the other day I had a conversation with a learned man from Virginia, who swore that it was useless to instruct Negroes in biblical truths as the race was biologically and morally incapable of true comprehension. I disagreed. I need not trouble your mind with the intricacies of it all, but no harm can be done by trying to convey to you some simplified version of the principle points. Not to mention, as I told the gentleman, that you and your race have a place in here." He punctuated his statement by jabbing a finger into the open book. "Yes, you do. And that is just what we've come to discuss. Let me see . . ."

William felt an ant bite into his big toe. He let his eye drop down to study it, just for a second, then tried to focus his gaze into the empty space just before his face.

"*And Noah began to be a husbandman,*" Mason began. "*And he planted a vineyard; and he drank of the wine, and was drunken; and he was uncovered within his tent. And Ham, the father of Canaan, saw the nakedness of his father, and told his two brethren without. And Shem and Japheth took a garment, and laid it upon their shoulders, and went backward, and covered the nakedness of their father; and their faces were backward, and they saw not their father's nakedness. And Noah awoke from his wine, and knew what his younger son had done to him. And he said, 'Cursed be Canaan; a servant of servants shall he be unto his brethren.'*" Mason held up a finger as if he expected William to interrupt him. "*And he said, 'Blessed be the Lord God of Shem; and Canaan shall be his servant. God shall enlarge Japheth, and he shall dwell in the tents of Shem; and Canaan shall be his servant.'*"

The man closed the book. "And from those three men all the people of the earth are descended. I and my kind from

Shem and Japheth; you and yours from the accursed Ham. You see, Ham's descendants . . ." He opened the book again, found the proper page, and read a long list of names that meant nothing to William. When he concluded he explained that those were the nations of Africa, from whom William was descended. "Your blood is not completely Negro, that is true, but you should be proud of it anyway. Some say that the Negro is not even a man, is another form of being entirely. I, however, cannot dismiss the words of the Lord. You and I are both descended from one of the Lord's chosen. My race, however, is blessed with mastery of the world, while yours is assigned a place just beneath me. Each race has been ordered in such a way to allow them to shine. You do see the logic in this, don't you?"

William nodded and mumbled, "Yessuh."

This was the divine rule of things, Mason explained. When this order was upset chaos was loosed upon the world. Think of all the so-called free Negroes in Maryland. Did they live wondrous lives with that freedom? Did they prosper and grow rich and satisfied the way the better of the white men did? Of course not, for such were challenges beyond their capacity, and it was the evil of the northern white man which led them to spread such fiction. He picked out a particular former slave as an example, a man whose freedom was purchased by another free Negro. For him, liberty only led to the basest of degradation. He took to theft and developed hungers that he hadn't known as a slave. He insulted white women and acquired a taste for liquor. He roamed the streets like some pariah of biblical times. Before long he was found dead, hung by his legs from a tree, his head bashed into mush by clubs, genitals severed from his body so that they were no longer a threat to female virtue.

Mason studied the downturned face of the young boy, searching for the effect of his words. "That would never happen to one of my Negroes. That will never happen to you. You are protected so long as you are faithful to me. You will always be protected from the anger of other white men, from the poisons spread down from the north and from your own baser nature. I take your welfare as a matter of honor. Understand?"

"Yessuh."

"Good. I have always been very happy with you, William. You are a fine boy, despite the misfortunes of your parentage, and I trust you will always obey me as you should."

Three days later William was hired out to the family of an Annapolis shipbuilder and his life of toil began. In truth, he saw nothing akin to logic in the man's words. As a boy of eight he didn't try. He sat there wishing that the interview would end, knowing that his mother would ask him about it later, angry at himself because he knew he couldn't lie to her. It wasn't until much later, when he heard such theories repeated, that he sought to make some sense of them. He never did. He wasn't even sure that he understood what Ham's crime had been in the first place. Was Ham cursed for seeing his father's own depravity? Why would God honor the wishes of a drunk, a man that woke groggy from overconsumption? Was it simply that Ham had looked upon him and saw him as he really was, while the other sons turned their eyes away? Was he cursed for knowing the truth about the man from whom the entire world was descended?

THE BEGINNING OF HIS THIRD WEEK as a fugitive found William a lean, ghostly version of his former self. His food was long gone. He had to tighten the cord that held his trousers up. His face took on the gaunt qualities attributed to the starving and the holy. His eyes retreated back into his skull. The flesh of his nose became a thin veil over the contours of the bone and cartilage beneath it. He was taken by a hunger he had never known even in his worst days, then pushed beyond it to a numb place that was the backside of hunger. Strange visions assaulted him. Or perhaps he was seeing normal things but only now finding them strange. One morning he awoke with several millipedes curled into balls and sleeping within the crescent of his body's heat. Another afternoon he leant to drink from a stream, but paused with his hand cupped above the water, shocked by the sight of an enormous, spotted spider gorging itself on a fish twice its size. And one evening while paused to survey the land ahead, he looked down to find a half-dozen daddy longlegs climbing up his trousers.

He was also struck with occasional bursts of prophecy. He had dreams in which whips fell from masters' hands and writhed as serpents on the ground, scenes of white men en-gaged in the most desperate acts of self-flagellation, glimpses of tails poking through trousers like the curled barbs of swine. There were visions of Dover as he had last seen her, memories so distant he distrusted them. She appeared to him in a frac-tured prism of images, a mosaic in which each part of her appeared with a singular clarity. The ringlets of hair curled against the base of her neck. Her eyelids flickering as he pleasured her. The slack weight of her breasts against his cupped palms. Her canines pressed against her bottom lip in anger. He awoke once to the image of a young girl spinning away from her playmate, her head thrown back in laughter. Though it had not been a dream of Dover, it brought her to mind. He always remembered her sternness and strength, but that girl brought back a memory of her laughter as well. She had a wonderful laugh, a joy that came from low in her throat and rose up through her body with a physical force that tossed her head back. Yes, she had quite a laugh, but she had shared it rarely, at unpredictable moments.

Though his mind was full of images, it didn't mean he lowered his defenses. One evening, in the small hours of the night, he realized that he was being followed. He didn't see his pursuer, but he knew someone was behind him, just out of view. He doubled his pace. He climbed into a wild land measured by tree-lined ridges and sectioned by streambeds. He dropped down into a ravine and fumbled his way over boulders and through water-pocked rock slabs. He tried to manifest his fear in motion, to feed off the adrenaline building within him. But by the time he mounted a wide plateau of white pine his apprehension had mixed with anger. The person was still following him, a shadow that he couldn't shake free. So he decided to change his tactics.

He jogged into the fragrant pine forest, bent over beneath the branches. The dawn light was just strong enough to bring out the colors and textures of the pine's rough skin. He chose one of the trees at random. He grabbed at the dry nubs of the broken, lower branches, wrapped his thighs around the trunk and cinched his heels against it. He heaved himself upward until he found another handhold. In this painful way, he inched up the lower portion of the trunk. When he got his arms around a sturdy branch, he kicked a leg out to the side, hooking the branch with his ankle. He straddled it in a second, and the very next he was reaching for the branch above. The pine allowed for easy climbing after that, the branches spaced as if for just such a purpose. He perched on a branch halfway up the tree, stilled his breathing, and waited.

His pursuer crested the plateau at a limping shuffle,

breathing heavily, a sack slung over his shoulder. There was no stealth or guile in his progress. Viewed through the screen of branches, he moved with a strange, wide-legged gait, his legs bowed out to either side of his body. He passed below William, ducking beneath the branches, muttering curses so steadily they seemed to be a necessary feature of his progress. William couldn't see the man's face or hair, hidden as they were by the brim of his hat, but his voice had a throaty cadence, a richness that William recognized. The realization stunned him, for in the various forms he had envisioned his hunter, this was certainly not how he had imagined him. In the few moments it took to conclude this, the man faded from view, leaving in his wake a silence greater than the one that had preceded him.

William sat for a few minutes. He looked around him from tree to tree, but there was no company with whom to confer. He leaned to study the ground below, as if some further information might be offered in that quarter. Strangely, it was. A smell rose up, pushing aside the pine syrup and replacing it with an even stronger odor, pungent, repulsive, and delicious all at once. It was the scent of overripe cheese. It went to the back of his brain with a force that set his mouth watering. He shook his head at his own stupidity, but began the climb down anyway. On hitting the ground, he set out after the man at a lope. He had long ago discarded his sack, but he still carried the corn knife. He pulled the weapon from under his shirt as he ran and strode with it out to his side.

When he caught up with the man, he was standing on the far side of a dry creek bed, under the full force of the sun. He was bent over, alternately contemplating the ground and peering through the low-slung branches ahead of him. He scratched his butt cheek, then lifted his hat and fanned his face. William moved toward him, crooked a little to the side as if

ready to bolt to the left at any moment. The needle flooring
gave beneath his feet, not completely silent, but muted enough
not to betray his approach.

As he grew nearer, so gaining a clearer picture of the man's
narrow back and thin arms, William's demeanor changed. His
posture grew more erect, his strides more forceful. The lines
around his mouth twisted like a man preparing to spit. Whether
he thought out the actions that followed or not was unclear.
They happened fast, fueled by a sudden overflow of anger.
He switched the knife from one hand to the other. Without
catching his step, he bent, snatched up a small rock in his free
hand, cranked his arm back past his ear, and snapped it forward.
The rock flew with an audible hiss. It hit the man at the base
of his neck and sent him stumbling forward onto all fours. He
scrambled like that for a moment, then remembered himself,
stood up, and turned around. He stared wide-eyed and mute as
William strode toward him, knife once more in his favored
hand.

The other man was a thin Negro. He pulled his straw hat
down tight around his head, beneath which a mass of curly hair
struggled to get free. He stood on crooked hips that set the
whole of his upper body on a slope, like a person carrying a
bucket in one arm. His clothing was as bedraggled as that of
any field hand, although his shoes were of a better make than
the coarse brogans allotted to most slaves. He rubbed the back
of his neck viciously, as if whatever thing had done him harm
was there to be wiped away.

"What'd you do that for?" he asked.

"Why you tracking me?"

"Tracking you? I ain't tracking you." The man's features
were a mismatched collection of parts, eyes canted at diver-
gent angles, forehead exceptionally wide, tufts of hair dotting
his cheeks. He used the whole of his body when speaking,

shoulders jolting around in the sockets, neck thrusting forward and back in the effort of it. "I caught sight of you a ways back," he said. "Was wondering if maybe we couldn't travel on agether. I don't mean you no trouble. You can be damn sure of that." He held up his hands to show that he was unarmed, with intentions as plain as the whites of his palms. "What I mean to say is, judging by the look of you we're in the same particular. You a runaway too, ain't you? Only ask cause I'd confess the same about myself."

William switched the knife from one hand to the other and back again.

The man shuffled back a few steps. "You looking to stick me with that? After I come up on you like a civilized body? I didn't make you for a culprit. Figured you for a Christian, at least."

William wiped the sweat from his eyes with his free hand. "What difference does that make?"

As if this question established some confidence between the two, the man explained that in his experience Christians made for the best company. And that was all he was looking for, a little companionship in his travels. He had more supplies than the good Lord should've provided him and he thought it best to share with others in need. "You can smell that cheese, can't you? Got a stink to it, right enough, but it's fine going down."

William sucked his bottom lip, weighing the demands of his hunger against the prospect of traveling with this man. It was a hard call. "Don't know that I need company. Where'd you come by that food anyhow?"

"Stolt it."

"Then there's men hunting you."

The other shook his head. "Naw, I don't reckon. I ain't hardly worth the trouble. Got a weak constitution, they say."

"That may be the first honest word you spoke."

The man took no offense at this. Quite the contrary, he nodded and smiled. "Anyway, we ain't properly met. Name's Oli. And if that don't impress you maybe some rock candy will. Got me a whole bag of it."

William cursed under his breath, lowered the knife, and motioned for the man to retrieve his sack. "Let's get some cover. For a spell, at least, while I think what to make of you."

Four

The hunt began as easy work. The hound found the fugitive's scent with little difficulty. Her only confusion lay in separating the hunted's scent from those of the other trackers who had already followed his trail. Once this was dealt with, she bounded away with Morrison in pursuit. They followed the path from the slave's hovel and through the woods, down a creek and up under a bridge and on again. The rain began soon after. When the hound hesitated the man thought this was the cause. He urged her forward with an encouraging whistle and a rough pat on the shoulder. He took the lead for a moment, sure that the hound would bound past him, renewed by his touch. But the dog was of another mind. She spun in circles, scenting the air, and finally concluding that the trail led to the west. The man almost called her back, for the signs of the other trackers were clear to see, heading north in line with the slave's progress thus far. But he held his tongue, for the hound was already some distance away.

When he burst through the vegetation and onto the beach, the storm struck him full in the face. Rain pelted into the Bay and jumped back up toward the sky. Water careened sideways as much as vertically and struck him like a hail of stones. He set his feet wide apart and shaded his eyes with his free hand. The hound moved up and down the beach in desperation, oblivious to the storm. When she caught sight of the man, she met his eyes and then turned into the face of the storm and howled out across the water. The man understood the message, but was little sure of what to make of it.

The rain had abated by the time Morrison returned to the plantation. He stood before the planter and told of his progress so far, of his hound's conclusions and of how he had tried to convince her that the scent was still there to be found. He had even roped the dog and dragged her along the path laid by the others in the hope that she would find the scent again. He had asked her to see reason and to overcome her stubborn inclinations. He had even offered her a bribe in the form of a twist of smoked meat. While the hound accepted the meat as her due, she wouldn't be led away from her beliefs, and so the man acquiesced.

That boy went into the water, Morrison said. That's one fact you didn't share with me.

That's hardly a fact, Humboldt said. He was sure that the boy in question was scared to death of water, just like they all were. He said that the rain had just scuddled the scent. He paused and looked between man and dog and added that perhaps the hound wasn't much of a tracker.

Morrison studied the dog. She studied him back. Don't believe she's the problem here, he said.

Again the other man countered, saying that all the other slave hunters had turned their hounds to the north and were halfway to Delaware by now, and probably right on the boy's heels. He said that there wasn't anything else for it. A nigger don't just disappear. And a nigger don't swim across the Chesapeake Bay. I've known three men in my life who could swim, he said, and not a one of them had a drop of black blood in him.

Morrison knew what he knew and now that he had men-

tioned it he had no more doubts. He proceeded cautiously, not wanting to share too many of his thoughts with this man, but needing some aid where his local knowledge failed him. He asked if the fugitive might not have crossed the water by boat, but Humboldt doubted this. There hadn't been any boats in that immediate area, nor had any gone missing. He didn't doubt that there were Quakers and other godforsaken sons-a-bitches who would help a slave escape, but he was dead sure that none of that element had gained access to this particular boy.

So there it was, Humboldt said. He hadn't stolen a boat, hadn't been picked up by a boat, and he sure as hell hadn't swum it. The boy ran north, he said. You get yourself in that direction and you might catch him. Otherwise you're wasting my time.

He turned to walk away, but the tracker asked him one more question.

Did he have any family across the Bay?

Humboldt spun around, annoyance in the crags of his forehead. No, no family, he said. But he did have a bitch he was hungered for.

A woman?

That's right, the planter man said, and, as an afterthought and a kind indulgence, he went on to tell him what he knew of her and her owner.

Five

The two men sheltered in the nook between the overturned trunk of a fallen oak and the base of one still standing. As Oli unwrapped the cheese, William swallowed hard to keep down the saliva that flooded his mouth. It was a frightful-looking block, slimy with the day's heat and dotted with fungal growth. But when Oli's knife bit into it, the flesh of the cheese sliced open beautifully, white inside and so soft on his tongue that it melted almost instantly. With this came great mouthfuls of corn bread, smoked fish and fresh peas eaten raw and so crisp that they popped between the teeth. They drank from a large skin of watered-down beer. It had little to recommend it over creek water, but William drank it down all the same.

Oli enjoyed talking. As they ate he told a painful story of life on a Virginia plantation. He had been a sickly child, the only one of six to survive into his second year. He grew into a sickly man, never built for the hard labor to which he was put. His master had tried each year to sell him but was unsuccessful every time. Oli came to suspect that his master was planning some devious venture with him. He had been approached by a slave trader who was willing to purchase Oli cheaply for resale into the deep southwest, into the fabled bottomlands of malaria and dysentery, where owners hardly expected their chattels to live through a full summer. They get what work they can out of them, then write them off as little more than a footnote in a logbook on their deaths. Oli couldn't abide that prospect. That was why he had hit the road north, his eyes set on that Canadian horizon.

The day faded into dusk. Deep within the woods as they were, their hideout was almost dark as full night. The branches above them obscured the sky and unhinged the clockwork that marked the passage of the hours. For the first time in days William forgot to measure the progress of the sun. On Oli's prompting, they built up a tiny fire, which they contained in a small bowl and fed on twigs. William ventured down to the last creek they'd crossed and refilled the water skin. When he climbed back into their hiding place he found Oli grinning.

"You drink this?" he asked, holding up a bottle of an auburn liquid.

"Whiskey?"

"Yep. Been saving it up and this here seems as good a time as any. Go on and get a pull."

As William took a few furtive sips, Oli began a long string of tales about rebellious slaves. He seemed to have a library of such stories stored in his head, embellished, no doubt, with his own embroidery. He told of three slaves who stole into their overseer's cabin one night and bludgeoned him with clubs. They dragged him from his home, broke his neck, and spent the rest of the night arranging to disguise his death. One slave rode behind the dead man on his horse, scuffing the ground in a peculiar way, and then he tossed the man from the mount, loosened his saddle and tugged it over to its side. They then slapped the horse and sent it running. The officials ruled the white man's death to be an accident, though most of the slaves who lived thereabouts knew the real truth. In another tale two bondsmen absconded from their master's plantation on horseback, sharing a single pony between them. One of them had the shoulders of a bull and a bullet-shaped head that glistened with sweat; the other one's deformed torso measured only twelve inches from crotch to neck. The sight proved so odd to passersby that all let the couple ride on, more amused by the spectacle than inclined toward any action. There were slaves who stole away with chests of gold and those who ravished their mistresses and those who avenged old wrongs before parting. There were fabled gangs of Negroes who roamed the wild country of the uplands, stealing from white settlers and wreaking havoc wherever they passed. And there was Nat Turner and the swathe of terror he cut through Virginia, like an incarnation of every white man's nightmare. It was a crazy time they were living in, Oli concluded, and he didn't see any signs of sanity on the horizon.

Asked if he was really heading all the way to Canada, Oli's

eyes lifted and studied William for a moment. There was something in them that William couldn't read, but he imagined them to be the mirror of his own thoughts. Such a place as the land of freedom was too far away from the place of their birth. How could they know that that country would accept them? That the ground would feel the same beneath their feet and the air the same in their lungs? And what of kin and friends and familiar places never to be seen again? In Oli's answer William heard nothing to indicate that this other man hadn't had the same thoughts.

"Yeah," he said. "I don't reckon there's any way to be free but to be quit of this whole country. Ain't no place in it a nigger's safe. I know that for a biblical fact. Don't much matter to me, not having much kin to speak of. But how bout yerself? You hurting? Leaving your kin, I mean."

"Seems like that's why we were put here—to hurt."

"That's a biblical fact, right there."

William smirked. "A biblical one, huh?"

"Been my experience that that book's a hard one to dispute."

"We may be of two minds on that."

"Ain't no two minds about it . . ."

"I'd just as soon not talk it to death," William said. His voice was edged just enough to quell Oli's response. But, having spoken sharply, he lifted the bottle and scented it and nodded to his companion. "Think I'm starting to feel kindly toward this whiskey."

The evening hours passed, and the two men became more fluid in their conversation. At first, William tried to speak sparingly, not caring to share too much of himself with a stranger. But as the night wore on the other man's talkativeness proved infectious. The whiskey spread out through William's body, loosening his tongue, lowering his guard. Oli didn't seem like such a stranger after all, and it felt good to talk to someone after all his time alone. He spoke of his home in Annapolis, of the various chores he worked at, of Kent Island and of St. John Humboldt. He admitted that the scars he wore across his back were fresh wounds, administered by Humboldt just before he ran away.

"Came out after me in the fields," he said. "This a couple days after I heard word that my woman had left Annapolis. Humboldt came out and asked why had my work slacked the last few days."

"What'd you say?" Oli asked.

"Told him I didn't know. Couldn't recollect. Didn't know what he was on bout."

"Bet that didn't sit with him." The small man passed the bottle.

William took hold of it and lifted it straight to his mouth. He closed his eyes at the sting of the stuff, although already it wasn't so sharp as it had been at first. He confirmed that his denial had not sat well with Humboldt. "Ain't nothing I could've said would've pleased him. He wasn't looking for no answers. Said he already knew what the problem was. I had myself a case of nigger love. That's what he said, 'Nigger love.'"

"Hit it right on, didn't he?" Oli asked.

William cut him with his eyes, a warning but not a firm one. He handed the bottle back to him. Oli asked what happened next, but William shrugged it off. No surprise. The overseer had pushed him to his knees and rained blows of rawhide across his back. "He beat me," William said. "Whatchu expect him to do?"

"And he done all that damage? Made you bleed and all?"

"Well . . . He ain't the only one beat on me. I was there on my knees, this big white man above me, tearing my hide, cursing at me, talking bout the slave girls he'd had, bout the things he did to them. It put a rage in me. Not just the beating, but the way he was talking. I put out my hand and grabbed a hold of that whip. I knew just then that he was an evil son-a-bitch, and that I could've snatched the whip from his hand. Could've turned it on him and beat him down. Could've bitten off his nose and spat it back into his face. Could've done anything, I was so full of hating him."

"You do that?" Oli asked. "Bite him I mean?"

"Naw. Just held the whip twined round my arm. Just held it ready. Just waited to see what he would do, and to see what I'd do. But he didn't do nothing. Just had me get up and walk back to the plantation."

"He didn't beat you no more after that?" Oli asked.

"Naw."

"Didn't? What'd you spook him? Put the fear of nigger in him?"

"I said *he* didn't beat me. But he got him this other boy, a big slave named John, to beat me. Worked me over good. Near killed me, that beating. But when I woke up I had me a plan, and I done followed it ever since. So these here scars ain't nothing I'm troubled about. They just the reminder of the day I got the sense beat into me and became my own man."

He held up his hand and motioned for the bottle. When he had drunk from it again, he went on to tell of his swim across the Bay, a feat which prompted Oli to call him the swimmingest Negro he had ever heard tell of. He told of his fatigue and of the rain and of the cold. It was easy enough to share these things, but he gave only a few scant details about Dover. When he fell silent and Oli rambled on, William recalled her face and the parts of her body he knew so well. It was unbelievable that he had once held her beside him and spoken to her of the casual events of life, that he had run his fingers over her features and placed his lips against her skin. It seemed stranger still that she had invested him with some similar affection, that she had touched him and whispered in his ear and invoked him to do things to her in lovemaking that he wouldn't have conceived of otherwise. He tried to find solace in these moments, but he only grew more uncomfortable. Perhaps things had never been as he imagined. With the alcohol slipping between the cracks in his recollections, he began to see a darker significance to all of his memories of Dover.

He recalled the first time he had ever seen her. In the August fury. He was kneeling between two rosebushes, shears in both hands, working the gardens on the edge of the Masons' estate. The tool was too large for the close and dangerous work, and he had to crane at awkward angles to make the appropriate cuts, all the time avoiding the plant's thorns. He was concentrating on the work, imagining perfections to the plants' forms and trying to make them real. A woman's voice roused him from these thoughts. She sang a tune just quietly enough so that he couldn't pick up the words. He recognized the melody, though he couldn't place it. It was beautiful, this voice, and unfamiliar. He stood up, but in so doing placed his back against the thorns. He cried out and lurched forward, knicking his chest. He slashed out with his arms and cut tiny cat scratches in them as well. By the time he freed himself and turned toward the woman she had stopped to stare at him. He was robbed of speech. They shared a long moment, but in the end she turned and continued on her way without having said a word to him. They never broke that silence. And try as he might, he couldn't find any more grace or dignity in the moment. Their first meeting was painful, embarrassing. Dover had robbed him of something. She had impaled him. She had walked away with a piece of him, and he had still not recovered from the loss.

He hardly noticed when Oli handed him another bottle, a smaller one this time and more finely constructed. He took it in hand and listened as Oli told another story. He would never remember bringing that bottle to his lips. He was too full of other memories, too confused at the way the world shimmied before his eyes and too focussed on the strange waves of euphoric nausea that rolled through him. He had to concentrate to single out the true Oli from the two or three phantoms that shifted in and out of sight. Though he stared hard at him, he wouldn't recall anything different in Oli's eyes. It was only when he felt himself losing consciousness that he realized he had consumed that second bottle on his own, while Oli drank only from the water skin.

WILLIAM AWOKE KNOWING that he had been hearing the voices for some time. He had sensed movement around him. His body had been pulled this way and that, rolled and dragged and handled. But for all the motion he was only vaguely involved. The sensations were muted, distant. It hadn't occurred to him to respond to this world until a splash of moisture on his face jolted him awake. He opened his eyes on a skewed and unfocussed scene. His hands were aching and numb all at once. He tried to bring them up to his face, but his arms were yanked to a halt by chains. He tried to sit up, but he couldn't find the balance to do even that. His head was full of rocks that ground against the side of his skull at the slightest provocation, the pain of it blotting his thoughts.

The pale face of a white man came into view, lean in the jaw but heavily browed. His skin was red and peeling from the summer sun. Old pox scars were evenly spaced over his cheeks and down his neck, and he bore a dimple in his cheek that must've been an old puncture wound.

"You gone and slept in your own sick," the man said. "I hate to see a grown man like that."

Pieces of the previous day flew back to William: the other black man, the weak one who told stories, the scent of cheese, the banquet spread before him, two men atop a single pony, a mirage of three faces mingling and merging, whiskey and laughter and . . . And they'd been found. Slave catchers had tracked them down and come upon them while they slept. The understanding flooded upon him in its entirety. They had been caught, he and the other one, the frail one, the runt with the crooked spine . . .

But then he realized that Oli was standing just beyond the white man, a few feet away, hat mounted once again above his mass of hair. William tried to focus on him, but his image wavered before him, real enough to render identity but no details. He was standing there, not chained at all but just standing, watching. William thought of his knife, but knew in an instant that it was gone.

"Oli, see that there's a space for this one in the wagon." The white leaned in closer, lowering his face down to within inches of William's. "Sorry to wake you like this. I know it ain't civilized, but we got some distance to cover to get us back to camp. You may be a little cloudy right now on the particulars of what's transpiring here, but I'll tell you this much so there's no confusion bout it. You're plum in the shit, boy. Hope you enjoyed your taste of liberty, cause it's over. Finished and done with. It's as official as Waterloo. You're back to bondage. My nigger Oli made sure of that."

The man didn't try to make William rise. Instead, he just dragged him by his feet. William's shirt rode up his back, the undergrowth of ferns and twigs scratching across his skin. It wasn't a long journey, however. The wagon was near at hand. The two men hoisted him and dropped his dead weight alongside boxes and crates and a soft thing that he slowly realized was the carcass of a deer. The wagon moved off, weaving its way through the trees for a few minutes, then dropping down into a steadier route of even grooves. He realized that they hadn't camped in the wilderness in which he had thought they had. A road ran just over the next ridge, no more than a quarter mile from where they'd slept. It was on this road they now traveled.

As the morning passed and his head cleared, William's eyes searched the wagon for a weapon or some sort of key, anything that he might turn against his captors. He even considered the antlers of the deer itself, wondering how much force it would take to snap one off, imagining the bloody damage such an instrument could inflict. But the two men had left nothing that he could really use against them. So he devised plans wherein he used his bare hands as weapons, his fingers like prongs to gouge out the white man's eyes, his fists like mallets to smash the bridge of that black man's nose. But his hands were cinched so tightly together that they soon went numb. They ached with a strange, gnawing pain, and try as he might he could not free them. Each time his schemes came back to the same conclusion. It was useless. He was caught, and it was all his fault for being such a fool.

Eventually, he gave up on escape and just lay in the bed of the cart through the afternoon, on one side and then the other, then upon his back. He turned again and again from thoughts of Dover, for he felt they might drive him mad. He watched the canopy pass above, the designs cast there and the play of the light through the dusted underbellies of the leaves. One of the deer's hooves marked the edge of his vision. It rocked in gentle circles just strong enough to upset the flies that tried every few moments to land on it. That dead limb became an animated creature, complete of itself, its movements a diatribe directed at the sky. Occasionally, Oli's head appeared. William knew his features, but he felt that he was looking at a stranger that somehow wore a familiar face. His hair still bunched in wild curls beneath his hat, but he didn't smile anymore. He looked William over with the impartial eyes of a doctor checking a patient's condition. Satisfied, the head would disappear without ever speaking.

Camp that night was a cluttered scar in the forest, a jumble of cooking supplies and stray tools. The white man built up a fire, laying a complete tree across the kindling. The green wood hissed and spat as the flames charred its midsection. Oli yanked William from the wagon and pulled him to his feet. He led him a little distance away and made him sit against the base of an oak tree. He ran another length of chain through his wrist irons, around his torso and then around the tree, securing it with another padlock. He didn't speak through any of this, and one would barely have recognized this taciturn jailer as the same talkative companion of the day before.

William sat with the weight of the new irons heavy on his thighs. Just as Oli began to turn away, he said, "Every damn thing you said to me was a lie."

Oli nodded and chewed this over. "Lied some, yep."

"Were you never a slave?"

"Oh, for damn sure I was. Twenty year of my life. Mostly like I told you. A slave till Mr. Wolfe done bought me." He glanced toward the white man. "Bought me when wouldn't nobody else have me. Now we partners. He treat me all right. He the first one ever did."

William stared at him, his features tense, trembling with anger. His hands itched to leap forward and pound the stupid expression off the other man's face. He only held himself back because he knew the chains would hold fast and he would look like a greater fool for the effort.

"What you looking so evil for?" Oli asked. "We all gotta work. I just done chosen mine. You got caught up in it. It's you own damn fault. You the one couldn't hold your liquor."

William spat.

The moisture fell short and Oli ignored it. "Reckon you'll just have to go back to working for massa. Ain't nothing you ain't lived through before."

"It ain't about that! Don't give a damn bout working. I'm talking bout something else, bout a whole life . . ." William caught his breath and looked down at his wrists. He blinked, and with his eyes still closed he said, "You ever think I wasn't running from something, but *to* something?"

Oli watched the man for a moment before answering. "Can't give too much thought to that. Way I see it, you're just one nigger in a hundred. Each one of them hundred got they own woes. Each one got they own special reason why I should give a good Goddamn bout them. But how many a them would spare water for me? Tell me that. How many a them? This here's a hard time we living in. Ain't even the hardest if you believe the Bible. We all gotta do for ourselves. Reckon my doing took issue with your doing, but that's the way the Lord seen fit to arrange it. Niggers could say the same bout white folks. Womenfolk could say the same bout men. That's the way it is, and I tell you what . . . I'm one humble nigger. Ain't bout to change the way of the whole world. Just staying alive. And you're doing the same. Member who chucked the rock at who. Member which one of us done pulled a knife on the other. You memorate that, cause I sure as shit am gonna." With that, he spun and strolled away toward the fire ring and the company of the white man.

THE WAGON TRAVELED all the next day through a poor district of ramshackle buildings. Some of the structures perched at the edge of the road as if intent on impeding the infrequent traffic. Of the ones that sat at a distance, they tended to be cluttered with abandoned implements of iron and wood, pieces of things that never formed a whole but which seemed necessary features of the homesteads. Canines roused themselves from the underbellies of shacks, lifted their heads and called out. Toward dusk they paused in a town composed of two stone buildings fronting each other on either side of the road. Wolfe climbed down and bought a few supplies in the general store. William sat in the back of the wagon, returning the hard gazes of the people who walked past. Wolfe was back in a few minutes, and they were off again at a pace brisker than before.

With the town still on the horizon behind them, Wolfe stopped the wagon, climbed down, and moved around to the rear of it. The wide brim of his hat cast his entire face in shadow, but the sunlight reflecting up from the roadside lit his features with a strange underlight. He chewed tobacco, an action that set all the sharp components of his face to motion. He waved a piece of paper before William, then motioned that he should take a look at it.

William stared at the man.

"You probably can't read, can you?" When William still failed to respond, Wolfe sent a stream of brown spit sideways from his mouth, cleared his throat and began to read the notice. His voice was halting, although so too was the style of the notice. "Says here, '*Runaway, from my plantation on the night of June 2, a mulatto named William, aged about 22 years, about five feet ten inches high . . . Had on when he went away a fancy-made cotton shirt, pantaloons and boots, some touched by the whip upon his back in due response to his overproud behavior . . . will make for a free state . . . also may try to contact a Negro woman . . . Twenty dollars will be given for securing the above mulatto . . . I dearly wish to get him again.'* "

Wolfe ran his fingers across the front rim of his hat. "What I'm pointing out to you is that we got ourselves a crossroads here. Should I, one—return your ass to the care of Mr. St. John Humboldt and collect myself that twenty dollars . . . Normally, I wouldn't mind doing that, but I've had some dealings with that man before and they left me a little sour on him. He don't honor his word, is what I mean to say. Plus, that's a few extra days haulage to get you there. Or should I drop you at a friend's over in Baltimore, a slaver I do business with on occasion? He's got a shipment heading southwest end of the week, and I bet he would pay me the same as Humboldt without causing me half the time or trouble. He would move you out so fast Humboldt would never be the wiser. What do you figure?"

"Humboldt don't own me."

"He don't?" The man checked the notice from several angles. "Who does then?"

"Why you asking me? Ain't asked me nothing fore this."

Wolfe smirked. "Just think it a kindly gesture on my part. I have my moments, you see. Anyhow, Humboldt filed the notice. You want I should take you back to him?"

"Rather you kill me."

The man thought this over. He shoved his fingers in his mouth and worked the wad of tobacco there. He pulled the leaves out and studied them. "Well, no, it don't say nothing about payment for a dead nigger. That wouldn't do me no good." He flicked the tobacco away and spat out the remainder of the leaves. Only when he was satisfied that his mouth was clear did he again look to William. "Fine. Humboldt can go screw himself for all I care." He crumpled the notice and tossed it into the bushes.

They camped about four miles from the town and were on the move again before sunup the next day. William slept little during the night, but in the early hours he found himself lulled by the movement of the wagon. He fell asleep as the sun rose, and only awoke when the wagon trundled to a halt. The day had grown heavy. The sky was overcast with a haze of gray that floated just above the building in front of which they had stopped. From the roadside it was an innocuous frontage of red brick, with a stone archway that at first seemed more like an alleyway than an entrance. It might have been a post office or some such structure of local government.

Oli prodded William down from the wagon. They walked through the archway and down a dark stone corridor. They passed several doorways and another branch of the hallway that was filled to the roof with clutter. They paused outside a small room in which Wolfe was already seated and conversing with two men. One of these came out and put William through a cursory inspection: eyes, teeth and breathing. A moment later he was on the move again. Another white man took over from Oli. He pushed William before him to the end of the corridor, through a small courtyard open to the sky. In turn, he passed William on to another man behind a locked gate. From there, William shuffled forward into the confines that were to be his temporary home. He turned and looked behind him, as if he expected some farewell from Oli and Wolfe, but the two were nowhere to be seen.

The walls of the enclosure were some twenty feet high, rimmed across the top with shards of glass that reflected the sun in jagged, multihued shapes. All else was shades of brown: the skin of the men and women in all of that color's various permutations, the dirt of the floor and the ragged earth tones of the captives' simple clothing. What little shade there was to be had was cast by the eastern wall. Under this, the majority of the slaves huddled, a couple dozen in number and of both sexes. Some stood leaning against it, a few sprawled out beneath it, but most just sat within the line of its protection, watching William. Their faces were lean and sunken, hair matted and speckled with bits of dirt and twig. In these sorry details they were no different than many field hands that he had seen. It was their eyes that were different. They were eyes driven mad by the tedium of waiting, by days spent in chains contemplating a future bondage, without even the distraction of work or family or nature to ease their minds.

William stood in the center of the enclosure. The gate clanked shut behind him and a silence fell over the place, broken by the muted friction of his chains as he stood. He felt all those eyes on him. For a moment they seemed as strange and unfamiliar as the eyes of white men viewing him on the auction block. Having exhausted the bare spaces of the walls, he dropped his gaze to his wrists and the iron that bound them, as if all of his problems hinged on those links of metal.

He might have stood like this indefinitely, had not a movement roused him. He looked up. One of the slaves rose from his prone position and propped himself up on one elbow. He motioned with his cupped hand. He said something, so softly that at first William didn't make it out. He thought on it and the fading words ordered themselves in his mind. The man had asked him over, had instructed him in simple words, to come get some shade. With that simple phrase and gesture William saw them anew. He realized that he recognized them all. He might not know them by name or face or blood relation, but they were his people after all. They wore the same chains. He walked toward them and took his place among them.

Six

Morrison and the hound sailed from Kent Island aboard a thirty-foot whaleboat. They were the only passengers and formed, along with the skipper himself, a crew of three. The vessel was open to the air like an enormous canoe, with a single mast sunk into its center. It was a slow craft by design, but tacking against a weak breeze it made hardly any progress at all. Man and dog watched the far shoreline appear and disappear, seeming, through the passing of hours, to actually be getting farther away. A haze settled across the water and features that were once clear became less so. Toward the late afternoon the skipper gave up on sail power. He asked Morrison to bend his back at one of the oars while he worked its twin. The work was strange to Morrison. It fatigued his back and shoulders in a way that he was not accustomed to, and their progress was as slow by oar as it had been under sail. The hound watched the men's exertions with opinionated eyes.

Once ashore Morrison looked back across the water at the far shore. He thought, and not for the first time, that if the fugitive had in fact swum for freedom he had probably found it at the Bay's murky bottom. Annapolis had changed since he had left the place years ago, and he didn't find the house he was looking for until that evening. He stood before it, contemplating the lights in the windows, studying the wealth signified by the well-kept gardens, the white façade and the black faces of the servants who passed by the windows. He thought about making his inquiries just then, but decided against it.

That night he stayed in a tiny room in a tavern near Church Circle, a place that brought back memories he didn't care for. He tied the hound outside and heard her barking late into the night. He purchased a bottle of whiskey and drank it down entire and lay on his bed with the ceiling spinning above him. He fumbled in his bags and came up with the crumpled letter. As he read it over, the words moved on the page, reordering themselves, incoherent. He mumbled that he should just burn the thing and be done with it, just burn it and get on with his sorry life. But he could not make himself rise to carry out the wish.

He woke up with a head like a metal drum and all the world pounding upon it. The letter was pressed to his chest, crumpled further but not destroyed. He gathered his things and greeted the hound and was again at the gate to the same estate by eight in the morning. He hallooed the house, spoke his request and got an audience with the widow herself. She answered his questions shortly, only addressing them at all because runaways were an ever present scourge upon the institution of slavery and all efforts must be made to staunch the flow. Or so she said. She even proposed calling for the woman in question, but Morrison stayed her. Better he just get the woman's description. Better that he follow her unbeknownst.

And that's just what he did. The woman left the house via the back entrance. The tracker gave her a good lead and blended his own progress with that of the other pedestrians. He nearly lost her once, when a wagon blocked his path and he missed which avenue she had chosen from a choice of three. He chose one at random, picked up his pace, and found that he had chosen correctly.

The walk took a little over ten minutes, but in that space of time one world merged into another. The large houses disappeared, as did white faces and swept roads and any inkling of grandeur. The woman wove her way into a territory of decrepit shacks, largely empty as the occupants were at work. Stray dogs came out to address the hound and the man kicked them back, all the while keeping an eye on the woman's form. She stopped at a hut that was little different than the ones near at

hand, constructed from materials that had seen better days
in other structures long ago. An old woman appeared in the
doorway. A swarm of bandy-legged children followed her,
clothed in shirts that hung down to their knees. Morrison could
just hear the woman's voice, not the words but the mirthful flavor
of them. She bade the young woman to enter.

Morrison motioned for the dog to follow him into hiding.
Together they found a place of thick shrubs just off the path that
afforded a decent view of the house. They had scarcely settled
down in the bushes when the hound grew agitated. Her nostrils
flared and quivered and her eyes darted about the woods along
the far end of the house. Her front legs pawed the ground before
her as if she could rake the object of her interest closer. Morrison
had seen this before and knew that she had caught the fugitive's
scent again. He shushed her quiet, for he hadn't thought it would
be this easy. When the dog continued, he slapped her flat-handed
on the head and tightened his grip on her collar.

The woman reappeared within a quarter hour, shouting a
goodbye over her shoulder. On this second appearance Morrison
experienced a strange sensation, a sensation he rarely felt as his
life was so solitary, and one he shouldn't have felt for this woman
for they had no relation between them. The woman carried the
same bundle and walked the same way as before, but somehow she
looked different. She moved with a grace he hadn't noticed before.
He found himself wondering if she bore any resemblance to her
sister, thinking that if she did then he could understand the fugi-
tive's ardor. He watched her to the distance.

In his attentive gaze he forgot the hand over the hound's
muzzle. Feeling the pressure released, the dog tried to pull the
man forward. But he held on a moment longer, his eyes fixed to
the point at which the woman had disappeared. He almost wished
he had reason to talk to her, but she had already led him back to

the trail and so she had served the use he had required. The hound craned her neck around and bared her teeth. The man watched the space where the woman had vanished and still did not release the dog. It was not the first moment since he had entered the Bay region that he had hesitated in his mission. But he could not turn away from this and he knew it. He flexed his fingers. The hound lurched from his grasp, loud and hungry and anxious, again on the runaway's scent. Morrison rose and followed. He was on the trail again.

Seven

The pen's mortar walls and hard-packed floor caught the day's fury like an oven. William sat baking, his body—like those of all the captives—covered in a film of sweat and salt and dirt. Through the hottest hours of the day, they did little more than swat at flies, watch the progress of the clouds and scratch at insect bites. Though their jailers were rarely seen, they were somehow a constant threat. The only noticeable lookout was the guard posted on the balcony of the main building overlooking the pen. He was sometimes visible, looking down at them with disinterest, but most often he propped his feet so that they alone were in view from below. They fed the captives corn-flour gruel, a tasteless, textureless substance. To drink they all shared a bucket of whiskey-tainted water that was refilled several times throughout the day. The alcohol was added for its antiseptic qualities. For William, the faint taste of it brought up a roiling nausea that was hard to contain. They also had to share a single toilet—a large basin set in the center of the compound. Men and women alike were made to squat above it, in plain sight of all, open to the sky above.

Despite the languid stupor of the day, it was impossible not to make eye contact with someone, not to nod a greeting or maybe even to voice a question. By this means William came to know those around him. The man who had called him over was a Louisiana slave named Lemuel. He had been sold four times in his life: twice in the confines of the Delta, once up into Delaware as a result more of gambling debts than of a business transaction, and then to the slave traders who now owned his life and future works. He guessed that the figure would rise to five very soon. He only hoped that he didn't end up anywhere near his birthplace, for it was a place no slave would want to see twice. His life in that swampy delta had been one of constant hardship, labor unending, heat and insects and cruelty, a life of cane and cotton that marked the seasons in catalogues of the dead.

"I wouldn't wish it on any man," Lemuel said. He sat beside William, with his legs crossed before him. His eyes were the same reddish brown as his skin, and they tended to move slowly, settling on one object and studying the full shape and function of it before moving on. He had a crescent of a scar above his eyebrow. It was an old wound, swollen like a brand scar. He sometimes touched it when he spoke. "Not even my worst enemy. You ever seen a thing bit to death by skeeters?"

"No."

"I have. I'm telling you, stay clear of them swamplands."

"You don't mean a person, do you?" William asked, the image of a man covered in pinpricks already fixed in his mind.

"Didn't say a person. Just said a thing. But if it could happen to a thing it could happen to a man too. We ain't all that different. Now don't take me the wrong way. There's a beauty down in that country too. I remember sometimes lying up at night, listening to the God-almighty racket of frogs, one louder than the other, smelling all the smells what come to you when it's dark. Yeah, there's a beauty in some of that. Just in listening. In tasting the world and breathing it in. That's true, but I'd just as soon not set foot back there again, all things considered."

One of the others was a runaway named Dante. He had been caught well into Pennsylvania, on soil some called free but which gave him no protection. A pack of hounds had ripped the flesh of his forearms and left the wounds raw and oozing. He sat near enough to share in the conversation, though his thoughts always began and ended in tragedy. He seemed to have given up the will to live, and made no attempt to swat away the flies that plagued him. William watched him askance, finding it difficult to look at him, but harder still not to. His eyes were drawn again and again to the man's wounds. He shooed the flies away when he could, although he did this covertly, as he somehow sensed the man would be annoyed to be the subject of pity.

There were two among them who kept to themselves. They made an odd couple, although no one thought it wise to comment on this. The more noticeable of the two was a giant of a man named Saxon. He was naked from the waist up. His britches were torn down the backside in a manner that exposed his privates to the world when he walked. His body was a thing to be marveled at. He must have weighed twice as much as any of the others, and he bore the weight evenly distributed about his frame. The muscles around his neck bunched and quivered when he moved. The flesh around his shoulders and biceps was scarred by stretch marks. The other man was quite inconsequential in comparison. He was a mulatto, honey-complexioned, with short legs and a slight pouch-belly, despite his otherwise lean form. He and Saxon shared only each other's company. They spoke in low tones that seemed so foreign as to be another language. At moments they were as still as statues. Other times they rose up from the ground, smacking parts of their bodies with the palms of their hands, striking out at the air as if warring with swarms of unseen insects.

They were a mystery to William, until Lemuel explained that they were Gullah people from the Sea Isles of the Carolinas. They lived isolated lives of incredible labor. They'd formed a culture unique unto themselves, with their own language, their own customs, their own blending of Christian and Moslem and tribal African faiths. It was said that they practiced black arts as powerful as any Haitian magic, blood rituals that called upon the undead to aid the living. Watching those two, William could well believe it. He found, despite himself, that he was curious about what they might know, what tools of evil they might have at their disposal.

"Now, I ain't saying there was never a good body come off them islands," Lemuel said, "but they got they own ways and not all of them ways is Christian. Listen at night and you'll hear them trying to work themselves up a voodoo to get themselves free. It never has worked, far as I can tell. But they sure keeping the faith. Whatever faith they got."

William watched the two men. They sat on the other side of the pen, touching at the shoulder, eyes closed and heads tilted up toward the sun. "Wouldn't turn the Devil down," he said, "not if he could get me outta here."

"You wanna be careful getting in bed with Satan," Lemuel said. "Tell me this, you ever met a white person you thought belonged in Heaven? You haven't, have you? Maybe some child, but that's not what I'm talking bout. Talking bout a full grown adult. Man or woman, don't make no difference. Ain't many of them getting to Heaven, not by my tally. If them white folks ain't in Heaven where is they?" The man pulled his eyes away from the two men and set them on William.

"Hell, I suppose."

"That's what I make of it, too. They in Hell. Now, do you want to spend forever with a bunch of evil white folks? It's hard enough just living this life in they company. Naw, I wouldn't get in company with the Devil. There's got to be a better way. It'll be shown to us one day. How'd you get yourself up in here, anyway?"

William lowered his head and studied the ground. Just the act of the man's asking reminded him of Oli, of his own loose tongue and the events that followed. He tried to answer the question vaguely, saying he was running and done got caught. But Lemuel pushed him for details. William answered one question at a time, and in so doing soon found himself well into his own story, one that seemed long and sordid already, blurred between dream and reality and plagued by mistakes.

When he concluded, Lemuel sat for a moment nodding his head. "Well, you done made a mess of it," he said.

That wasn't the response William had expected. He tried to think of some way to refute the statement. He picked a twig and bent it into a strained curve. Finally, he just said, "You can go to hell."

Lemuel took this statement seriously and answered in a different tone than before, softer, more open. "Don't think I'm littling you. That ain't my intention. You living a world a pain and I know that pain. All us round here know it. I ain't littling you. I'm just saying you slipped up. Had freedom in your path and first chance you got you gave it away for a meal and a little whiskey. It hurts, don't it? That's some expensive whiskey—the kind that costs a man his freedom."

William snapped the twig and tossed the two ends away. "Don't tell me what I lost. You don't know the first thing bout it. You wouldn't talk that way if you'd ever gotten a child in a woman." He made to rise, but the older man stayed him with an outstretched hand.

"Now, that there—I'll tell you what it puts me in the mind of," Lemuel said, "the time Abram asked God why he didn't have no children and what was to become a him being childless. Come on now, sit yourself. Ain't gonna harm you just to listen. Now, Lord took Abram outside and told him to look up at the sky and count the stars. Said, '*Look now toward Heaven*,' and if he could count all them stars then he would know how many children would come from him and how fruitful his seed would be on into eternity. I'd tell you the same, I would. I say look up and when you see them stars know that you too go on. They your children, and your children's children and on like that. You may never put your hands on them and pull them to you in this life, but you can look up and know they out there waiting for you and some day you'll be together with them. That's what I do. Cause, nigga, I got more children out in the world than I can number on my fingers. And not one them would know my face to call me papa."

William stared at the man. "Don't know whether you're coming or going," he finally said.

Lemuel grinned. "That's right. That's the way I like it. Keep em all guessing."

William didn't rise again, but he did turn away from Lemuel and sat with his back to him. From this angle his eyes fell on a pregnant girl. She was tiny, with a child's round face, still incomplete in her body's development. As with Dante, William tried not to look at her, but his eyes kept wandering back to her. She sat within the shadow of a tiny alcove, a space offered to her in kindness. But she was never comfortable. Her belly seemed to be the center of her, all thoughts and pain and emotion contained in that great swelling. She rolled her body from one side to the other, sat up and then lay down, all the while squinting out at the world.

Later that evening he lay listening to the rhythm of the girl's moaning. It began slowly and almost faintly enough to ignore. But as the dusk faded into night and the moon rose her cries did as well. The compound was as still as ever it had been. Even the two Sea Islanders were silent and motionless. This evening, it seemed, was too sacred for the invocation of spells. Into this calm the woman's calls rose up and reached out like open hands. They grabbed the listeners by the throats and held them until the moments of agony passed. The light of the new moon was so bright, and William's senses so heightened, that he could see the girl and the women who attended her. She stood with a woman at either arm. She hung between them in the peaceful moment, limp and breathing. But when the contractions returned her body tensed from head to toe and she bowed with the wave rolling over her.

Dante, sitting nearby, said, "That baby gonna kill her." He sat with his damaged arms cradled in his lap, but his eyes were fixed on the girl, watching every second of her labor. "You think she all right?"

"She all right," Lemuel said. "You never heard a woman give birth before? It's always a God-almighty pain."

"But she just a little thing," Dante said. "Big boy-child might bust her. My momma died in the bearing. Not me but the child after me. Got stuck up in there the wrong way. I re-member the night it happened. Was a summer night like . . ."

"Hush, boy," Lemuel hissed. He touched his forehead with his fingertips, found the scar and then pulled his hand away, as if he were checking that the old wound was still there. "We don't need to hear that mess. Not right now. You set your mind on better thoughts than that."

They were still for a few minutes. As if invited by their silence, another contraction took hold of the girl. The muscles of her bare arms stood out as she clenched her aids; the contours of her neck flexed when she tilted her head to the sky; her teeth glinted like tiny weapons raised against the night. William didn't speak, but he found the display just as disturbing as Dante. It was hard to imagine Dover going through such pain, frightening to think that in life there was always the threat of death. He wondered who the father of the girl's child was. It was clear he wasn't within this pen. But what sort of man was he? Had he loved that girl-mother as one does a wife, or had he simply used her?

For all of the noise and pain the girl's labor was actually quite short. William didn't see the conclusion of it. Clouds hid the moon and the women circled the girl, blocking out his view. He turned his eyes to the sky and tried not to listen and not to think and not to care. But then the moment came and the woman's cries stopped and silence lingered, a thing as black as the night and as full of danger. Then a new cry floated up into it, that new being's plaintive call, its high-pitched, trembling complaint. When that moment came tears appeared and crept from the corners of William's eyes and fell to the ground. He felt for that woman, for that child, for the small part of God's heart that allowed for such moments, a feeling which he didn't name but which was as painful as it was joyful. He was full to the brim with an emotion just kinder than rage, and with a longing for his own loved ones, the desperate hope that someday he might hear the same cries and know that in them he was perpetuated. In this he was not alone, and his tears were not alone.

WILLIAM'S MOTHER HAD TOLD HIM the story of his birth many times. It became his first memory, an event he relived over and over again through her perspective. Until he was old enough to refuse, Nan would lie with him in bed, arms close around him, her long, black hair tickling his shoulders and neck. Although the palms of her hands were as rough as any field laborer's, the skin along the undersides of her arms was of a softness he would never forget. She spoke quietly, telling him what it was like to have had him within her, to have felt him moving against her from the inside. Some women, she said, gave birth right in the fields, labored as they labored, only pausing long enough to push the child out of their body. "I's too soft for that, baby. You hurt me something crazy. Took hours to get you out." She remembered every minute of those hours, the way the pain gripped her, the way the crown of his head pushed her open, wide, wide like she had never been before, and never would be again. She said that she dreamed of being in labor years afterward, and she always began those dreams in fear. Who or what was this creature within her? It could've been anything, so unnatural seemed the pain of its coming. "But," she said, "them dreams never turned bad. Every time it's just you. Every time I see you come up out of me I know it could only ever be you. You a gift from your daddy to me."

He was sure that no other boy-child had ever been told such things by his mother. It embarrassed him even before he understood why. But she often embarrassed him with her love, and confused him with the righteous complexity of her thoughts. To his young mind she seemed to be a swirl of contradictions. One moment she spoke of the bonds between loved ones as all-important; the next she demanded self-reliance in his every act and deed. One morning she would preach acceptance of their position as slaves; and yet by the evening she might become a fount of verbal disobedience. She sometimes found beauty in the work of her hands, in the splendor of nature, in the sunset-light waving across the fields. Other times she punished her fingers for giving their gifts up for other people's pleasure, crushed flowers with her bare feet, tossed up curses to the power that spread such rarified light across a land so filled with grief.

The evening after his interview with Howard Mason, Nan returned from work and called William to her. She took him by the hand and walked with him back to the strange structure they lived in, a shack built around the base of a tree just beyond slave row. She sat him down, took the apple from his hand and set a piece of corn bread before him. She asked what Mason had said. William repeated the man's words as best he could, jumbling the biblical lore completely, but honing in on the substance of the man's point.

"And whatchu think of all that mess?"

"Dunno," the boy said. As his mother was silent, he added, "Had him a Bible he read from."

"A Bible, huh? That's just a book writ down by some white men to explain themselves to themselves. Don't be fool enough to study on no Bible. I'll show you what to study on."

She grabbed him by the wrist and pulled him through the woods. She led him around the far corner of slave row, within a stone's throw of Fishing Creek, through the grove of stunted cherry trees, and on to the plot of land reserved for the Negro dead. It was an area no different than other wooded patches, but to William's eyes the place was one of unnatural threat. To him, the trees seemed particularly gnarled. They twisted into shapes that were nearly human. The boughs above cast a thicker darkness, and the tall grasses caressed his legs. He knew the lore of this place as well as any child, the tales of headless beings, of angry slaves walking the earth undead at certain hours of the night, of spirits called forth by the living to wreak havoc on their enemies.

"You see this here?" she asked, pointing at the spot that William knew to be his father's grave. "This here your daddy. He in the ground just here, in the nigger plot. But he wasn't no nigger, was he? What was he?"

William's gaze touched on his father's weathered cross, a bone-white thing that seemed to be fashioned of the same material as the skeletal remains it marked. He stared at it like he was watching it for the minutest movement, searching for signs that the being buried below it was stirring. He dreamed of just such things sometimes. The earth peeled back on itself and up rose a gaunt, worm-eaten person, ivory-skinned and glowing in the night. He called William's name and labeled him as kin and demanded some blood penance of him, a ritual never completed but which began when the man's fingernails pierced the skin of his wrists and began to peel the flesh away.

"What was he?" his mother asked again.

"White man," he said.

"That's right. He was a white man. What's he doing buried with all these slaves then?"

William didn't answer. He knew that she was about to tell him whether he answered or not.

"He here cause he was a good man," she said. "Cause he loved me like a wife and you like a son. He wasn't afraid of that love. Had his own mind and spoke it. If you got a true mind in you, you don't need to read from some old dead men's words. You speak up with your own mouth and speak what you see and what you know from looking at the world around you. You hear?"

Nan knelt down beside him. She took both of his hands in hers and forced him to look up at her. Her skin was just a shade darker than chestnut; her eyes cast of the same color and quality. There was a fullness to her features—a pout to her lips, a roundness to her high cheekbones. Her face, before her son's, had been tempered by a clash of cultures. She told him, as she had done many times before, that his father had been a good man. He had seen the world with clear eyes. He had loved and been good to her and had abandoned the privileges of his race to luxuriate in that love. He was a foreigner, yes, but this was a country being built by foreigners. He had come here poor as any slave, but he had chosen her over his own prosperity, had found a greater reason for living and had so produced him, William. If he had lived their lives would have been different. She wouldn't have had to tell him these things because he would've seen his father and known him with his own eyes. That's the first and main thing she wished she could change about the past.

"But there ain't no curse on you, at least not a curse put on by God," she said. "You got good blood in you, boy. Never disbelieve it. The blood of a man what loved you before you were born. Got good blood, on your father's side and on mine. Look at me . . . Ain't I beautiful? Ain't you proud I'm your momma? Tell me, you proud of me?"

William fixed his eyes on her collarbone. He wasn't scared anymore. He wasn't thinking about ghosts or spirits or death. His mother's question replaced those things. He wanted to pull his hands from her grasp and step back, for the air close to her was hard to breathe, as if she were sucking it all in and away from him. But even as he thought this his view of her collarbone went blurry. His eyes flushed red and his bottom lip began to tremble, alive with an emotion he hadn't known he had within him. One second he wanted to run from her; the next he knew that he would never, never do that. She was everything that he had ever been, ever needed or loved or ever would, and of course he was proud of her. "Yeah."

"Yeah what?"

"Momma . . ." He tried to hide his face against her neck, but she wouldn't let him.

"Tell me, yeah what?"

"Yeah, I proud."

Nan tilted the boy's face up toward hers. Tears tumbled from his eyes and streaked his cheeks. She studied him for a moment, then pulled him to her. He never forgot the things she said, nor the feel of her arms around him, nor the smell of her skin. He didn't doubt that she loved him or that she was something special or that she had lessons to teach. But at a base level behind all of that, he did doubt her story of his father. There never was such a man. There never could be such a man. No man he had ever known was so created. He knew the truth. His father was a ghoul, and Nan was only trying to shelter him from the shame of it.

Eight

From the slave quarters the hound followed the trail with little difficulty. Her great canine nose snuffed up the faintest traces of scent from leaf matter, ground or even out of hollowed depressions filled only with still air. She ran through the marshlands eager and loud. She darted through reeds and across boggy ground and through woodlands bordered by farms. She was nearly distracted more than once. But, ever mindful of her position, she kept her nose down and tried to ignore the signs of other sport, markings of other canines, smells of as-yet-untried victuals. For his part, Morrison trudged along at a wolf-run, walking at times and jogging at times and kicking up into a run when his body allowed.

In the evenings the two sat beside the tiniest of fires and shared out their food and ate like equals. This land brought back memories that the man did not care for, bits and pieces of his first days on this continent and the hardships that time had brought. And his thoughts sometimes went even further back, all the way to the land of his birth. He had been born in northern Scotland in the early years of the nineteenth century. In his youth he had a family about him that he loved dearly. A younger brother like a shadow behind him, a wee sister who tottered on her pins, a mother grown gaunt by her troubles, and a father who slept sitting up and breathed loud in the night, whom he adored with an unreasoning affection. Theirs was a hard life as tenant farmers in a land of stony soil, a country of wind and of rain that came sideways like a stampede. They were chilled in the summer and cold in the changing of seasons and near frozen in the winter. But for all that it was a beautiful land, a tragic country that bore the scars of men's sins across its flesh, peopled by a spirited race that he seldom had reason to be ashamed of.

In his fourteenth year the landowner compared the profits offered him by his tenants with the profits offered by filling the land with sheep. The four-legged creatures paid far better, and such simple arithmetic was all he needed to turn his mind. Men came upon the family one morning, armed and angry and quick in their work. They set the house to torch and pushed them out with the things they could carry. It was as simple as that. After that, they worked where they could, lived how they could. They farmed a sorry plot, a rutted and sandy landscape that provided never a flat spot, but instead torqued and pitched at ever more bizarre angles, the purpose of which seemed only to crash down into the sea in new and unusual ways. Morrison and his brother fished straight from the cliffs and climbed the crags in search of bird eggs and even waded in the pools prying limpets from the cold rocks. But they never ate enough, never slept enough, and the wee girl's nose never stopped running. It ran so steady and undisturbed that her upper lip grew painful to the touch. One morning they awoke to find her cold and calm and finally forgiven. In the weeks of mourning after this, the father too gave in. The mother and her two boys made their way to Aberdeen and collapsed there amongst the granite foundations of the place. The mother became a gaunt wraith of a woman, a simple, pale sheet of skin thrown over her bones. She got what work she could gutting herring, but it was no use. She had no spirit within her anymore. Eventually, she too lay down and did not rise except for the exertions of the two remaining sons, who carried her away and aw her into the ground themselves.

In their days alone in Aberdeen the two brothers had been all and everything for each other, for in that place there was little of the kinship they'd known in their youth. It was a fight for survival, each to his own, one man pitted against the next. This was a lesson the boys learned quickly. They awoke each morning as if they had shared the same dreams. They labored each day at the same work, wore the same clothes as if each item was held in trust between them, and they ate together from the same bowl in the evenings, trying with their loud slurping to make the food more than it was. At night they slept one entwined around the other, finding in this lover's embrace just enough warmth to see them through to the next day. And it was there in that tiny room that the two brothers devised their plan and set about to see it made real.

In Morrison's twenty-fifth year the two brothers earned the money for their fares. He was no longer a boy. He was a man and had seen things to make him old beyond his years. When he quit the land of his birth he did so with a bitter heart. He asked God to damn the place, for the sea to swallow it, and for each and every *landowner to choke on his own bile. They journeyed afoot to Greenock and boarded an ancient ship so frail it had to be bound together with a great chain that ran from the deck under the hull and back again. It was not meant for human cargo. It had made the eastbound journey from America loaded with lumber. And as she made the crossing afloat they decided to up the wager and sail her back. But there was no wood to head that direction. Neither could it be tea or cloth or spices, as the hull of the ship was awash with water and so valuable a cargo would be sorely missed if it went to the bottom of the sea. So they sailed north and loaded her full of a coarser freight, the teuchter, the Highland Scot, for if they were to perish who would mourn whom wasn't already in mourning?*

When the ship first floated free of the dock it groaned and protested. The vessel left behind all memory of land and climbed through a range of waves and troughs. Morrison tried to rock back and forth with the ship's movements. For the first hours, he thought he had found the rhythm of it, but then discovered that he was working against it. He moved this way, while the ship moved that. And when he tried to find reason in the thing and change his time he found that there was no time. There was no reason. That was the trick of it. And so the sickness began. It was a new sound in the darkness—the retching, the coughing and the moaning. Filth dripped from the chins around him. It fell heavy on the boards, rushed upon his nostrils and sent him heaving like the rest. And these were not the only trials on that ship. There was the hunger. There was the pickpocket who rooted in the younger brother's jacket with little care because he deemed him already dead. There were the lice that swarmed across them and the rats that stayed hidden until the passengers had no strength to beat them away. And there was the catalogue of the dead, those who went into the sea with prayers carried away on the waves.

Seven weeks after beginning their journey they laid eyes upon the coastline of America. But in truth, they never reached their true destination, the Cape Fear of North Carolina, the place to which many of their Gaelic-speaking kinsmen had preceded them. Instead, they were put ashore in a quiet cove of the Chesapeake. The hatch opened and they were summoned up at musket-point and put to land along the quiet, wooded shore. The two brothers stood on the beach with the others, some thirty-five of them, watching the long boat row back out to the ship. They were left with no explanation, no provisions, no directions. They knew only that it was American soil beneath their feet, and that the great bay before them bore a name none of them could yet pronounce.

Of that original group only twenty found their way to the settlements. The rest dropped off along the way of one fever or another, from hunger and fatigue, weakened by relentless mosquito attacks, skin blistered by the southern sun. The two brothers dragged each other through the marshland. They pushed through reeds and walked over ground so boggy that they sank into it with each step. They spent the nights sitting back-to-back, looking up at the stars and trying, through their own conversation, to drown out the din of unknown insects. Through much of the trek the younger brother wept. Morrison wrapped his arm around him and propped him up and the two took some measure of strength from each other. And it was in this way— connected at the shoulders—that they returned to the world of the living. They saw one fisherman sail past at a distance on the water, and then another tacking into the wind. Then a farmer and his dog rose up from the landscape as if they'd just climbed out of the earth itself. They stared at the newcomers with all the wonder they might have shown at the Second Coming. This was how the two brothers arrived in this country and laid eyes on their first *friendly face. It was quite a memory, one that hadn't dimmed with the passing years, one that the tracker was daily amazed to discover anew.*

As they continued the hunt, Morrison and the hound circumnavigated Baltimore, moved away from the Bay and up into a hilly country cut into plots of woodland and farm and occasional towns. They followed the fugitive's scent through a range of pine forests and down onto a road and along it for a good distance. Around noon a couple weeks into their search Morrison bounded up behind the hound, who had stopped still in the middle of two deep wagon ruts. The canine stood dejected and ashamed, and the man knew that she had lost the scent.

Nine

The march began that Friday. The slaves' chains were checked and rearranged in the morning light. William was bound by a short length of iron links between his ankles. His arms were likewise fastened together and connected by the wrists to Lemuel. They all wore collars that were chained to the persons in front of and behind them. They were forced to march in two groups of ten, shuffling close behind the person before them, with their arms tugged to the side by the pull of the person next to them. They were pushed to move quickly, but the chains hampered their steps and often somebody stumbled, causing momentary havoc in the lines. William struggled to keep from stepping on the ankles of the woman before him, but soon the woman's bare heels were thick with congealed blood. Try as he might, he couldn't help but kick her with the hard toes of his brogans.

They were driven by five men: one who walked in front, three on horseback spread throughout the line, and one other who drove the food wagon. One was a Frenchman who spoke a languid dialect of Southern English, punctuated with French inflections; another was a stringy man from whose beard perpetual streams of tobacco-stained saliva dripped; the third, the man who drove the supply wagon, conveyed his thoughts primarily through profanity. The fourth driver was a tall boy with reddish hair. He pulled up the rear in silence and looked as though he was suspicious of all men, white or black. They were poor whites who took from this job a poor man's pleasure—that of trafficking in the souls of those even less fortunate than themselves. They were quick to curse a slave's slow progress, quick to cuff and to kick and to threaten. And they were thirsty men. They pulled hard on their jugs and came away from them squinting and blurry eyed from the alcohol they contained. William was sure that if it hadn't been for the sweat and the toil of their work, each one of the men would have fallen down drunk from the amount they consumed. As it was, the drink only blackened their moods. They complained of headaches and damned the sweat that stung their eyes and sometimes stumbled over irregular ground, but they never tired of refilling their jugs.

Among them, only the leader carried himself with a military bearing. He sat straight-backed in his saddle, rifle near at hand, watching all with eyes keen to seek out dissent in either the slaves or the drivers. If he tolerated the men's drinking, it was because such was the way of these people. It was a drinking country, and they were the drinkers of the nation. He alone surveyed all with sober eyes, and this seemed enough to satisfy him. The slaves were bound and bound again. This journey was routine, the chattel below him not so different than other animals he might be asked to herd.

The wagon driver sometimes fell behind them, but always passed them during the course of the day and had camp started for the evening. In what appeared to be a gesture of mercy, the young mother and her infant were allowed to ride in the wagon. The woman was naked from the waist up, chained by the wrists and fastened to eyebolts in the wagon bed. She was barely more than a child herself, with slim shoulders and small breasts that were round and taut with milk. Her eyes studied her baby, never lifting to meet the gazes of the other slaves or to take in the world as a whole. She sat cradling the child, nursing it, speaking to it in quiet tones that William couldn't make out. He couldn't see the baby, wrapped as it was in a stained cotton blanket, and he found himself longing to see the infant's newly formed features. He wondered if a child born into such a world showed any sign of understanding it. Did he or she know what life held in store for them, or was it always to be a cruel surprise?

By midday the voice of an older slave in the other group had become familiar to them all. He spoke encouraging words, hummed them almost, as if the simple directions he gave were hymns meant for a church gathering. He begged them to find a rhythm to their marching, to walk in time with one another, to feel the same breath within them and to share it between them. He urged them not to fight the march. "Lord no, don't fight it. Don't fight each other. Instead be the many limbs of a single being." His words must have helped, for in listening to him William realized the day was passing.

They camped that evening near a wooded creek well populated with frogs. The creatures set up a ruckus as the day dimmed and carried on long into the night, a croaking chorus with no discernible rhythm and yet somehow musical. The drivers, having doubly secured the slaves, plied themselves with even greater concentrations of liquor. They drained the whiskey keg straight into their tin cups and took the spirit undiluted. They bantered among themselves for some time, while the slaves sat just a few feet away, each hoping that the night would pass without further incident, each knowing that was unlikely. And indeed, before long the men's revelry turned to distraction and desire. They chose a woman from among the slaves, unchained her and pulled her from the others. William looked away as they shoved her toward the back of the supply wagon. He set his head down, his temple flat on the dry ground, eyes open and staring out at a canted world. He was relieved when Lemuel began speaking, a low whisper but close enough to be heard.

"One time . . ." the older man said. "This was back a good few years now. Had me an errand to do one afternoon." His voice was softer now than William had ever heard it, though not from stealth. He didn't speak as if he sought to conceal his words, but he seemed to have little breath with which to pronounce them. It was a cool afternoon, he said. He had come up a hillside and stood at the summit with the breeze against his face, the sweet kiss of it something he felt was meant for him alone at that moment. He dropped down into the next valley light on his feet, happy almost. And it was this joy that caused him to alter his normal course. He left the road and cut out through the woods, losing himself within the tree trunks. Only a momentary excursion, but one that reminded him of what it was like to experience the world with free eyes.

"That's how come I found them. Was three Negro boys and a girl."

He hadn't known what they were doing at first, but as he drew nearer it became all too clear. They couldn't've been no older than eleven or twelve. The boys had her pinned to the ground. From their seminude states it was clear that each planned to use her sexually. She struggled against them, but the boys were strong and fervent. One grabbed her by the hair and hitched up her skirt and fumbled to find his way into her backside. The sight sent Lemuel into a rage. He ran toward them and kicked that boy with a brogan hard into his face. He grabbed another and yanked his arm loose; tripped the last and sent him sprawling. Before he knew it he had a piece of half-decayed wood in his hands. He was lashing at the boys, throwing fists and jabbing, momentarily intent on killing them all, perhaps even the girl for the part she played in this.

"There I was beating them," Lemuel whispered. "Crazed about it. Like I wanted them children dead. Like the crime they was doing to each other was worse than any done to them. That's how it felt."

But then, in the length of time it took for him to raise his hand in the air, he realized that even in this crime these children were each a victim. They were acting out scenes they'd witnessed before. They were using violence and sex as men had taught them, as much a part of the institution in which they were bound as chains and whips. They were criminals, yes, but in their crime they punished themselves. "And I knew they would hurt themselves like that forever. Not just them boys, I mean, but all of us. All of us that have to live with these things."

Lemuel was silent for a moment, but the pause seemed to make him uneasy. "So how do you live with that?" he asked. "Tell you what I do. I make for myself a string-together life. You take all the fine moments of your life. Eating honey from a cone. Cool stream water on your naked toes. Fireflies lighting a summer evening. Two children tagging and chasing each other. You take them fine moments and you pull them close and string them like a necklace of shells. In the bad times you hold on to them and remember all the reasons God gave you life in the first place. It's what you hold onto that makes a life, so hold onto joy and let go the rest. Understand? Let go of nights like this, put it behind you and wait for the better times."

The two lay in silence, and before long that silence was once more punctuated by the sounds that Lemuel's voice had blotted out. Sometime later, William felt the pull of the chains around his feet. They were yanked and shifted as the woman was refastened. He didn't turn to look. He wanted to. He wanted somehow to reach out with his eyes and comfort her, but he didn't trust himself to convey the message properly. Instead, he shut his eyes and prayed for sleep to numb him.

He awoke later in the night and asked, "It's what you remember that matters?" He was surprised at himself, but the question escaped him before he knew it. He wasn't even sure that Lemuel was awake until the man answered.

"That's what I believe."

"Then which thing you remember better? Standing on that hill with a breeze on your face? Or the sight of them boys on that girl? You remember the joy, or the anger?"

The older man didn't answer.

THE NEXT DAY WAS A REPEAT of the one that came before, distinguished only because William had memories of that previous day and therefore this must be another. That evening they camped in a fallow clearing next to a cornfield. Bats appeared in the fading light, first a single bullet and then another, then a whole storm of them cutting the sky with their erratic, reasonless flights. Late that night he woke to a beautiful star-filled sky. He lay staring up at it, for a moment forgetting the discomfort of his fetters. He listened to the chorus of breathing around him. So many nasal voices exhaling up into the air, blending with the night calls of insects. It reminded him of Dover's house, where, like now, bodies lay close to one another.

When he first noticed the other noise he realized it had long been part of the night, a background sound indistinguishable from the rest and nearly disguised. But it was different. It was a quiet grinding, occasionally interrupted by the clink of iron on iron. He rose up on his elbow. His eyes went first to the guard on duty. It was the tobacco-chewer. He sat leaning against the base of a tree, a shotgun cradled in his lap. The brim of his hat shaded his face from the starlight, and for a moment William thought the man was staring at him. But as he didn't move or respond in the slightest, William realized he was sleeping. The sound continued, a little louder now that his head was raised. He craned his body around and looked over toward Lemuel. That's when he saw them. The two men lay half-prone. Even in the dim light he knew who they were: Saxon and his companion. They seemed to be engaged in some delicate work, the little one especially. He leaned in closer to the object than Saxon, and his shoulders moved backwards and forwards, like a man working with a tiny saw.

As if feeling the touch of his eyes, the two men stopped their work. Their heads turned toward William in unison. There was little expression in their faces, neither threat nor surprise, nor any message that William could discern. He held their gazes for a moment, then looked away and lowered himself back down as if to sleep. A few moments later he heard the noise again.

He closed his ears to it and looked up at the sky. He tried to think of nothing, but instead found himself thinking of many things: a flock of pigeons that had once darkened the sky from horizon to horizon in passing, a child from his youth who'd been his companion but was lost to him now, the shape of Dover's back viewed from the side, with candlelight warm on her contours. He remembered all these things and many more, but eventually his mind settled on the limbs of the tree that had supported his childhood house. Nan told him that the tree house had been his father's idea. That white man had dreamed it. He pleaded with Nan's master for permission to build it, striking a bargain wherein he gave much of his own labor into the man's service. He became a slave of sorts, so that he might live as man and wife with another slave. Though he knew little of housing construction, he set himself to the study of it. He couldn't pay for proper lumber and made do with cast-offs from the mill. No two boards were ever of the same length or thickness. He accepted oak or pine or even lesser woods, and he used what tools he could borrow or rent. They were rough implements whose functions he learned or invented to suit his needs. He worked early in the morning and late in the evening, constructing around and into that great tree a strange, squat structure that seemed part of the tree itself. It was filled with cracks and weaknesses and was lopsided in a variety of ways. But for all that it did have its own charm. It didn't take life too seriously, and yet it had as its central pillar a living tree so old it predated white settlement of the Chesapeake. Off to one side were the glistening waters of a harbor, and in the opposite direction lay the Bay itself. In summer what breeze there was found its way to the house, and in winter there was just enough shelter to break the force of the gales. The house suited Nan and she loved her white man for having been its architect. She used to tell her boy-child that if fate had been different he and his father would have fished together from the beach. On starlit nights they might have sat on the shore and watched the play of light across the water. If fate had allowed them a little peace, life just might have been tolerably beautiful.

But William couldn't feel the same way. As much as he loved his mother, he could not share in her adoration of this man. He had no image of him, no drawing or engraving. They had never spent those idyllic evenings fishing together. He was a man composed of nothing save Nan's words. And on this her words were not enough. They lived in a world divided by race. Of course, he knew of many violations across the color lines, but these were crimes of lustful owners upon the owned. That was very different to the tale of love between the races that his mother claimed. There was nothing in it that he could twin with the world around him.

William tried to roll to his other side, but was trapped by his chains and couldn't complete the motion. He shook his head to clear it. Yes, he wanted the memory of that house, but he wanted nothing to do with the man who had built it. He lay there thankful that the man had died seven months after completing that house, starved to death by his own frozen jaw.

THROUGHOUT THE MORNING of the third day a haze hung in the shallow valleys. Only the insects seemed undeterred by the humidity. Their calls rose with a staccato brilliance unparalleled by the visible landscape. They seemed not to belong to this land. Yet they were as integral a part of the countryside as the dust-fine dirt and the tilled fields and their distant workers. They marched through a town of slack-jawed inhabitants who watched the slaves pass from the shade of porches and storefronts. At the far edge of the town a white man sat in a wagon with an old Negro in the bed behind him. The Negro watched the group passing with somber eyes. Before they progressed he spoke words of encouragement and a reminder that the Lord awaits them all and will judge them all in their season and that patience and faith are the things He looks for foremost. The white man turned on hearing this, brought the butt end of his whip down on the speaking man's head and commenced to beat him senseless. The coffle marched on.

Around midmorning they climbed the bare back of a

ridgeline and entered a woodland of crab apple and sugar maple. A few minutes into the shade the Frenchman, who walked ahead of the group by some fifty yards, stopped and stared at something at his feet. He lifted his rifle high, held it a moment, then slammed the butt end of it down on the ground. When the tobacco-chewer reached him, he reined in his horse, leaned over its shoulder, and peered down. The two exchanged some words. The first of the slaves bunched up behind them and slowed. The leader ribbed his horse forward a few steps, leaving William with a perfect view of all that was to follow.

"What is it?" the leader called, but the others were not to have time to answer.

The little man bound to Saxon twisted his wrists and shed the cuffs from both his hands. He reached for the chain attached to his neck and ripped it from his collar with one yank. From where William stood, it seemed he had rendered the iron of his cuffs suddenly molten, with no more strength than soft clay. It made no sense, such a simple action but one so profound in its effect. The links dropped into a swinging arch, free on one end. They were soon snapped taut by Saxon's wrists, to which they were still fast. The giant held his arms stiff-limbed before him and swung them up just as the tobacco-chewer turned. The links wrapped around the white man's head and yanked him from the saddle. He hit the ground hard on his shoulder but didn't come free of the stirrup. He dangled there with a leg entrapped and the horse in a frenzy. The white man's head snapped and jerked with blows from the horse's hooves. His hands slapped at the stirrup but could make no sense of it. An instant later he was hiding his face. The next his arms hung limp around him. The little one used the Frenchman's moment of confusion against him. He was behind him in a second, even with his feet still bound, and he took him out at knee level, laying him flat on his back. William couldn't see just what he was doing to him—crouched down as he was, staring wide-mouthed, full of terror and euphoria both—but he seemed to have the white man gripped about the neck. Another slave, the one who ate dirt, hobbled over to the two, pulling a portion of the line with him, and prepared to jump on the Frenchman's lower body.

The leader pulled his rifle from its scabbard and lifted it to sight, an action that inspired motion in all the slaves. They pressed themselves against the ground, squirming and pulling each other in chaotic directions and therefore moving nowhere. The leader's first shot tore into the dirt-eater's shoulder, taking with it the workings of the shoulder joint and leaving his arm dangling limp from what flesh remained. The boy stood stunned, staring at his injury, until another shot took him in the chest and ended all such contemplation. The white man was shouting out to all, white and black both, commanding order and action and calm. He might have prevailed even then, but Saxon swung his chains up into motion again. He was a good twenty yards from the horseman, but he moved with startling speed. He dragged those connected to his neck chain in his wake. The teen just behind him fought against him for a few futile seconds. Then he moved forward crouched just behind the big man, his eyes flashing with fear.

The leader backed his horse and tried to stay calm. He balanced his spent rifle on the horn of his saddle and reached for his revolver. He had trouble getting it free. All the time his mount backed and shied and Saxon came on steadily. The white man got his revolver free, but as he brought it up to aim his horse reared up and his shot went wide. The horse found this more disturbing yet. It twirled. The man's head became entangled within the low branches of a tree. As he fought to free himself he misfired again. The horse balked, yanking the man to the side of the saddle. So he was when Saxon reached him: arms fighting with the tree, legs frantic in their grip on the horse, he losing at both efforts. The black man swung up his chains and caught the man's torso. The horse bolted, snapping the man's forearm between two branches before he gave up the saddle. He hung for a few frantic seconds in the air, then fell. Saxon was instantly on top of him.

The little man rose to his feet and pulled the Frenchman up with him, the latter barely able to stand. Saxon stepped toward him as if to steady him, but instead brought his two fists down hard across his face and smashed the bridge of his nose. The man dropped to his knees, shouting for mercy in the name of God. This only fueled the black man's rage. Saxon turned, snatched up the tobacco-chewer's rifle and dropped to his knees. He placed the weapon at the base of the Frenchman's throat, stared into the white man's face for a few seconds, then pulled the trigger. A spray of dark moisture sprang from the top of his head, followed by larger bits of solid matter. They all surged up in silhouette, caught before the background of the green summer afternoon. The Frenchman collapsed. Saxon threw down the firearm and began rifling through his clothes and pockets. Finally, he pulled a knife out of a sheath tied to the man's ankle. He measured its weight in his hand. He tested the edge, then leaned close and tilted the point of the knife into his flesh.

William wanted to look away. There was a wild beating of hooves behind him. He knew without looking that they came from the boy's horse, riding not into the action but away at breakneck speed. He tried to make his eyes move, to turn his body, to twist his neck. But his whole being betrayed him. He watched as Saxon sliced the man's flesh in-line with his jaw, behind the ears and up along the edges of his scalp. He stared as Saxon tossed away the blade, wormed his fingers beneath the edges of the cut and ripped the man's face from his skull. He stood and lifted the flap of flesh on the palm of his hand, like an offering to God. His forearms dripped with the mingled blood of his victim's face and of his own wrists. Then he spoke for the first time.

"Next time they come for me I tell them Saxon not a nigger," he said. "I say, 'Look, look my white man's face.' " He held the Frenchman's face against his own for a second. When he pulled it away his eyes touched on William. His mouth cracked open and he laughed, creating an image William would sleep with that night and many more nights to follow.

With the white men dead, the other slaves searched among their corpses and came up with the keys to unlock themselves. Freed of his chains, Saxon leapt into the saddle of the leader's horse. The mount spun beneath him, wheeled and bucked for a moment, then fell still and accepted him. The little man likewise mounted up. Together they bounded down the lane beneath the low canopy of trees. William followed them with his eyes until the path turned and they disappeared. He stared after them at the space into which they vanished, experiencing a quick progression of emotion: fear, awe and disbelief, wonder and a physical revulsion that twisted his insides into knots. While he stood transfixed the rest of the slaves made fast their escape. He caught movement from the corner of his eye, heard the sounds of bodies crashing through the woods. Within a few moments they all had vanished. He stood alone on the pathway. His chains hung from his wrists. The empty sockets that had once contained Lemuel bumped against his shins.

It took him some time to find motion. In the end the same creatures that had first caused the men to pause spurred him on. He spotted their movements, faint and tiny though they were. He stepped forward through the slashes of blood on the ground, until he realized what he was looking at. Snakes. The Frenchman's rifle butt had smashed the head of a pregnant garter snake, killing her and pinning her flattened skull to the packed soil. But life had not ended with her death. She had been fat and ripe for birth, and her children squirmed out of her still warm body. One after the other: four and then seven and then more than he could count. With their tiny, dead eyes, they were perfect miniatures of the mother. Their motions seemed otherworldly and unnatural, crawling as they were out of a corpse, tongues tasting the air, hungry already. William turned from them and found himself on his knees, heaving up bile from low in his stomach.

AFTER FREEING HIMSELF, William covered several miles before he reached the shores of the lower Bay. It was well into the night, a still evening, close around him. He followed the ragged shoreline to the northwest. Eventually, the woods gave way to geometric shapes of thicker darkness and ground worn smooth by traffic. He crept into the town, keeping to the darker regions, moving the heavy soles of his boots with all the care he could muster. He heard voices off to the left, where the main body of the settlement seemed to be. He moved away from them, careful to slide from shadow to shadow along the shore, never even opening himself to the starlight. In this way he crept along the edge of town and out to the far reaches of the docks.

He still had no clear thought when he stepped onto the planking of the pier. It was lined along most of its edge with cargo. He looked for some sign as to whether it was newly unloaded or was waiting to go out, but he couldn't tell. He sunk between two crates and took his weight off his legs. Once settled, he looked out across the river at the dancing lights cast from the far shore. He could just make out the shape of the houses over there, dwarfed as they were by the thick jumble of trees just behind them. The water was calm; the night sounds muted. The tide lapped at the pylons of the pier. A fish jumped, its body caught in a sliver of silver, a splash of white, then tiny rings echoing across the surface. Strange how tranquil the world could be, the same world that had created the day's bloody scenes. Images that had been kept at bay through motion came back to him. The eyes of the maddened horse, the way the beast's teeth snapped and its hooves smashed crescents into the skull of the man trapped beneath it. The black hole of Saxon's laughing mouth. The Frenchman's brain shot through, with a fan of crimson hung like a sheet upon the summer light. The same man's face upheld and eyeless upon Saxon's palm. The serpents. William closed his eyes and pressed against them with his fingertips as if he could blot out the images with pain.

When he looked up again a shape stood out that he had not noticed before. There was a ship docked at the end of the pier, a medium-size brig, with the short, stout build that marked her as a cargo vessel. There was no light about her, no sign of crew or watchman. He thought this over. He had reached the northern point of the land, and he had no heart for swimming any more. He was sure his legs would pull him straight to the bottom. But if he could climb aboard that ship and find a place to hide . . . There would have to be hidden depths to it, crates and boards and black spaces into which he could twist himself and not be found.

The decision was made. He crept aboard and stole his way far down into the belly of her. He wedged himself in against the backbone of the ship, tight between a moist wooden beam and the corrugated side of some crate. It was a most uncomfortable bedding, and yet he was asleep almost as soon as he closed his eyes. It wasn't until he felt the ship move early the next morning that he wondered where the vessel might be taking him. But by then it was too late, and he had to ride it out. Yes, the boat was moving, but if he rode it out, he thought, if he slept through it, perhaps somehow he would awake to a world less ruled by chaos.

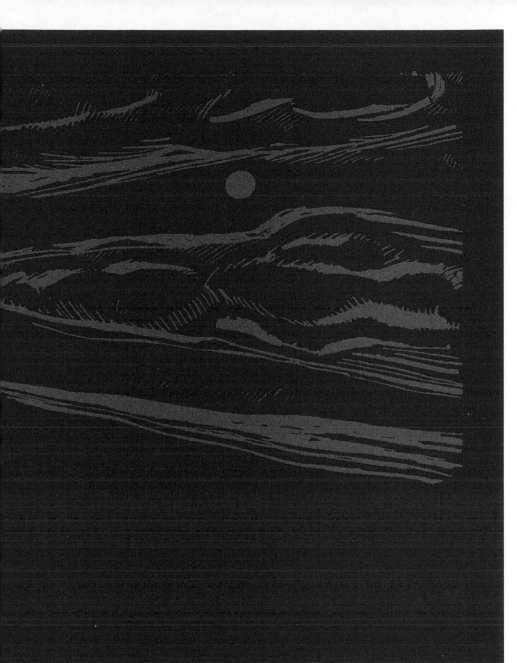

PART TWO

One

*In the weeks after they lost the runaway's scent Morrison and the
hound continued their search by other means. They traveled the
busier roads and stayed in the larger towns. Morrison tried to
think out some logical route for a fugitive across the land's features. He spoke to men on horseback, hitched rides in the back
of wagons and walked along beside fellow pedestrians, asking
everyone about the man he was hunting. He stopped in boarding-
houses and stables, spoke to farmers and even posed his questions
to children. It was hard for him—all this conversing—for he
was not a man for many words.*

    *Something in the process reminded him of his early days in
America: having to learn the landscape, asking strangers for help,
sleeping in barns at the fringes of civilization, the hunger of a
search for something elusive. It was years ago now, but he had not
forgotten. Those first months were as hard on him and his brother
as anything that came before. Their first work was butchering the
carcasses of dead horses at a glue factory. It was coarse work.*

Neither of them had the stomach for it. Neither was adept at treating the parts of a once-living animal like so much fodder for the vat. The younger brother would wake up lashing out at his bedsheets, troubled by dreams of vengeful horses rising up from soup in which they boiled. They quit this work within a fortnight and cleaned chimneys instead, Lewis squeezing himself into small spaces as if he were an urchin of the Glasgow slums. This work singed the clothes and clogged the lungs. Twice the younger brother got himself so wedged in the confined spaces that the older joked that he was stuck fast, at least until the owner saw fit to kindle a fire beneath him. They quit that work before long and found employment as hewers of wood, and then as haulers of manure and, finally, as diggers of graves. It was lonely work, forlorn in its purpose. But it was steady.

As winter set in it was more than that. With the first frosts came new harvests of the dead, the young and the old mostly. The two brothers bundled themselves as best they could against the cold, sewing stray swatches of wool inside their garments, lining their jackets with the cheapest material they could purchase, Negro cloth. Lewis went so far as to wear a triangle of wool on his head, atop which sat a crinkled straw hat which was held in place by a ribbon that ran under his chin. It was a most awkward headdress, and the older brother looked at it with skeptical eyes. But when other laborers poked fun at Lewis, Morrison fashioned for himself a similar hat. Bearing it proudly, he challenged any to offer their jests. They did not. Warmth cometh before pride, he confessed, but pride is a right close second.

By December the ground was a frozen corpse. It was a thick skin that fought against their shovels. Day long they labored at a work that the younger brother called another form of butchery. It was hard on the hands, wearing into them till they were blistered, callous mallets, wooden fingers so stiff one had to flex them with quiet concentration. The younger brother developed a pain in his *torso that sometimes sent jolts like sheet lightning fanning across his back. This was no work that suited him. But it was a life, Morrison said. A life leading to grander things. And that was the way it was between them. Every doubt the younger brother voiced the older shot down. Every fear he unveiled. Every longing for things past he disdained.*

But behind his assured words Morrison's mind reeled unhinged. This land was bursting its seams in a way that had no parallel. It was a land of many tongues, many faces, many nations being boiled down into one. And this did not seem possible. How does a nation contain within itself the English beside the French, Germans beside Swedes, Catholic and Calvin and Quaker all intermingled? How could they exist at the edge of a continent already peopled with men of such a different hue and temperament? And what sense could one ever make of the strange bondage held over the race called Negro? Morrison kept these thoughts mostly to himself, but Lewis couldn't help but speak of his amazement. He admitted that from the first moment he'd laid eyes upon these black people he longed to touch their skin. He wanted to verify beneath his own fingers the nature of the stuff, to confirm that its form and function was the same as his own. He would speak to his brother late at night, asking aloud why God had created humans in such different hues, wondering if there wasn't some puzzle in it, a riddle that mankind was yet to solve. Morrison never answered such questions. He kept his fingers deep within his pockets and told his brother to think of other things. They had enough troubles of their own. Leave the accursed be.

This was why Morrison complained to their employer when a Negro man was partnered with them at their work. He asked him did he think that he and his brother were nothing but slaves? Were they to work the same ground as a black man as if they were equals? This employer was not swayed to sympathy, making it clear that he and his brother could both be replaced if the terms didn't suit them. So Morrison returned to digging. He didn't speak a word to the black man, only gesturing roughly to communicate. But Lewis seemed happy to talk to the slave. Overhearing his conversation, Morrison learned that the black man had been hired to this labor and that his wages went into the hands of his master. Lewis found something in this to remind him of his homeland. He asked his brother if that didn't sound like a Lowland custom, growing rich off the labor of honest men? But Morrison would not be brought into partnership with the Negro. That evening he berated his brother. Did he really think they were so like these niggers? Did he believe they shared anything in common with that flat-faced, mumbling creature? Must he talk with them as if they were equals, for if he acted so then other men would believe so and they'd never fare better than slaves. To most of this the younger brother was silent, and in his silence were the first inklings of dissent.

Early in the new year the Bay froze fast, trapping within it boats and bringing much trade and commerce to a halt. As such, it was a bad time, but as with all aberrations of nature it also invited men to moments of mirth. The brackish water made a strange ice, ridged and translucent and somewhat soft to the touch. It gave way beneath their feet when the two brothers ventured on to it. They stumbled and clutched each other, shouted nervously and listened as the stuff cracked. They had never seen the likes of it before—frozen seawater. They walked out dangerously far, looking back over their shoulders as the black line of the shore grew thin. The younger brother joked that they could run all the way back to Scotland.

The older brother said, Aye, but you'd be daft to try it. Daft and alone you'd be.

But even as he said this he wasn't sure what actions might or might not be called sane. He looked to the distance, at the white, lumpy carpet of the Bay, to the shoreline and the sad conglomeration of houses there, structures he still believed could be blown away should this land ever produce a storm like those of the North Sea. It was a sad picture. That shore was not a shore worth the name. It was a pathetic melding of sand and water. It was hard to tell where one ended and the next began. The land never rose but for the smallest hills, never dipped but for the shallowest of depressions. It was a land meant for the till, aye, but it was a sorry sight compared to the country that bred these brothers. How different was that homeland, where the black waves cast their full bulk upon the rocks, where the two forces engaged in battle. There the sea was the muscle of nature and the shore was a craggy stone wall thrown up against it. The interaction between them was a grand confusion of sound and spray and motion, constant through the day and night. That place was built in bold features, where the land never tired of change, rising from loch to glen to mountain. That was a land. It was harsh in many ways, but one could never mistake it for a sandy rise in the water. And once having seen it, one could never forget it.

Lewis pulled at him then, and the two slipped on the ice and laughed and tried to scrape up chunks of it to throw at each other. In action thought was reprieved, dreams deferred, life moved on. Motion pushed them on, and this, Morrison thought, was good. Neither realized that objects in motion couldn't stay so indefinitely. They must, at some point, collide.

Two

William knew they were coming. He had heard them move about near at hand more than once. He could distinguish them from the rats by their voices if by nothing else. But this time they were closer than before. He tried to slide himself further back between the crates, but there was no place to go. His spine was twisted, his body at a cant, the space so small he couldn't even sit with his shoulders straight. So he paused and waited for them, patient, watching the light of a lamp creep across the beams above him in strange fits and starts.

When the two white men appeared, William just stared at them. They said something. He knew that they were speaking because their mouths moved, but he couldn't hear their words. For a moment he couldn't hear anything. The world had gone quiet. He just watched the men's puzzled faces, knowing that they were questioning him. Eventually, one of the men reached down toward him. His outstretched hand hung in the air, beckoning. William reached up and met the man's grasp.

That's when the spell was broken. The man's palm was callused, warm and very real. Reality spread out of it, down through William's forearm, up his shoulder and into his head, which cleared in an instant. This was no dream. They hoisted him up onto his stiff legs and led him through a maze of crates, wooden beams and shadows. He stumbled in the dark and found himself leaning on the man beside him. He tried to pull away, but just fell against the other man and progressed along supported by one or other of them in turns. They reached a ladder that William ascended by wrapping his arms through and around the rungs. They walked the length of the next level, mounted another ladder, and then pushed through a series of narrow doors.

Light pierced to the back of his eyes. Fresh air slapped his face, salt-tinged and moist. The world came alive with sounds. Nothing was muted. Sails snapped in the wind. Waves sliced open before the ship's bow. Seagulls cried their rude calls one to another. And he heard the voices of men, harsh at times and gay at others, men hard at a type of work that gave them joy. As his eyes adjusted to the light he saw the visual manifestations of those sounds. He was on the brig. But instead of a dim shape in the stillness of the harbor, the ship was at full sail through a white-capped ocean. Studding sails stretched far out on either side of the vessel, billowed by the wind, driving them onward. The coastline was some distance off to the left, and to the right the water stretched to the horizon and beyond. They were no longer in the shallow waters of the Chesapeake. This was the open Atlantic.

The two men grasped him by either wrist and the muzzle of a gun pressed into his abdomen. They led him forward. He took small steps, thrown off balance by the heaving of the ship, his head dizzy and vision swimming. They walked around crates and between giant coils of rope, beneath the mainmast and through the taut lines strung vertically and reaching up into a web of angles and shapes and lines. They drew up before two other men, just behind the foremast. One was a small fellow, compact of structure but tightly built. His golden hair kicked out from his head in strange angles. When he saw William his hand went to the hilt of his dagger, a slim, curved weapon that dangled from his waist belt.

The other man turned and took William in with little visible sign of surprise. He was older and wore an intricate sailor's hat, bent brimmed in the style of an earlier time. His face was craggy-featured, rough and multitextured. His eyebrows perched above his eyes, two thick lines drawn in coal. A similarly bushy beard spread downward over his jowls. His eyes were large even for his wide face, more bulbous than usual. William's captors addressed this man, explaining where and in what condition they had found him.

The smaller man moved before they had finished speaking. He strode the space between them in two quick steps and punched William across the mouth. William reeled away from the blow, but was set right by the two men. "You'll soon see you've made a mistake, my friend." He signaled something to the men. One of them moved off, but the other one, with the gun, kept his grip on William.

"Captain," the small man said, "we'd be within our rights to hang him ourselves."

"Without a trial, Mr. Barrett?" the captain asked, his voice unhurried and nasal.

"What trial did his like give those men?" Barrett stepped forward and grasped William by the chin between his rough-gloved fingers. "What trial did you give those men before you rose and slaughtered them?"

"Please, Mr. Barrett, give me a moment." The captain motioned the younger man aside and examined William from head to toe, taking in each feature of his body and clothing, lingering long on his tattered breeches and on the sad state of his brogans. He reached out as if to touch William along the jawline. William lifted his head before the man made contact with his skin. "You don't have the countenance of a murderer," he said, "but I of all people know that looks can be deceiving. God gave us the good sense to know the difference between the lion and doe, and he wrote the laws by which we punish the criminal among us."

One of the other men returned, bringing with him the familiar clinking of heavy iron. William set his jaw against the sound. Tired and exhausted as he was, he would not stand before this man like a slave on the auction block. He set his gaze to the distance to show them that he was far away from all this, someplace else entirely, a place they could never own. For the first time it occurred to him how much there was inside of him that no white man could ever know. There were regions within him upon which no claims of ownership had hold. He thought about Dover and that rage of hers, and he felt closer to her than he had since that day in January.

"Forgive me if I sin against you," the captain said, "but I have my ship and crew to protect. You understand . . ."

The captain motioned the man forward with the chains. William stared straight before him as the man clamped the iron over his scarred wrists. He watched the distant shoreline, a white line of sand behind which dunes rolled out of sight.

"I am not wholly without sympathy for your situation," the captain said. "I abhor the institution that has enslaved you, and I even believe that the spilling of white blood may at times be justified. But, for the moment at least I must treat you as a criminal. You may, at will, make a case for yourself and I will hear you out." The captain paused and expressed with his folded hands that he was ready to listen. "Have you anything to say in your defense?"

William didn't answer. He didn't want to listen to or engage with the man at all, let them do with him what they would. Given a moment's peace he would again try to escape. And if caught, he would again escape. And if he was not meant to find Dover then he would die in the effort. Even if he was to die here he would not show an ounce of fear, for he had seen white men killed. He had seen their flesh unmasked and looked beneath it. If he never saw Dover again, at least he would die knowing she would be proud of him. She would find him beautiful in his anger.

"You are one of the fugitives from that coffle, one of those that rose in Virginia and massacred their keepers?" When he didn't answer the captain sighed. "Perhaps no white man has ever asked for your thoughts before, but that's just what I'm doing. I'm giving you the opportunity to speak for yourself. You would be wise to take it."

Though William tried not to listen—not to engage with

the man at all—the strange cadence of his words reverberated in his head. He gathered that the man knew of the massacre and knew that he was a runaway, but he couldn't place what the man's attitude to these things might be. If he had called for a rope just then it would've made more sense. If he knew the things he appeared to, then William would only live until a noose was fastened around his neck. Did he have anything to say in his defense? He had a million things to say but not one that a white man would care to hear.

"Sir," the small man said. He crowded behind the captain.

The captain's voice stayed calm. "You are one of those fugitives. You stowed away on my ship in such a way as might have compromised me to the authorities. Am I correct? Do you deny any of this?"

William pressed his tongue against his teeth.

"Your silence leaves me no choice," the captain said. "Barrett."

The small man sprung toward him, spun William around and shoved him toward the port side of the brig. The railing hit him at waist level and his upper body pitched forward. The water slipped past with incredible speed, the sleek back of the ocean and the ship carving into it. Barrett held him facing it for a few moments, his fist clamped around his collar. "The captain said talk!"

William wanted to wrench himself from the little man's grip and look upon the captain again, to hear more of his questions and more of the voice in which he spoke them. He opened his mouth, but where and how to begin? What could he say that would stay the moment and grant him more time to think? Barrett pushed his elbow into the small of William's back, making him gasp, a sound that came out like a curse.

"You hear that?" Barrett asked. "He sassing us. Listen to him."

The captain moved in close to the two men. "I am sure you can perceive the extent to which Barrett is willing to go with this questioning. We must have answers, and if you'll give us none I'll give Mr. Barrett permission to submerge you. Do you understand? He'll bind your feet with a long rope and toss you overboard and you will learn what it's like to drown. It's not at all pleasant. You lash out in the water trying to find some purchase. But the water is a thing with and without substance. You beat against it but it cannot be mastered. Your exhaustion is like none you have ever experienced. We pull you on like a fish on a line. You would cry out, but your head is beneath the water. You may lose consciousness, if you're lucky. If you're not lucky you'll be very aware of the moment the water rushes in on you, filling your insides and choking the life out of you. And at that point Mr. Barrett would haul you back aboard and ask you the very same questions. Now . . ." He turned William's face toward his. ". . . let us avoid all of that. Tell me, are you a murderer?"

William shook his head.

"You have no blood on your hands?"

For the first time that he was aware of, William vocalized his answer. "No."

The captain asked the next question in simple, deliberate words spoken close to William's ear. "Then give me the words . . . Speak so that I may know the truth."

"I never murdered anybody. The others did that."

"Typical," Barrett spit. "Typical answer! Shall I dunk him, sir?"

"No. We don't have time for that." The captain drew himself up, folded his arms behind him and considered William from that posture of authority. "This is not a court. We shan't hear this matter out here. He pleads innocence. That's enough for now. See that the prisoner is locked away securely. We'll turn him over when it suits us." Barrett looked ready to protest, but the captain stopped him with a raised hand. "That's my mind, now see it made true."

With another motion of his hand the captain spurred several men into action. They wrestled William out of Barrett's grip and began to drag him away. For the first few yards he walked as guided. He closed his eyes and let them lead him. The image of the shoreline came to him and he was filled with an urge to dive into the ocean, to swim for that shore or drown in the effort. He opened his eyes and saw the passage into the ship approaching. He jerked his arms free of the men that bound him and strode forward, turned and made for the edge. He lunged for the railing, but just as he touched it his feet were kicked out from under him and the men were upon him, grappling and kicking him. They hauled him up and dragged him onward. He tried to yank himself free, twisting to see the captain and to talk to him, suddenly willing to plead his innocence. But the captain was out of his view. As they dragged him to the portal his arms banged out against it to stop him. He yelled out Dover's name, but his cry was snatched away by the wind across the deck. Then the ship swallowed him.

WILLIAM SAT FUMING in his cell, wrists chaffing beneath the chains, buttocks sore from pressing against solid wood. It was a tiny room, too short even for him to stand, just wider than his outstretched arms. His chains were secured to a ring in the floor, though it hardly seemed necessary. There was not a chink of light to be seen in the cell, no moving air. It was a chamber of black, dripping wood. His captors had set a bucket near the door for him to relieve himself. But he didn't need it. There was nothing inside of him to come out. At first he dreamed of escape. He imagined how he would manage it, scenes of blood and gore not natural to him but being learned. But his anger didn't last. It seeped out of him and into the darkness around him. It was a relief almost, to give up hope, letting thoughts and schemes slide away, replaced by a numbness inside that mirrored that around him. How much could a man take? How much until he could give up with honor? Perhaps he was failing Dover and the child, but how much could he take before giving in?

When the door opened he snapped upright. A single candle shone through the crack. A moment later a face appeared beside it. For a second, William thought the candlelight was playing tricks on him. The face it illuminated appeared to be black, only the whites of the eyes clear and bright in reflection. The face vanished. The candle wavered. Then the door swung open and a man stepped in, candle in one hand, plate of food in the other. For some seconds the person's face was hidden, but when it turned toward him again he realized he had not been mistaken. It was an ebony facade, that of a Negro, darker than he, with hair that—if the image in the candlelight could be believed— sprung from his scalp like black worms several inches long. For a moment William thought the face feminine. High cheeks sloped to a narrow, hairless chin. Eyes were wide set and al- mond shaped, tilted upwards at either end. But there was something masculine about the person's movements, quick and assured and not the slightest bit nervous with their proximity.

The person set the metal plate before William, placed the candle next to it, and squatted a few feet away. He was dressed as any sailor, in dark breeches and a cotton shirt, but it was to his strange, angular face that William's attention was drawn. His lips were a dark pucker below his nose. A series of black lines cut diagonally across his cheeks, scars or tattoos it was hard to tell. Despite the intensity of his visage, William felt no threat from it.

"Eat," the man said. In a single word his voice conveyed its foreignness. It was spoken from the front of the mouth, just the play of the tip of his tongue on the backs of teeth.

William felt for the plate. Steam rose up from it and slipped across his features. He couldn't smell it, but he knew what it was when he took a mouthful, hominy. He ate several mouthfuls, slowly, remembering how to eat. Before long, he forgot the man in front of him. He felt the food slide into his mouth and move around his teeth and slip down inside him. It woke a life down there that had been dormant for a long time. After he had scraped the plate clean of hominy he noticed the strips of meat lining the edge.

"Is venison."

William's head snapped up.

The man repeated the word. "Ven-ni-son." He smiled and nodded his head, asking if William understood. He motioned with his hands, a pronged gesture that looked to William like that of a rabbit jumping. But then the man held them above his head, creating strange limbs there with his fingers. When William still looked confused, the man dropped his hands and thought. Eventually, he said, "Doe."

"Doe?" William said. "Oh, you mean to say 'deer.' " He had never eaten venison before. He tasted it. It was richer meat than he would have imagined, and thicker than seemed possible from such lithe animals. He glanced back up at the man's grinning face. He seemed to be waiting for a response.

The man nodded and then asked, with no preamble or change in the expression on his face, "Who Dover?"

For a confused second it felt like the man had pulled the name from his head, had somehow robbed him of it. But as he stared he saw no guile written across his features, no evil intent, no sorcery. He simply asked a question and awaited an answer. William remembered that he had screamed her name on deck. He must have heard it then. "She . . . She's my woman."

"Your woman?" the other said, teasing out both words as if further meaning could be deciphered by saying them slowly. He nodded and said no more.

William continued eating. His seething anger was gone. It lingered back at the far wall of his conscious mind, but his thoughts were clear. Perhaps the food had helped. He wanted to ask this man who he was, what he was doing on this ship. Somehow—and it was not just because of his color—he seemed out of place. He seemed to hold serenity within himself, a peace with his physical body and patience with the quiet moments he was spending here in this dark cell. William decided he would speak again when he had finished the meat.

But just as he did so the man scrabbled forward in his squatting position and scooped up the plate. He motioned that he would leave the candle, and then he paused beside the door, looking at William once more. "The captain is here," he said. He stepped out of the door, and the white man appeared in his place. He must've been standing just outside the whole time.

The captain entered the cubicle and set a lantern down near the door. The black man handed him a bottle and two wooden goblets. The black man glanced at William and then, at a nod from the captain, pulled the door fast behind him, leaving the two men alone.

The captain looked at the boards beneath his feet, taking some time before lowering himself down to sit. He shifted around into several positions before settling on one, legs folded before him, back straight. The captain watched William for a few moments, taking in his face and clothing, body and then face again. He pursed his lips as if to comment on his appearance but then thought better of it. He uncorked the bottle and filled the two goblets. "I am sure you are thirsty," he said. "I have taken the liberty of bringing some wine for us to share. I've nurtured a great thirst all day." He placed one of the containers within William's reach, then tilted his own and drank.

William didn't respond. He fixed his eyes on an area of shadowed darkness, trying to calm his heart, the pulse of which he felt in his palms.

The man wiped his mouth and took note of this. As he replenished his goblet he began to speak. He talked in that odd, meandering voice of his. He first detailed the weather of the past few days, then discussed the winds and how they favored them, even described the sheet lightning he had seen dancing across the distant sky the night before. William barely took in a word of it, waiting instead for him to get around to what he really had to say, some decision about his fate, some news of when he was to be handed over. But, if the man did have such news to disclose, he was slow in getting to it.

"What do you think of Adam?" the Captain asked, indicating with a nod that he referred to the black man beyond the door. "I bought him, you know. He is as free as any man now. I paid silver for his liberty off the coast of North Africa. A trader in Tunis approached me, you see. I had been drinking, searching for amusements. I did quite a bit of this in those days. It gives a traveler heart, and we need heart in foreign lands. But, as I was saying, my mind sought amusement, and this trader made it known that he had boys to sell, boys who could be used for whatever purposes a demented mind might think of." He paused and studied William. "I was curious, you see. The trader said he was taken from a pirate ship off the coast of Madagascar, but he may well have lied. I don't even think Adam knows where he was born. In any event, he had suffered horribly in his short life. Not worked the way you may have been, but used for a different purpose. The trader had him stripped, and put on display each portion of his body. He was made to bend and contort and . . . It was very degrading, for both of us. I paid the boy's price without haggling over it. I took him out of there, not to use as that trader suggested but to walk him to freedom. Do you understand why I did that? Some acts of men degrade all of mankind, not just the individual. I had watched as that boy was made to display himself, and that was a crime in its own right. I had the silver, and I sought to absolve us both. I was clear headed when I did it, and I shall never doubt it was one of the better actions of my life. He is not a slave, I tell you. He is free to go where and when he pleases. That he stays with me I consider a blessing of sorts. He and I have spoken many hours together. He is a good listener, and I am one who seems to need to talk. As I have just proven."

The captain smiled and tilted his goblet. "Please, do have a drink." He lifted William's goblet and handed it to him. "I speak of Adam because he spoke of you. He observed you on deck, and he's of the opinion that you are falsely accused. He says you are not a murderer, not yet at least. I would like very much to hear you speak it with your own voice. Speak to me, for the moment, as a free man. You are afloat on the sea, not bounded by the laws of your home state at present. So speak to me."

William said nothing, just stared at the wine and the vague reflection on its surface.

"Your reluctance is understandable, of course," the captain said. His somber expression showed that he acknowledged no humor in this understatement. "My wife always thought that I was insensitive. She said I pushed my nose where it need not be. But I have always argued just the opposite. I push my nose because I am overly sensitive. I ask questions because I have some interest in my fellow humans. Do you not think the world would be a better place if more men acted in the same man- ner?" He paused for an answer. When he got none he mum- bled, "Not that I hold myself up as a model to other men ... Do you know that we were boarded in Virginia? And again yesterday along the Eastern Shore. The first time we had no idea you were aboard, and the searchers were halfhearted in their examinations. Yesterday was a different matter. I don't know why I did it, but I denied your presence aboard the boat. My first mate, Barrett, nearly collapsed with anger. It is fortunate for both of us that, despite his failings, he takes orders as a sailor should. And as sailor myself, I should attend my ship."

The captain rose and dusted the seat of his trousers with his hands. He picked up the lantern and opened the door, pausing in the corridor. He glanced back in at William, who still sat with the goblet in his hands. "Soon I will ask you of Dover," he said. "Please consider this."

With that, he closed the door, and William was again in darkness.

Three

As the trail grew colder, Morrison began to prowl the Negro quarters of any town that had a population large enough to merit such a section. He tried as best he could to engage the Negroes, both slave and free, in useful conversation. This proved largely impossible. The black faces never lifted toward him. They stared at the ground, spoke in monosyllables and seemed to misunderstand each question he posed to them. And yet from the fringes of their company he heard them exchange a free and animated flow of words between each other. They told jokes, exchanged threats and insults, all spoken with tongues nimble as rabbits. At least, until they spotted the white man among them and fell dumb.

Morrison wanted to tell them that he had once walked and conversed and mingled in every way with people of their many colors. He would have explained that he had worked beside them in his early days in this country. He would like to have spoken to them of his brother, who had recognized the Africans' humanity before he had and who had taught him so many things in the short span of his life. It was his brother who returned to their shared room one night with a black man's blood on his fingertips. He had taken to night wandering, for he was finding it hard adjusting to this land and said he hated staring at the walls. Only exhaustion helped him. The best way to produce it, he found, was midnight rambling. On this particular evening, Lewis burst into the room with his hands held out before him, begging Morrison to wake, beseeching him to light the flame, light the flame. He was thick with mud up to his knees and across his chest and arms and even up into his hair. But he ignored this. It was his hands and the manner in which they were fouled that troubled him. He held them close to Morrison and asked him did he see it? Did he see the blood? Did he know that this was a land of blood, that it flowed in the streets like mud? The elder brother calmed the younger and got him to tell his tale.

It was a forlorn night, damp with the residue of spring rain. Lewis walked it alone until he turned onto a lane and saw the three men at the far end of it. He would have stopped and slipped away before they saw him, but he was propelled on by the desire not to look criminal. He quickened his pace and carried on toward them. One of them held a torch, while two others went to work on a fourth man, a Negro whom Lewis had not seen at first. The moving light of that torch rendered a scene of surreal barbarity. The black man crouched on all fours, while two of the men beat him about the head and back with short clubs. They pushed him low into the mud and stamped upon his back. They lifted him up and punched him one after the other. His blood mingled with the mud and their hands had difficulty grasping him. This drove them to new furies. One of the men hefted his rifle up to shoot him. But he changed his mind, grasped it by the barrel and swung it at full length in a wide arc. It hit the black man at the apex of its swing, the stock end catching him across the face. It shattered his cheekbone and sent his body sprawling in pursuit of his flying teeth. He lay there in that outstretched position, sinking into the mud.

As they turned to go the man with the rifle fixed his eyes upon Lewis and studied him as if noticing him for the first time. The man's features were boyish and smooth. He nodded and half-smiled. You know what they say, he said. A nigger's a halfpenny to kill and a halfpenny to bury. He motioned to the half-submerged form in the mud. Figure this here one's a full cent. With that, he turned and walked away, rifle over his shoulder, pointed up at the sky, his gait loose and contented.

The younger brother stood for a long time, staring at the Negro's form and watching the brown stuff closing around him, as if the earth were accepting back its own. He couldn't move. He couldn't think. He couldn't make sense of the rifleman's handsome face, not with the vision before him. He could find no way to explain it, no plotting for how he had stumbled upon this and what course of events had brought it about.

Then the man moved. It was no great motion. It was little more than an exhaled breath, but to Lewis it was proof that he still lived. He pushed his way toward him through the mud. He rolled the man over, slipped his open palm beneath his neck and tried to stay his lolling head. The man opened his eyes. The bloody mud parted and two orbs of smooth moisture reflected back the starlight in the clearing sky. He looked at Lewis with an expression that he was at pains to describe. There was no emotion in it. It was not sadness or fear or resignation. It was none of these. His eyes were two questions, and Lewis knew he had failed to answer. And that was all. At some moment those questions turned to hollow notes that never changed pitch or tone but simply went on. The man's eyes stared up at him but they did not see any longer. They did not blink and did not move. They were dead things and no longer portholes to the man's being, the bare materials of life without the substance.

Lewis slipped away and walked home with trembling steps, sure once again that this was all wrong. This place was not their home, and yet... Mute the colors and wash them out and cast the world in a different cadence... Do that, and this country was not so different than the one that had created the brothers. And that was the thing that truly frightened him.

As he held his sobbing brother, Morrison knew that he didn't cry simply for that unknown black man. He cried for any such moment for any person. He cried for the things we do to each other and because the eyes of that stranger in death were no different than the eyes of his loved ones. It was memories such as these that Morrison would have shared with the dark people he met now, confessions he would make to the ears of black men only. He would've told them of the next time his brother came home with tales of a colored person, a woman this time, a tale of joy instead of sorrow. But as he walked the backcountry roads of Maryland posing his questions, he spoke of none of these things. Such a dialogue was impossible. Words alone could not bridge the gap between him and these people. Perhaps only actions could. This was, after all, the true test of the mission before him.

Four

When the captain returned he didn't ask about Dover. Instead, he talked at length of the strange things he had seen at sea. He spoke of storms that in their fury beggared belief, of calms that left one feeling the world had died along with all the living beings in it. He told of a creature from the deep reaches of the ocean, a many-limbed thing with a beak for a mouth and an eye so big around that both the captain's palms failed to cover it. He spoke of flying fish in the Caribbean, flocks that came so thick across the deck that his men once dove for cover, fearing that the ocean was throwing up silver daggers against them. He said the sea was abundant in its bounty at times, munificent out of all reasonable proportion. But it could also be frigid and bleak, callous and utterly indifferent to mankind. It was a strange love affair he had with the sea, a lifelong marriage of sorts.

William sat listening, his fingers around the goblet, rubbing the wood of it with his thumbs. Perhaps the dark chamber that they shared helped call images vividly to mind, internal colors and motions and panoramas. Or perhaps it was the cadence of the captain's voice, so controlled and even, words pushed like pearls of thought, things with their own undeniable life. Or maybe it was just that William's mind hungered for distraction, for contact with another human, for dialogue, even though dialogue had gained him so little in the last few weeks. For any or all of these reasons he was entranced by the white man's words. He lost himself in them while they were together, and they lived on when the captain departed. He saw daggers thrown up from the sea, placed his hands across that great creature's eye, watched the sun burn its way into the rim of the world. All of this without leaving the low chamber of the ship.

Their third meeting followed much the same pattern, except that the captain tried to shift the discussion over to William. Where had he come from? Had he fled a wicked owner? Had his life been the living hell the captain imagined slavery to be? Was he true to this Dover? Was their relationship a marriage of sorts? William didn't answer except in gestures, mute requests that he not be questioned. He wanted to listen, but he still couldn't get himself to speak. To open his mouth was to reveal everything. It didn't seem possible to utter words without betraying all of his troubled history. The man was asking him about the forces that shaped his life, the agony and the wonder both. There was no middle ground in talking of such things. He could give all or nothing. So he asked for more silence.

The captain turned the conversation to thoughts of his wife. She was of Irish stock, he said, so fair of complexion that her skin was almost translucent. Though frail of health and temperament, she bore him two children, a son and daughter. The son was bright, red haired like his mother and, like her, somewhat fragile. His daughter, Esther, had more of the sea-man's blood in her. She was so impetuous that she had never crawled. She had climbed up onto her spindly legs and stum-bled about the world like it belonged to her. It was strange, he said, to think back to those precious moments. Painful to think of all the time he spent on this vessel, moments that would have been better spent in the company of those three loved ones.

"I remember one summer afternoon walking with Esther," the captain said. "We'd been some time wandering the grounds of an estate in Baltimore, and found ourselves far from shelter as storm clouds began to build. To get back we decided upon a route through the woods. It was thick with bracken, thorny bushes and the like. It was difficult, and I was soon of a temper.

I slashed out at the bushes, for they seemed to knit themselves against us. They snapped back at me and scratched my face and returned each of my aggressive gestures in turn. I was working myself into quite a state, beyond all reason, the sort of anger one only directs at inanimate objects. Then Esther called to me. I turned and met her gaze. She looked at me, pity in her eyes, and said, 'Father, be courteous, or the forest won't know you from a ruffian.' She pushed past me and led the way forward, no curses, no slashing. She just slipped through the vegetation like one might through a crowd of civilized people. It was most remarkable, a grown man following his daughter's lead through a wood. I thought her very wise that day, and time has not dimmed the impression. She shaped me in that moment, and I've never quite trod the earth in the same way since."

The ship creaked in the silence following the man's story. William shifted where he sat, rotating his wrist so that the iron lay against a different portion of his skin. He realized he had forgotten his chains for a few moments. Strange, for he had rarely ever done so before. He had even slept with the knowledge of his bondage in his dreaming mind. But here, for a few moments, the captain had lulled him into forgetting.

The tallow candle sputtered and smoked as it neared death, and the captain leant forward to light another, a small nub left over from the previous day. "A man who doesn't know the joy of fatherhood is a poor man," he said. "A man who has not been challenged by fatherhood's trials is a weaker man than one who has. I learned from my children, much more than I ever wished to. They are all three years dead now. My wife, my son and daughter . . . all taken by consumption. They were taken when I was at sea. Consecrated and given over to the Lord while I sailed a favorable wind up from the Sea Isles. To me they are remembrances. To me they are as they were, as I would have them be.

This is my grand delusion, but I learn from it still. I never asked you, do you have any children?"

William thought the question over before deciding to answer. He ran his fingers over the coarse, damp grain of the wood below him. "I don't know," he said, just three words but enough for him to know that he had committed himself.

The captain looked puzzled, but only for a second. An expression of embarrassment washed across his features. "I understand. I forget the barbarities of slavery."

William knew that he didn't understand, and it suddenly mattered to him that he did. "What I mean to say is I might have a baby now . . . I mean, I ain't seen Dover to know."

Ridges stood out on the white man's forehead. He touched his bulbous nose with his fingers. He looked ready to inquire further, but he didn't. It was just this silence that encouraged William onward. He didn't look at the white man. He tilted his head and kept his eyes on the shadowy beams above them, but when he spoke he did not hesitate.

"That's why I ran off," he said. "Found out she was carrying my baby. She woulda been carrying it for months before I heard of it. When I found out nothing was the same, couldn't never be the same again. I had to get back with her. Couldn't just go on living. That's why I ran, Captain. I didn't do it just for my own sake. I sure didn't kill nobody. I'm just trying to get back with Dover and that child." He paused and inhaled a long breath, as if he hadn't done so since he began speaking. He could hear the yells from the men on deck, strange for he had never heard them before. "I dream of her all the time. Every time I close my eyes, seems like. It almost don't seem right . . . How much I think bout her."

"That's love," the captain said.

William glanced at him, trying to read the man's face but

finding it no different than before. He didn't address the comment directly. "In them dreams she sometimes carrying our child. But them times she always at a distance. The far side a field. On the shore when I'm in a boat. That type a thing. I never have seen that baby's face. Seen the shape of it, but never have looked on it properly."

"And do you want to see that young one's face?"

"More than anything else that's what I want." He hadn't known that he believed this before he said it. The words almost surprised him, how easily they slipped out of him, how fully formed and undeniable. Yes, he yearned to reunite with Dover. Yes, he hungered for freedom, for vengeance. But these paled in comparison to a bone-deep longing that he couldn't explain, that began and ended and went on forever in the possibility of that child. To look upon that face, to kiss that face and to know that child was he and Dover made immortal, to see that child walk and to hear it speak the wisdom of innocence: these were all the things he wanted. He had never known it as completely as he did at that moment. "It's a hard thing to reckon on," he said.

"Yes, it will be that," the captain said. His gaze drifted away from William and hovered somewhere in the space between them. He wrapped his fingers around the wine goblet and lifted it, testing its weight and the give of his wrist in supporting it. "I have been wondering if you would tell me something of your plans? How would you make a life for yourself if your labor was to be your own? The land to which you were running is a much freer one than the one you came from. But it is not without its share of snakes as well. The captain changed position and drank the rest of his wine. "What do your people think of Northerners?"

William picked up his own goblet when the other man

slapped his down. As if prompted by the question, he took a quick sip, choked on it and spent a moment coughing. "I . . . I don't know, suh."

"Sure you do. Have you not passed all your life thinking about it?"

William made as if to drink again, but thought better of it. Despite himself, he came close to answering the man. It was hard to refuse his questions. He almost responded that yes, every slave child hears of the free North, hears tales of the white people called "abolitionists," a word they all knew but rarely said aloud, and never within the hearing of white men. But what are they other than distant notions that the childish mind conceives of fanciful images? Perhaps they glow with a light of holiness that no Southerner has. Perhaps they float above the earth and look sadly to the south. Perhaps they have wings. He had imagined them as all of these things. Yet he had met more than one Northerner in his life, and they had seemed no different than any other white men. They ate the same food and shat the same stink, and more than once a visiting businessman had bedded down with one of the house servants and spent his lust the same as any Southerner. He had no delusions about Northerners, but he didn't try to explain this to the Northerner questioning him.

"The South sticks to their ways because they pay, my friend," the captain said. "There is little more to it than that. And the North . . . Well, different things pay up here, that is all. Most Northerners are no more moral than your former masters. They are just different. An accident of circumstance. My brother once stayed with a Southern gentleman in Savannah. On his return he told me in detail of the rituals of his stay. His room was tidied and swept and the bed turned out in preparation for him. He told of the maid—and he did not fail to notice how comely she was—and the way she met him in the evening with a wash basin. She would bend and take off his shoes and make sure his every need was cared for. In the morning, when he rose from bed she was there again, sliding his slipper onto his foot before it touched the ground. When he spoke, she listened. When he commended the dawn for its beauty, she agreed. In everything, she was his servant; he was her master." The captain turned and looked at William. The man's eyes were intent, gentle, his lips glistening from the wetting of his tongue. "My brother is a good man, but he found this short stay quite intoxicating. No Northerner has that sort of luxury, no matter how rich he is. It's the grandest of delusions, and that is why the South will never give it up except by blood."

For a long moment after this statement William was unsure what he meant. Only after studying the man's face did he understand that he meant white men's blood. And this was a more frightening thing yet. White blood taken by white hands, for the sake of black people? It would never happen. William stared at him, wondering if he was crazy, for no sane man would speak thus to a slave.

The captain returned the stare. His face held its frank expression as though at a test of wills. They shared the silence a moment, then the man cleared his throat and spoke on. He pitched his voice a little lower, with a hint of resignation, but he still didn't look away or soften his visage. "When you stowed away, you brought more than just your person into my ship. I thank you for it. It was good that we spoke, but this will be our last meeting together. This afternoon we entered the Delaware. It is a full moon tonight and, as my crew knows these waters well, we will sail for a few hours after dark. There'll only be a few men on deck, and I'll keep them occupied as much as possible. During this time you will make your escape."

William's eyes flicked away from the man and then back,

as if he had disappeared and then rematerialized in the space of a second.

"Don't look at me with awe, William. You've held things back from me and I from you. I'm no great man. I'm no altruist. In my youth I aided the slave trade. In my manhood I gave vent to desires that shame me. Now, in riper age I must live with the memories of my mistakes. This is just one act I offer you. But I won't mislead you. This hardly amends a life ill spent. I wrestle daily with the question of whether that's even possible with a million acts of kindness. I wonder if they even are acts of kindness when I can't stop thinking about my own soul and the old sins that stain it." He stretched out his hand. "Go find your loved ones, and do a better job with them than I did with mine."

William reached out toward him. He felt a sudden need to speak, but his mouth had gone dry. The captain grasped the tips of his fingers. He held them a moment, and, on that confirmation alone, he turned and left the room.

Adam appeared a few hours later, carrying a satchel that he set down in the corner. He spoke in motions, instructing William to raise his manacles. He unfastened them, a slow process, as the key was roughly cast and the lock of a primitive design. As William rubbed the raw flesh of his wrists, Adam retrieved the satchel. It was a leather pouch with a drawstring closure, soiled with some greasy substance layered on long ago to waterproof it. He opened it and displayed some of its contents: items of food, a cotton shirt, a bottle of some liquid. He thrust it into William's abdomen and said, "Follow."

William stepped into the maze behind Adam. Dark as it was, some faint traces of light filtered down into the ship. But this only served to disorient, casting the slightest indications of shapes, skewed angles and highlights that delineated the darkness all the more. He followed primarily by sound, but the man led him like an expert at such work. Each time William thought he had lost his course the other would rap his knuckles on a beam, whistle or simply scuff his foot across the boards. Each sound might have been coincidental, except that they came always at the right moment. Before long, William stepped into the bright light of the full moon. He hadn't even had to climb a ladder, and yet still the blue light and open air was unmistakable. He was on deck, with Adam close beside him. The man's hand clamped around William's elbow. He tugged him back into the shadows.

Two sailors stood against the railing a few feet away. Their backs were turned, and, judging by the casual way their conversation continued, they had noticed nothing. William felt Adam next to him. He could smell him and hear his breathing and sometimes feel the touch of his dry fingers. But the man just stood unmoving, ordering William to silence with the force of his own example. Five minutes later, one of the men ventured off toward the bow. And soon after that the captain's voice was heard, calling to the other. The remaining sailor said something under his breath as he sauntered away.

Adam pointed toward the railing. "Go."

William was into the moonlight and across the deck in an instant. He placed a foot up on the railing and looked back into the shadows out of which he had just come. At first, he saw nothing save an empty black space, a shadow that framed no man but was simply a void. Something in this caused him pause, a feeling that Adam's disappearance had been too complete, too abrupt. Something left unfinished. But then the African's hand darted out of the shadows, lit in bone-gray, a black man's hand rendered in highlight. With it his body was given substance. Of course he was there, waiting, watching, and, now, directing with a single pointed finger. William obeyed.

He turned and peered overboard. At first he thought he was meant to jump, but then he noticed a thick, knotted rope trailing from the deck down into the water. He clamored over the railing, tucked the neck of the sack under his armpit and began to shimmy down the rope. It was a bruising effort, trying to move silently as the hard knots of the rope dug into his thighs and chest and chin. When the bay began to lap at his knees, he clenched the neck of the sack tight in one hand and let go of the rope with the other. He went under, swirling and tumbling with the force of the water upset by the brig's hull. A few moments passed like this, with no notion of up or down, the water so chilly it sucked the air from him, his eyes open to the salt tinge but seeing nothing.

He hit the surface gasping. His legs kicked out to steady him, spinning him in circles as he tried to make sense of the world from this new level. The ship was already moving away. Its shadow blocked the view to the west. He watched it, eyes flitting from one section of the deck to another, listening for any cries of alarm. But none came and with each passing moment the winds and currents pushed him and ship further apart. He turned toward the shore and swam, doing the best he could to hold the leather satchel above the water, a free man for a third time and, finally, within shooting distance of his goal.

Five

Morrison and the hound wandered two weeks without the slightest sign of the fugitive. Their luck changed one afternoon as they approached a small town west of Baltimore. The hound loped beside the man with her nose low to the ground. She had walked like this for miles without hitch, so the man took note of it when she paused. She raised her snout in the air. Whatever she smelled up there sent trembling waves of excitement from the base of her neck, over her back and down her thighs. Tilting her head back even further, she let up the howl that had long since become a signal between her and the man. She bolted toward the town. She didn't wind through the traffic of the street, but instead followed the most direct route. She grazed the hind legs of a mounted horse, cut a circle of children right through its center point and bounded across two front porches.

But her final destination was none of these. It was a wagon, parked near to a general store and unattended. She leapt into it and patrolled every corner of it. By the time Morrison reached her she knew she had come up empty. She tilted her head and howled, lowered it and searched the small space again. The man stood panting behind her, staring without comprehending. The hound swung around and met his gaze and in the exchange something clicked for the man. He called the dog down, calmed her, thanked her and led her away, avoiding the curious gazes of onlookers. The two stationed themselves a little distance away and sat watching. And they were soon rewarded.

A Negro stepped from the general store carrying an oblong box, which—judging by his posture—must have been quite heavy. He loaded it into the back of the wagon, then peered back toward the store. He seemed to consider re-entering, but then chose instead to lean against the wagon and study the day.

Morrison approached the man with his rifle shouldered. He halloed him from a few feet out, came in smiling and explained that he was looking for a runaway slave, all before the man had the chance to move or speak. He described the fugitive as best he could, his origins, recent whereabouts and physical characteristics. The black man listened to all of this with his head nodding, his features twisted with the outward contortions of deep thought. He was a misshapen creature, but in his eyes were glistening hints of guile that Morrison didn't fail to notice. When he had heard all the man had to say he shrugged his shoulders.

I can't even start to help ya, he said. I don't have no truck with runaways. They ain't kindly my kind of people, if you understand me.

But Morrison was sure he could be of some assistance. Had he not seen this fugitive? Or had he not heard of any that had? It was information he might be willing to pay for.

You might be what?

Willing to pay.

Is that right? The Negro looked back into the store. Let's us talk a minute over yonder. He led Morrison a little distance away.

You say you got money to stake?

Morrison answered him by pulling a bank note from the inside of his vest.

The black man studied it close to his face, turning it over front to back. He licked it with the tip of his tongue, rubbed it with his thumb and checked it for scuffmarks. There were none. I mighta' heard something bout that nigger, he said.

Is that right?

Yessir. I ain't seen him myself, but he's been hereabouts.

Do you know where he went?

Well, let me jog my rememory a bit. The man bit his lip and screwed up his eyes. You say this here information is worth money to you.

You got the cash in your hand.

As if surprised by such an idea, the Negro checked his hands, palm and backside, making it clear that no such note was on his person.

Don't try to play me, Morrison said.

The Negro considered this, looking from his hands up to the man's face and then glancing back at the store. He lowered his hands. So, you say you're looking for a nigger?

You gonna tell me something or am I gonna have to take that dollar back?

Just then a white man emerged from the store, arms laden with supplies. He scowled as he stepped into the sun and snapped his head from right to left until his eyes focused in on the two men talking. He didn't take his eyes off of them as he walked to the wagon and placed his parcels in the bed. He set his hands on his hips and called the black man.

The man excused himself, saying he would be back directly. He shuffled over to the white, a strange, straddle-legged gait that moved him with surprising speed. The two men spoke beyond Morrison's hearing. He had just begun to walk toward them when the white motioned the black up into the driver's seat and struck out toward Morrison at a fast walk.

What the hell you talking to my nigger for? he asked, planting himself just a few inches from the tracker. You got a question for him you got a question for me is how I see it.

That's fine, Morrison said. I'm looking...

But the other way I see it is that I ain't got no interest in answering any questions. You hunting some nigger, I know that. Who ain't hunting a nigger? I done hunted niggers all over this state and over a few others as well and one thing I learned from it is it ain't no good answering questions. You might differ in your opinion cause you're the one with the questions to ask, but that's the way I see it. Now, we gonna go and you gonna leave us be. If you don't I'll be happy to stick that rifle up your asshole and fuck you full of lead. And I ain't a poet. That there is a promise. It's as simple as that.

The man spun and began to walk away.

Your boy's got some of my money, Morrison said.

The man didn't even turn his head to answer. Be glad that's all you lost, he said. He mounted the wagon up over the bed of it and plopped down in the seat beside the black man. They were trundling forward before he had even settled himself.

Morrison looked to his dog and frowned. Aye, well...I believe they know something, he said.

The dog looked down the path at the back of the wagon and seemed to ponder this possibility.

Morrison's plan was simple enough in concept, but he had no idea if the reality of it would prove likewise. He only needed one thing from town and that he bought at the general store. He didn't even leave the town till dusk, but still he didn't have far to travel. He came upon the men in the dead of night, the hound silent at his side. He stood at the edge of their camp taking in the scene. The two men slept atop their bedrolls on the ground: the black man with his mouth open to the sky, the white man on his belly, with his arms thrown out to either side as if to embrace the earth. The dying embers of the fire tainted all that followed with a crimson underlight.

Morrison slipped forward silently, low to the ground. He went to the black man first. He stood on the outside edge of the fire-light, set down his rifle and positioned himself with both hands just inches from the man's face. He glanced at the hound and saw that she was ready and then he began. He set the tip of a finger and thumb upon the black man's eyes and yanked them open. His other hand flipped over and tipped a powder into the man's eyes, a mixture as thick and red and as hot as live coals. The man started to howl, but Morrison was up and away from him, rifle once more *in hand. He leapt across the edge of the fire ring. Just as the white man began to push himself up, the tracker caught his chin with a closed fist. The man collapsed and Morrison was atop him, one knee pinned against the man's spine and the muzzle of the rifle set against his temple. The man scowled beneath the pain of it, hissed and spit as best he could.*

The black man howled and lashed out at the air and wiped his eyes with his fists. The hound dodged and feinted around him, barking and snarling and snapping her teeth. The man came up with a pistol aimed vaguely at the two other men. But before he could find a target the dog clamped down on his forearm and raked her teeth up and down the bones there. When she let go the man fell to the ground, groveling and pained and cursing. He did not rise again.

Morrison turned his full attention back to the white man. Now, he said, we have some things to talk about.

Six

The city dwarfed Annapolis, the only town William could compare it to. The place was a collage of smells and sounds like nothing he had ever experienced. He stumbled into it propelled by hope. He had reached the goal that had seemed so impossible, covered those miles of unmapped terrain and somehow found his destination. Now he would just find her. He only needed to pose the question to a friendly face. Or, failing that, he could plant himself at a busy spot on the street and wait. At some point, before too many days had passed, she would appear. Out on some errand, she would catch sight of him from a distance, walk closer doubting her own eyes, then break into a run that ended in his embrace.

But after walking the streets for several days, he couldn't believe she lived in such a place. It was a confusion of docks and piers, warehouses and factories. Smoke pipes belched plumes of slow rising filth. Soot covered windows. Sewers lay open to the air, their stink rising with the heat of the day. At first, he told himself he had entered the city via its most bustling district. He would have to measure its length and breadth and find some reason in it. His eyes flitted from structure to person to animal to the great tenement heights above him and the ash-laden sky. Foot traffic swarmed about him, people who moved with all the energy of ants at work. They dressed in fashions he had never seen, with hats and canes, with beards trimmed in all manner of shapes. They moved with a determination edged with threat. They shouted words that in the rapidity of their speech and in-flection seemed like a different language. There were white men who spoke with lilting rhythms, others that barked their words and still others who communicated with a code com-prised of gestures of the hands and arms, tiltings of their hats and scowls and grimaces. Coaches and omnibuses cut swathes through the traffic with reckless speed. Hooves churned past, the drivers red-faced, loud and heedless of the people to either side of the vehicles' whirling wheels. There were carts of every shape and description: decrepit things on lopsided wheels pushed by children, long, flat beds drawn by horses, piled high with sides of beef peppered with flies, calf heads sweating in the sun, fruits and vegetables, balls of dough fried in fat and coated with sugar. Amongst and between these, gangs of chil-dren prowled, dirty-faced and ragged as slaves and just as lean. A white boy-child with a single eye stepped up to William and spat a question at him, something so incomprehensible that William turned from him and moved away, that eye following him and seeing him and still somewhere out there now waiting for him.

The city's Negroes were also a puzzle to him. While most wore the clothing and demeanor of the working class, there were others who seemed to occupy each strata of society. Women and girls walked about in wide dresses, clutching satchels to their bosoms and lifting their hems above the filth. Still others mingled into groups of whites, talking and moving with mannerisms he couldn't twin with any other Negroes he had ever seen. They all, no matter the class or age or sex, had a demeanor about them that was unfamiliar. Their spines were set firm and straight. And there was something else, an intangible energy in the air around them that hummed like a tuning fork just before it faded to silence.

He studied faces and backs, shoulders and arms, trying to find even the slightest hint of something familiar. And, despite the strangeness around him, this was easy to do. The world and its inhabitants were full of pieces of Dover. His breath caught at the sighting of a certain hue of flesh. The image brought back a certain afternoon, when he and Dover sat together on the beach of one of the Bay's tributaries, talking of nothing in particular, but just sharing the day, learning about each other as a couple can only do once in their time together. A profile reflected in a shop window reminded him of the nights he hid in the bushes beside the house in which Dover worked, watching for her in the windows. And symbols of a more abstract nature took hold of him, as when he caught sight of a certain woman's hat, intricate and white and wholly unfamiliar to slaves. Dover had never worn such a hat. For that matter, he had never seen such a headdress on any black person. Yet the sight of it cut him to the core and left him breathless, shot-through with longing. Whether this longing was for something he had forgotten or for something he had never yet experienced he was unsure.

Though he moved surrounded on all sides by humanity, he avoided direct contact. He once collided with a well-dressed Negro, a man clothed in a black suit, vest and top hat, cane in one hand and some sort of ledger in the other. The man jumped back as if he had been assaulted, glaring at William with a look of loathing he had rarely encountered in other black men. The man looked him up and down, then he snatched a handkerchief from his vest pocket and proceeded to dab it across his jacket and vest. In an instant William felt himself awash in shame. He recognized all at once the pathetic sight he must be: the state of his clothes and his wild hair and speckled beard, the stains dripping from his armpits and neckline. He had never felt himself more a slave than he did in that instant, before that fellow man of color, never felt a greater need to explain himself. But the other man didn't allow him even this. He clicked his tongue and moved past him, cane held erect in one hand as a warning.

That night he ate the last of the hard biscuits from the ship. They rattled around inside him, measuring the girth of his hunger. He huddled between crates in the lee of a warehouse, the water near enough that he could smell it in the air. He told himself again and again that Dover wasn't far away. She was in this city. She had somehow made a home of this place, and if she had done that it couldn't be all that bad. But each time he said this he doubted it more. As he drifted toward sleep, he was half-aware of floating out of his body and up over the city. He hovered above it, suspended in the air with a view that took in the landscape in its entirety. How painful that view, to know that Dover was within an afternoon's walk in any direction. Or worse yet, that she strode down one street while he prowled the one just next to it. That she might sit in view of a window he passed, but that either, with their eyes otherwise occupied, might miss the other. He was so close to her, and yet he had never felt further away.

WILLIAM SPENT HIS FOURTH CITY NIGHT hidden among the bracken of an alley. Rats nibbled at bits of his exposed flesh each time he stilled, keeping him balanced on a knife-edge of fatigue and pain. He rose remembering his purpose and daunted by it. He crawled from the tiny lane an earlier version of the man that had entered it. The city air was so alive with smells that his hunger took on a life of its own and became his main obsession. His stomach churned and writhed at the slightest provocation, driven to frenzy by the scent of frying meat or the dry aroma from baking bread. There was so much around him and yet it was denied to him. He could stand a few feet away from a display of apples and pears and melons. He could imagine their textures within his palms and make out the slightest designs in their colorings and feel his teeth against those auburn skins. Yet there was a barrier between him and those foodstuffs. No one needed to remind him of this. It was nothing solid, nothing tangible, but it was a wall clearly enough, and he saw it evidenced in shopkeepers' stares, in the sharp jerks of their chins in directing him onward. He heard it in their tongues and felt it surrounding the people pushing past him when he paused. All the world was aligned against him. He knew this now and wondered why he hadn't before. And he was so tired, his body so heavy, the air so thick. He felt himself flagging and knew he needed to ask for help, but whom or how he couldn't imagine. Some friendly face . . . But had he seen one since he had arrived here? Each face was the same in that he had never seen it before. No kin to him, no one known or known of, strangers all.

By noon he found himself standing in an area of parkland, rimmed on all sides by the cobbled streets, busy with pedestrian traffic. He leaned against a tree and half-tried to blend into it, one hand massaging his temples. He didn't notice the two women strolling toward him until they were quite close. They were both dressed formally, one white and one black, and something in the look of the two of them struck him as familiar. The white woman's dress billowed around her with great frills and girth, and she carried a parasol for no apparent reason. The black woman walked with her hands folded across her abdomen, clutching a narrow purse in gloved hands. He listened to their voices as they approached, passed and faded. He didn't discern any one particular word, but he noted the tones they used, the delicate phrasing of the white woman and the rich, familiar tone of the black woman. They passed within a few feet of William without ever noticing him. They carried on toward the edge of the park, leaving in their wake a scent that flooded William with an image of pale purple.

He was moving before he had thought out his plan. He mustered his energy and stepped out behind them. His head smarted at the movement, but he walked past them, out to a cross street, spun and placed himself in the path of the white lady. He lowered his head, eyes cast downward, face meek and yet anxious to be acknowledged. He didn't move toward her, but his feet pawed the earth beneath him, like a horse nervous at the approach of a stranger. If the white woman noticed him she gave no sign. A few feet from him, she turned and smiled at another pedestrian, a man with a high black hat balanced on his crown. The two of them fell into conversation, leaving William poised in a strange pantomime with no audience.

The Negro woman had noticed him, however. She paused and, when the lady continued talking, she stepped back to William and looked him over. She was in later middle age, straight-backed, with wide-set eyes and a mole at the corner of her mouth. She wore a high collar around her neck, which she touched with the fingers of one hand before she spoke. "Can I ask what you were about to propose?" she asked.

William stared at the woman, momentarily losing his command of language.

The woman rephrased and repeated her question.

When he mustered the resources to speak, he said, "Do you know Dover?"

The woman frowned. She kept a little distance between them. "Who?"

"Dover. She a girl . . . Works for a family."

"What family?"

"Carr. The family's name is Carr."

"No," the woman said, "don't know any Carrs."

"You must know them."

"I don't know any Carrs," the woman repeated. "Sorry."

"Carr," William said again, a little louder, as if her hearing was in question.

But the woman shook her head. Her lips curved in a way that were somehow refusals in and of themselves. "You might try . . ."

"Sure you know them. You just ain't thinking right." He took a step toward her, his fingers held out before him like nervous spiders, trying to spin something in the air between them. "The name is Carr. They live in Philadelphia. This Philadelphia, ain't it?"

The woman's eyes flicked toward the white woman, seemed to edge toward her as if they intended to slide away. "Yes, but I've told you . . ."

He knew he was losing her. His words weren't right and he had to fix them. He wasn't saying the things he meant to. He had to calm her down. Calm himself down and explain. She didn't know him, didn't know who he was or what he had been through.

"This woman don't know you," he said, realizing as he mouthed the words that he was speaking them and that he hadn't intended to. Those words were for his thoughts, and now he had to explain that to her. Where were his wits? He motioned with his hands. The woman sprung back, her whole body tense and her face cold where it had been cautious a moment before. He stepped toward her, but again she leapt back. He tried to calm her, but his voice cracked and wavered and rose higher than he intended. The woman moved away. He would've followed, but he became aware of the many eyes focussed on him. It seemed all the city had stopped to watch him: the white woman with a gloved hand over the oval of her lips, a Negro, broad-shouldered and strong as a blacksmith, the Italian children on the stoop a little distance away, the carriage driver with his whip raised at the ready, the laborers standing with spades thrown over their shoulders, one of them with a smile wrinkling his lips. They all watched, and they all knew everything there was to know about him. They were all aligned against him.

That afternoon he stood outside a baker's shop, staring through the dim porthole at the loaves of bread aligned there. There was an ache behind his eyes that throbbed and pounded and jiggled like his skull was a loose-capped pot of boiling water. He decided that the pain came because his eyes were famished. Eyes can feel hunger just like the rest of him, he thought. When he moved he did so without thought, leaping the four stone steps down to the entrance of the shop in one bound. But there was no grace in his movement. He landed on a crooked ankle and stumbled forward and smashed his lips against the doorjamb. He came up face to face with the baker and recognized the man's intent. He turned as the man swung up a club. The weapon missed him by inches and splintered the doorframe in his place. He ran from there and didn't stop moving till he had no choice for the pain in his ankle.

The fifth night he beat away a pack of stray dogs and rooted through the rubbish behind a tavern, shoveling the muck into his mouth with his fingers. In the early hours of the next morning, he knelt in a park and retched up the vile concoction. He collapsed and lay sweating from the exertion of vomiting. But he found no rest. The heat within him built and no matter how still he lay his breathing was no easier. He fell into a fitful sleep. In that sleep he dreamt, scenes that filled him with a strange nostalgia, images of his home in Maryland, of the cabin of his birth and the fields of his youth and even the island he had labored on under St. John Humboldt. He walked through mundane scenes, everyday moments of the life that had been his. He tended the Masons' garden on a windy spring day, bees flying about him, loud and large and intent on their own work. He lifted and sorted tobacco, felt the leaves between his fingers and smelt the rich scent of it as it hung drying. He walked a landscape peopled with loved ones, his mother and her friends, Dover's people, Kate and his boyhood friend, Webster. He spoke to these people, exchanging words that suited their surroundings, talking about work or the weather or a myriad of other things that were forgotten as soon as they were spoken. But he never got close enough to speak to Dover herself. He caught glimpses of her from a distance: her at the edge of the field, her back as she strolled down a lane, and her with a child, his child, resting on her hip, both of them with their hands upraised, waving. He watched her with a vague unease, wondering if she was concealing something with her distance, as if her behavior was the only thing he found strange in this whole world.

He wasn't sure where he walked the next day for the city seemed to have little substance. He could barely stand and his muscles ached as if his bones were beating against them. His skin seemed to crawl with a rash that turned to dust when air touched it, floating up from him and yellowing everything. His hunger was gone. He was aware of that. He couldn't even remember food anymore, couldn't imagine wanting to put things in his mouth. His gums were loose and bloody—in a strange way a mirror image of the world moving past him. This was something he had never noticed before. He didn't move through the world, but it moved around him. He was the pivot point and the world was some great maze and there was a force moving it. He didn't need to move anymore, so he sat. Then he lay. He watched the sky and then closed his eyes and watched the world as seen upon a crimson screen. He was aware that he had soiled himself, but somehow it didn't matter anymore. God, he was hot. The world was baking. It was a furnace of red and orange and he was tired and wanted nothing more than to put that world to sleep. Let no one disturb him. Sleep was the only true good, let it come complete.

DURING HIS FITFUL SLEEP, his unconscious mind saw fantastic things. He moved from one strange reality into the next, separated by gaps of time in which he was aware of nothing save the fact of that nothingness. He found himself in amazing places but never doubted those places or questioned how he came to be there. He ran upon the bottom of the bay and did battle with marine monstrosities that he never saw completely. They were glimpses of fin and backbone and great eyes as flat as coins. Later, he prowled through the streets of Philadelphia, the buildings adrift as if floating, sliding into position before and behind him, a maze that was ever changing and incomprehensible. He watched a sky of deep maroon, the color of sumac in the fall, through which flew endless flocks of birds, tides of avian life fleeing this world in pursuit of others.

At these moments he was deep within himself and the outside world held no grasp on him. That's why he never noticed the woman who stopped to speak to him. He didn't remember shouting her away, nor that she returned the next morning and then again later that day. The third time she came with two adolescent boys who lifted him and carried him slung between them. William kicked at them as best he could. But he was weak and the boys were strong and soon many arms aided them. Palms touched him underneath, each contact a gentle one but so numerous that they held him above the ground and passed him along like he had no weight at all. In this way they bore him to the cave and lay him down and shut him in that quiet space and let his dreams overcome him again.

At some point Nan appeared beside him. The two of them met in the rainy woods from the first days of his flight. She sat beside him and looked at him sadly, her face the same handsome features they had always been, her hair just as long and radiant about her, the strands of white so fragile they seemed threads of spider silk. Her cheeks were wet, but whether from tears or the rain he could not distinguish. "What's become of you?" she asked, and hearing her voice he felt a child again. He felt ashamed though he wasn't sure how to answer her question. He said he got himself into a mess, was all, and she agreed, saying that he could say that twice and it wouldn't be a lie either time. She asked him was he too hot and he said he was and then she had before her a gourd of water which she dragged across the wet leaves and lifted, full and cool, to his lips. As he drank she spoke to him of things left undone. The small patch of land behind her cabin went untended. It had gone wild and overgrown and that was a shame, for she always kept a fine garden, hadn't she? That, and the roof was a mess. House never did keep the water out, looked like a blind beaver built it, didn't it? Somebody needed to mend that roof for sure, but she was past that type of work herself. Past it for sure.

She took the gourd back from him and pressed it down into the leaves. Water seeped up from the ground and slipped into its open mouth, filling it. They both watched this. Nan looked to him as if to say there was a lesson in this. She asked, "How come you did me that way?" William knew of what she spoke and tried to explain why he hadn't been at her burial. He was a slave, he said. He couldn't have come no matter how much he wanted to. He had not even been told of her death until weeks afterwards. But she shook her head and he knew that those excuses meant nothing. If it had been him going into the ground she would have been there. Nothing would have stopped her, not being a slave or being a woman, not even being old. Nothing should have stopped him, either.

"Woulda been there beside you to help you on," she said. "You doubt that?"

But he didn't doubt it at all.

"A son always knows his momma would lay down her hide for him," she said. "That's what's wrong with ya'll. You take it for granted. Think that's just how a woman is gonna be. Think you can act the fool and treat her cold. Then you get ashamed of her and stop coming around to see her. Think all her stories must be nonsense cause she only an old woman sick with love. You get to figuring you ain't gotta love her back proper. You forget she's the one made you and start to think you done made yourself. But that ain't true, is it? You always did love your momma, didn't you?"

He said that he had and to prove it he began to tell her all that he remembered. He spoke of the Bible and how white men twisted it to suit themselves and how he should never trust the written word unless he did the reading himself. He had a worth that couldn't be measured in any master's ledger. He had dreams and thoughts that corrupt men would never understand and that he must cherish for they were the things that belonged neither to massa or to God but were his alone. He would have spoke on, for he had so much he wanted to tell her. But he felt a hand on his forehead and it stilled him. It was not his mother's hand, for she had not moved, but it was familiar nonetheless and it was a comfort.

"Let me tell you this," Nan said. "I still remember you on the inside of me. Understand? I remember you fore you was you, when you was an acorn inside me, back when I could cup my arms around my belly and feel you kick me from the inside. That use to please me so. You can't even imagine," she said. "You can't even imagine."

Seven

Morrison found the runaway in a dank cell in a sheriff's gaol outside of Frederick, Maryland. The black man's captors laughed at his timing, for, they said, he was gonna hang like a side of beef in just a couple hours' time. Morrison asked if he could speak with him anyway. They debated this for some time, but in the end didn't see the harm in it.

We worked him over a bit, the sheriff's deputy said, but he's still got a tongue to talk.

It was hard to see the prisoner at first, but his breathing betrayed his presence, a moist rasp that befitted no human. As Morrison's eyes grew accustomed to the dim light he realized the state the man was in. He sat on the bare stone in the corner of his cell, naked from the waist up. His chest and shoulders glistened with a gooey substance only vaguely understandable as blood— for there was so much of it and the white man was unsure of how the man might've come to be covered in it so. He kept one arm at rest in his lap, though even the faint light betrayed the break that lamed it. The man's face was another puzzle altogether. One eye had been pounded till it had swollen shut; his nose was flattened across the bridge; holes had been punched through both of his cheeks, giving the impression that his tormentors must have shoved some long object clear through them. There was a swollen, sickle-shaped scar on his forehead. But this, at least, was an old wound.

The tracker could think of no easy way to begin this. He knew that men so close to death were the hardest to lie to. He didn't try. He asked him what he knew of the fugitive he was pursuing. The black man said nothing. Morrison described the man as he had been described to him, by appearance and temperament and history, and asked if he had been with the coffle heading south.

The black man offered no response.

I'm not out to do him harm, Morrison said, if that's what you're thinking. He and I have business... But it's not quite as you'd imagine.

Why don't you go on and get? the man said. He clamped his teeth at the pain and kept his voice level in its malevolence. He locked Morrison in the gaze of his good eye, an orb the same color and reddish hue as his skin. I'm fixing to meet my maker. Ain't got time for you.

Morrison thought about this. That's a lonely place to be at, *isn't it? he said. Seems too big a thing for most men to face, being that most of us are cowards.*

Hell, yeah, it's a lonely place. But what do you know bout it? Go on and get. I ain't telling you a thing.

Well . . . All right then. I'll leave you in peace.

Whatchu know of peace? You don't know peace. You ain't never gonna know it. You gonna sleep with the Devil, but you ain't never gonna get no rest. I wouldn't trade places with you if I could. Ain't nothing more I want from your world. You wanna do something for me? Then put the barrel of that there rifle to my forehead and end this. Otherwise go on and get.

They've been hurting you that bad? Morrison asked.

A decent man wouldn't believe it.

And they're not done yet, are they?

The black man looked through the bars at the white. This land contains a great evil, he said. You part of it?

Morrison hung his head and considered the question. He didn't lift it to answer but instead stared at the black stones of the floor. He told the captive that in his youth he had inflicted his will upon many of God's creatures. He had killed more than his share of beings, including other men. But with age he had become more and more haunted by his actions. The souls of men were troubled by violent deaths. They stalked at the backside of his mind's eye, always near at hand, voices calling for him to repent and quit such actions. He had done just that some time ago, but the voices had never left him in peace. They had become his own and he could not escape from himself. He concluded that he might indeed harbor some of that great evil within himself. He took no joy in this possibility, and if he could see a way to distance himself from it he would take it.

The black man was silent through all of this. When the other finished, he said, Killing and evil is two different things. The

Angel of Death is a warrior of God and his is a holy mission. You understand me?

Morrison nodded that he did. But he didn't think he could oblige the prisoner his request. That's a lot to ask a man, he said.

The black man was silent for some time, studying this sentence from all its different angles and then rejecting it. He told him to be damned then, be damned and do it away from him. Go on, get.

Morrison stepped blinking into the light of midmorning and walked toward the tree under which the hound sat. The dog rose when the man reached out to touch her head. She took a few steps in the direction she figured they were apt to take, but she turned back as the man did not follow. The hound stood looking back at him. The man contemplated the ground for some time, then lifted his gaze and took in the square and the hangman's platform at the far edge of it and the people milling about beneath it. He studied the mirth on their faces and their animated talk and the way they shared pulls from a whiskey bottle and the way a young boy snapped out a whip under the direction of an encouraging chorus. He looked down at the ground again. He motioned the hound back into the shade and bade her stay put.

He strolled into the crowd of men and shared a pull of whiskey when it came to him and made conversation. He asked what they had planned for the accused and this is what they told him. It was to be an afternoon of many amusements, to begin at noon. It would include whippings. It would include beatings. They would lay out the man's various limbs and take turns breaking them with a sledge hammer. They would urinate on his face, pour tar down his throat and they would cut off his fingers and bait them on fishing hooks. When all that was concluded, they would hang the man in keeping with the court ordered punishment for his crimes of murder, insurrection and treason. And they would do all this before an audience of the county's Negroes, so that they would see and understand the order of things and would never mistake which people God had chosen as his favorites. Morrison turned down the whiskey when it next came back to him.

When Morrison appeared once more before the cell the black man closed his good eye as if the apparition might be a trick of his vision. But upon opening it again nothing had changed. Thought you was gonna leave me in peace, he said.

The white man extended his upright palm into the cell. Thought you might care for a chew, he said. The other man stared at the tobacco with his good eye. He looked to the white man's face then back to the twist, so dark against his translucent palm. He licked his lips and reached out and took the stuff up with his fingertips. He nodded, a gesture like a thank-you but not quite.

Morrison nodded back. He produced another twist from his other hand and took a bite out of it. He chewed and looked for someplace to spit and then did so, covering the spot with his boot. If you don't mind I'll sit a while, he said. As the man voiced no answer, objection or affirmation, Morrison leaned his rifle against the wall and lowered himself onto the stool once more. Just give me a minute to get used to the idea. Go ahead and taste that tobacco, and then we'll get on with it. You've got my word on it.

The black man shut his good eye and lifted the tobacco gently to his mouth.

Eight

The scent was strong in his nostrils, sharp, head-clearing. There was movement around him. Hands worked over his body.

Someone's hip pressed against his side. A damp towel lifted from his forehead and the air touching his wet skin brought a new cool. There was a hymn, sung low, sweet and painful both, from deep within a woman's throat, which grew alternately louder and softer as she worked. And beyond her were walls that sometimes groaned and settled and a ceiling upon which steps could be heard. And further beyond were street sounds, carriages and voices, a dog that barked in clipped, high tones. There was a clock that told the hour, but he knew this was far away. He wasn't sure just when he had become aware of these things. It seemed, in fact, that these things had always been around but that he had only recently noticed. They hadn't mattered before. But now, for some reason, they did.

It was a strange feeling, remembering his eyes, recalling that he could open them, that there was a world to be beheld and they were the tool for it. The first thing he saw was the blurred, fleshy underside of an arm, bare to the skin, smooth, a hue like stained chestnut, dotted with freckles the size of poppy seeds. This arm was the entirety of his view for a few seconds and then it was gone. His sight flew upward into space, settling on the ceiling, unpainted boards with water stains radiating out from a few points like ripples in a pond. He stared at these for some time, not thinking about that arm or its owner, just focused on the grain of the wood and the manner in which water distorted it.

The humming stopped. "Thought you would find your way back," a voice said. At first, the voice seemed to have nothing in common with the hymn. It was solid where the tune had been ethereal; it had a matter-of-fact good nature so different than the melancholy of those notes. William didn't turn to the voice, and yet he was strangely prepared for the face that appeared before him. She was a colored woman, her face the same freckled complexion as that of her arm. Her features were weighty and generously rounded, not crafted for beauty and yet pleasant to look upon. She smiled, her teeth uneven and spaced with gaps but somehow merrier for it. "Yeah, you back for good this time."

She turned away and left him staring at the ceiling. He wanted to follow her, but he had forgotten how to turn his head, forgotten that such a movement was a possibility. Instead, he listened. The folds of her fabric as she moved, her flesh rubbing against the cotton, the dribble of water into a basin, a sound that he knew was that of a soft, wet cloth being squeezed between two hands. They were lovely sounds, and he realized he had been hearing them for some time.

A door somewhere slammed shut, the vibrations of it echoing through the house. The woman dropped the cloth into the basin, stood with it and moved away. William followed her with his eyes. The room was tiny, little wider than the cot upon which he lay, and the woman had only stepped away a few feet. She turned her attention to a small, dim window toward the far end, high up at the junction with the ceiling. She peered up at it, head craning side to side at something he couldn't see. "That girl's just now leaving the house," she said. "I knew it. She's gone and lost that job. I knew it by the way she wouldn't look at me straight. She's back to peddling her backside. Told Russell as much, but he said what's it matter long as she pays the rent."

The woman clicked her tongue off the roof of her mouth and turned back toward her patient. "Lord, William, if I didn't need them tenants to pay the rent I'd clear the house of them. Here I am trying to keep a decent home and they each and all got other things on they mind." She moved back toward him, her legs rubbing the side of the cot, metal basin balanced in her one hand. She sat down on a small stool, set the basin on her lap and dipped her fingers in for the wet cloth. "Bet you still a little cloudy, aren't you? You had a fever, William. That's all. Little yellow fever or something kin to it, but you done pulled through just fine. You ain't out of the fire yet, but the worst is behind you."

The woman's words resonated in his head, bouncing around and, at first, difficult to grasp. He had to force his mind to order them and narrow them down to a simple sentence. "I had a fever . . ." The woman agreed that he did, a damnable fever that she had been fighting for three days now. She went on talking, though he lost the direction of her words and had to close his eyes and try to start over. "Who are you?" he asked.

"I'm your angel of mercy in a time of need. Least I'm trying to be. Name's Anne Murphy. You call me Miss Anne and I'll answer to you."

He opened his eyes. "How'd you know my name?"

The wrinkles of the woman's forehead creased with amusement. "I know your name cause you told it to me. Told me all sorts of things. I won't even embarrass you by recounting them." She set the damp cloth in place across his forehead, just far enough down that the ragged edge of it cut the upper portion of his vision. The sharp scent of vinegar—that's what he had been smelling. "Naw, some a what you said I'll just keep to myself. You'd die of shame I told you half the things you rambled on about. Course, I am gonna help you find the lady of yours. But we'll talk about that when you're stronger."

William started to protest. He felt for the cloth and would have pulled it away, but the woman clucked an admonishment with her tongue. That was enough to still him. More than that even, the sound eased him, reminded him of something which he didn't try to place but which was a good thing. He lay back, and was asleep by the time the woman pulled the door fast behind her.

IN THE DAYS AFTER he regained true consciousness, William pieced together the events he had missed during his illness. Yellow fever was one of the many maladies rampant during the summer months. Anne explained that it had ravished Philadelphia just before the turn of the century like some classic plague of the Middle Ages, nearly halving the population. It had never been as bad since, but it flared up often, always during the hottest months, always without explanation. Anne had found William in an alley near her home and recognized his symptoms. She couldn't explain what had prompted her to take him in, except to say that she figured he was somebody's son. She had two boys herself and just did as she prayed others would do if one of her lot was in trouble. She hid him away in her cellar and nursed him through three days. He went in and out of consciousness, sometimes aware enough to converse with her, other times so far gone that he soiled the cot without noticing. She put aside all notion of propriety, bathing and caring for him as she would her own kin. William remembered almost nothing of this time, and Anne joked that that was fine, as a man might get embarrassed if he did recall such things.

The ordeal left William so feeble that he couldn't stand for a week after waking. Most of his time was spent in solitude, staring up at the ceiling and listening to the world outside the cellar window. At night, Anne's sons and her boarders returned. He was never sure just how many people lived in the floors above him, but he began to recognize certain voices. There was the short, polite speech of a young man who left early and returned late, and the deeper voices of the workmen who stomped into and out of the house. Their boots shook free dust particles that floated down on him, catching in his hair like dandruff. Children's voices came in a clutter of sound, intermingled with the quick patter of their feet. The girl Anne had speculated about had a strange cadence to her speech, beginning each sentence forcefully but losing steam as she spoke, the end of her statement dribbling away above him. Anne's eldest son had a rich, baritone voice. Her younger was shriller in his speech, quicker. Neither of them bore much resemblance to her, a fact William noted when one or the other of the boys brought him food and water. One was dark-skinned and short. The other was light of complexion, with wavy hair like that of a white child. They were the only others to care for him, and, as far as he knew, none of the boarders even knew of his existence.

Anne emptied his bedpan daily, something never commented on, just a chore she attended to without complaint. She shaved his scraggly beard with her own hands, her handling of the blade precise and without hesitation. It was strange to feel the air on his chin again, to finger the smooth, sensitive skin. Anne said a clean face suited him, his features being strong as they were and best viewed without disguise. Patches down his jowls and on his upper lip were remarkably pale next to his suntanned features. Anne commented on this, but William only shrugged and looked boyish and uncomfortable, nervous as if he were standing before her unclothed. She left the blade for him to use as he wished, and she brought him a replacement shirt. Though it was not new it was embarrassingly clean and well kept when compared with his own. Before parting with his old garment he plucked the medallion from the inside of it and slipped it in the pocket of the new shirt. He did this secretly, unwilling to explain the action to Anne.

Anne was also true to her promise to help find Dover. William didn't see most of her efforts, but she brought back word that she had sent an army of friends in search of her, using the Carr name as her primary reference point. She spoke to chambermaids as they hung linen to dry, to cook staff at the back doors to kitchens, over slatted fences and in alleyways and church pews. She sent inquiries out through colored coachmen and chatted longer than usual with the coal man. He was a grizzled man who had long sought to court her. He knew the back streets of the city and promised to find out what he could. Though her sources brought back many intimate details of the city's white citizens, no strong lead was forthcoming. The first Carr family they discovered was of very new money, with ties across the Atlantic. As far as she could learn, they had no female children of marrying age. The second family was not of the appropriate station to match William's descriptions; the third was a rambling group of dockworkers whom she likewise dismissed.

As the first week passed into the second Anne questioned him further on this family he claimed Dover was with. Was he sure he had got the name right? Did he know the white girl's given name, or, better yet, her father's? She tried to get him to remember something, anything else they could go on. She even asked him if he was sure they were from Philadelphia. Each of these questions left him ringing with doubt. He had emblazoned the Carr name onto his brain. He had formed it in his mind every day since he had heard it uttered, but as soon as he took that doubt on board nothing seemed as certain as it had before. He had never written it down, never spelled it out. He had never heard the woman addressed by that name and had no real proof of its authenticity. And that last question nearly floored him. Might he be in the wrong city? He searched back through that distant conversation with Kate and tried to see the words her lips formed. Even if he was not mistaken, Kate might have been. She knew little of the geography of this country or of the difference between Philadelphia and Providence, New

York and Boston. If this city was just one of many, his search
might have no ending.

One morning Anne's youngest son brought him a book
and a faded map of the city center. The map was about twenty
years old, but he thought it might still prove useful. William
thanked him, without asking how it might be useful. The
young man nodded and slipped out the door, up the stairs and
away into the upper house. Without opening it or reading the
title, William set the book on the floor beside his bed. He had
no interest in it. He did unfold the map, however, and lay it out
on his cot. He ran his fingers over the creases, as if the imper-
fections would flaw the map's details. He had seen maps of
Britain and France long ago when he had been hired to that
schoolboy, but that had been so long ago. It was hard to make
sense of the flat dimensions before him, the grid pattern etched
with hard edges, black ink against yellowed paper. He traced
the wavering lines of the city's two rivers and eyed the letters
of street names, finding nothing familiar in any of it. He tried
to twin the rectangles and squares with avenues he had walked,
buildings he had looked upon, but the effort was more frustrat-
ing than anything else. Before long he folded the map and
slipped it back inside the book and lay back on the cot. He tried
to feign indifference, but he was not indifferent. Within half
an hour he had retrieved the map and leant over it to try
again.

In the afternoons Anne always found time to come and sit
with him. She chatted about the day's events, the myriad dramas of the streets and the foibles of her own boarders, people
she spoke of frankly but also seemed to have a fondness for.
She didn't ask him much of his history, but she never seemed
surprised by it. She had known he was fugitive before he had
admitted it. Known he had been a slave. Known he had been

whipped and seemed to even know the designs of the scars on his back. And though she was ever kind, there was something disturbing in her knowledge of him and in his dependence on her.

"You know that girl has had three babies already?" Anne asked, speaking once more of the young woman she believed to be a prostitute. "Three babies and her hardly seventeen herself. One of them came out stillborn. Other two she sent off to her family in the country. Ask me, she should head back out there herself, but she got her own mind on things. Always thinks she's missing something."

She sat on the tiny stool beside the bed. One leg crossed atop the other to form a platform upon which she draped a shirt she was mending. She moved carefully with the long needle, leaning forward and straining her eyes in the dim light. William stood at the far end of the cellar, testing his legs. He paced a tight circle, lifted one knee to his chest and then the other, pressed his arms against the rough wall and leaned his weight into it.

"I tell you what, William, you best hope that baby of yours is a boy. A boy's a handful, but can't hold a candle to a girl for mischief." Her fingers paused in their needlework. She watched William squat and push himself upright. "Yeah," she said, "you're looking good. I might even let you out of this room before too long."

"I could work, you know," he said. "I expect you'll want some work outta me fore I leave. Just as soon start on it now."

Anne let her hands drop into her lap. "And why do you expect I'll want to put you to work?"

William, noting the tone of her voice lowered himself to the corner of the bed. "Well . . . All the things you done for me . . . Figure you'll want something back."

"Did your captain want something when he helped you?"

William cut his eyes. The question embarrassed him though he didn't know why. "Don't know. He mighta, but he let me go."

"But you think I want something from you?"

He didn't answer, just watched his hand where it lay flat against his sheet.

"Think about what you're saying," Anne said. "There you sit before me, what, twenty-some years old? You've been twenty years a slave to other men. Whipped and beaten and all that comes with being somebody's horse. You been through all that, but then you have two people do you a kindness and you don't know what to make of it. William, all I'm doing is treating you like a human being. That captain just did the same, God bless him. You want to be free, don't you? You want to be a man?"

"I am a man," William said. The words sounded strange and he wasn't quite sure what prompted him to say them, but Anne accepted them as they were.

"That's right. You are. All I'm doing is treating you like one. You think on that some and you might just learn to like it. This world ain't all evil. And I'll tell you another thing. Ain't one slave who's gotten himself to freedom without help. Not one. There's no shame in it. Just the way it is and the way it's gonna be for a little longer. You have any other fool thoughts you want to share?"

He did not and for a little while they sat in silence. Several times the woman flexed her fingers as if she would resume her work, but she did not. Outside a horse and wagon trundled by. They came on in a confusion of noise, whatever cargo they carried trembling like sheets of metal. The driver called out directions at the top of his lungs, as if he would command the streets and the houses and the people therein to all make way for his passing. The woman looked up at the black square of

glass that marked the cellar's one window. William paid no
heed. He lowered his head and let his brow rest on the prongs
of his fingertips. As quickly as it came the wagon was gone.

"You're not the first one who's had a long road to walk,"
Anne said. "I'm not preaching at you." She looked at William
and began to tell him a story, one that she said was from a
couple years back. It was the story of a certain man who had
long worked for the Underground Railroad just outside of
Philadelphia. He was a faithful conductor, known by many,
respected by all, who had himself come up from slavery years
before, leaving behind all his people and all he ever knew of
the world. That kind of work was not easy, and the man's out-
spoken beliefs took a toll on his life and health. His business
ventures often fell apart for no apparent reason. He was jailed
more than once for suspicion of aiding a runaway. Although he
was always acquitted for lack of evidence, those damp cells gave
him a constant cough that marked his presence at prayer meet-
ings. He was hounded by officials and constantly in fear for his
life, for the forces of slavery led forays into the North and this
man was well known to them. The fore-portion of his home
went up in flames one winter evening and was only saved by
a provident snowfall. His eldest son was attacked and beaten
within a whisper of his death, left limping forever after and shy
as a field mouse exposed to the night sky. But through it all the
man persevered in his work and ideals and helped numerous
souls to move deeper into dubious freedom.

One day a strange man approached him and asked for his
help. This man said he was a fugitive and that he was hunting
help on the way to freedom. The conductor was wary of his
inquiry, for there was something familiar about the man, something strange in his mannerisms, in the length of his arms and
the set of his jaw. He couldn't explain it, but he almost turned

the man away unaided. Almost, but not quite. He feigned
no knowledge of the railroad and cautiously questioned the
man. The runaway told where he was from and described his
escape in such detail that it sounded credible. Then he named
his parents. The railroad man just stared at him as though he
were crazy, asked him was he having him on. The runaway said,
"No suh. That's the God-honest truth. Otherways he can strike
me down where I stand." God didn't strike him down, and instead, the conductor stepped forward and embraced the man,
his brother, who he hadn't known he had until that very moment, a sibling met for the first time thirty-seven years after
his birth.

"And that's a true story," Anne said. "Every now and then
the Lord lets some light through. It's moments like that that get
us through. We gotta remember them stories, so in the years to
come when people write down our history it ain't all the sor-
rows alone. You understand me? Ain't no people in the world
that can live on a diet of pain. Pain may be the bread of a slave's
life, but there's got to be water as well. William, that man was
forty-five years without a brother. But on the day that man
walked in to him it didn't matter. He had his brother, and you'll
have your wife. You gotta remember her, conjure her, don't ever
let her slip from mind. And you have to have the sense to just
accept a helping hand when it's offered. You hear?"

William, without looking up, nodded that he did. Anne
clucked her tongue. She lifted her work and studied it a moment, then pushed the needle into the fabric. "Now them two
boys Cecil and Jack, they're good boys but not a lick a sense between them. Don't know why I put up with them. I tell you
about the mess they got in with that preacher over on Lombard?
All started when Jack seen the collection hat coming toward
him ..."

ON A STILL EVENING two weeks after his fever had abated, William sat in a corner of the cellar. His head lolled to one side and leaned on the unpainted bedrock of the wall. His eyes were open, staring with an unfocussed gaze across the rough stone surface. The wick of his oil lamp was nearly exhausted and emitted a steady stream of black smoke, a gloom that gathered like a veil across the ceiling. He was still except for the thumb of his left hand, which caressed the tips of his fingers in monotonous rhythm, like a man counting toward infinity. It seemed he had been in this city for years, and that nothing changed from one day to the next and that all the coming days offered the same. His mind wandered of its own direction, through a maze that commingled the streets of Philadelphia with those of Annapolis, which set his bunk in the basement atop his straw pallet on Kent Island. He saw faces from that long ago time and images that left within him a longing for the certainties he had left behind. All the people and places and memories that made up his life seemed so far away now. He was now coming to realize that the risks of this venture went beyond the physical, beyond even failure at finding Dover. He was gazing at the wall beside his cot, but what he was seeing was a future lived in exile.

He looked up when Anne walked into the room. Her mood was at odds with his. Her hair was pulled tight against her skull. But despite the attempt at maintaining her formality, humor tickled the corners of her eyes. Her gaze was quicker than usual in settling on him, warmer. She seemed ready to smile but then checked herself and frowned at the state of the lamp. She lifted the lamp from the shelf, held it close to her face and fiddled with it. "Had a visit from the coal man, Mr. Payton, this morning," she said. "That man is something else, bringing his raggedy self up the back steps like a suitor calling on me, a flower in hand if you can believe it. And me a grown woman old enough to be a grandmother." Her tone was lively, joyful almost, but seeing William's glazed expression she cut her mirth short. "He brought word. Word of your Dover."

William stared at her. He didn't actually question her, but Anne moved closer and proceeded as if he had. Mr. Payton had found a Carr family who lived in the fashionable area near Walnut Street. They had in their employ a young Southern Negress. This woman had returned with the youngest daughter of the family from a failed marriage to a Southern planter. He had a street name and number at which they lived, both of which Anne whispered as if fearing being overheard. Those were all the details Payton could acquire, but, Anne said, this may be the answer to their prayers. She placed the lamp back on its shelf, burning cleaner but still giving a dim light. "It's her, William. I can feel it."

"Near Walnut . . ." he said, a phrase not a question or a statement, but something in between.

"That's right, rich folks up in there. But listen here. You can't just go over there and knock on the front door like a gentleman caller. You don't know the state of things over there. Don't even know for sure that Dover's there; don't know if there's men looking for you or what. So promise me you won't do nothing until I've found out more. Payton said he would see what he could find out. Let's wait on that."

"You want me to wait on it?" William asked. When the woman nodded that she did, he rose and walked the short length of the room.

"It's the best for now. I'll go over there myself if I have to, but you don't know what might be waiting for you there."

William stood at the far end of the room, facing the window. Somebody passed by out there, a shadow darkening the pane and then moving on, not a solid being but just the suggestion of one. "You want me to wait on it?" he asked again.

"I do. I brought you the news and I expect you'll take my advice along with it. Tell me what you're thinking, William, your face is a mystery."

He reached for a tin cup and poured water from a jar beside the wash basin. Then he set the cup before him and stood again, without ever having lifted the cup to his lips. "I don't know what I think. I wanna hope, but I'm afraid of hope. I'm afraid of what hope is doing to me right now."

"I hear you," Anne said. She rose, stepped nearer and set her hands upon his shoulders. "I just brought you good news, William. Remember joy. You just have to leave it for the morrow, you hear?"

William thanked her, but he did not say if he heard, or if he would leave it for the morrow. He held his thoughts behind clamped teeth. As soon as the woman left him alone, he began planning.

Nine

The gift that Morrison offered the prisoner was that of a quick death, a flight straight into the arms of a colorless God. It was only right to honor the wishes of a doomed man, although the white townspeople didn't see things in like manner. After the single rifle blast, the Scotsman made his escape by the most direct of means. He walked out. It wasn't long before the townspeople discovered his actions. They ran the man and his hound from the town with deadly intent, a mob angry at being denied its pleasures. Morrison carried a scar above his eye from where a youth

slashed him with a plow point tied to a piece of rope. It would
have knocked him unconscious save that his legs kept him
moving and movement kept him sentient. The hound would for-
ever after limp on chill days, as the deep bone-bruises on her hind
legs would never heal completely. She would sometimes dream
of the frenzied townspeople and their reasonless rage and wake
up to her own yelping. Despite the wounds inflicted upon them,
the two travelers covered many miles over the next few days.
The man walked in a frenzy of thought, mumbling to himself.
This land contains a great evil, he would say and this troubled
him, for all around were the signs and symptoms of that evil.

    He moved through the country like a child seeing it for the
first time, collecting images piled one on top of another, a strange,
internal collage of the world's dramas. The black bodies of labor-
ers in the fields shimmered in the heat of midday. A white child
stood naked in the dirt beside a fence post, pot-bellied and thin-
limbed, with turquoise eyes that would have been beautiful had
they not been portholes to simmering belligerence. An itin-
erant preacher shouted the gospel from atop a crate in a town
square, the gathering crowd loud in their affirmation of his
words and he sweaty and red-faced from the effort of it. A hump-
back watched him from a storefront. When he looked too long
the humpback opened his mouth and spat and asked him was he
as dumb as he looked. A slave woman led her children past him
on the road, one child trailing behind the other, three in a row,
each holding the one before by the tail of his shirt, the one in the
back naked from the waist down. This last image reminded the
tracker of a picture he had once seen in a storybook, but he could
not remember what book or where. He was not sure whether the
storybook characters had been human or some other animals
entirely. These scenes were not new to him. They were of this
land and he had seen such things a million times. Perhaps, he

thought, the wound in his head had weakened him, for he had
known even smaller scratches to be the death of better men
than he.

The waning days of August found the tracker once more on
Kent Island. He met Humboldt coming down the road. The two
men stopped and looked at each other. The planter said he figured
Morrison hadn't had much luck. Morrison didn't disagree.

Yep, the planter said, I know you didn't cause I got a suspicion that the boy is holed up in Philadelphia, the Godless place.
I'm sailing there directly. Humboldt said that he was tired of
all this shit waiting, tired of sad excuses for trackers who couldn't
find their own mother's teat. He had a lead and he was gonna
follow it.

The man began to walk away, but paused when Morrison
asked if he might accompany him. Why? he asked. Did I say I
was taking on hands?

No, but I thought you might take on another gun.

The planter thought this over. He asserted again that there
would be no pay in it, but Morrison waved this away. Why you
want to go so bad? he asked.

Just like to see things completed, Morrison said.

Yeah, I know the feeling, Humboldt said. Nigger's not even
my own property and here I am chasing him down. Sometimes it
just gets personal. Come on then. He began to walk and as he did
so he continued to talk, reminding Morrison that there was no
guarantee of real pay for his services. He would just have to see
what circumstance brought his way. To this he added one further
bit of information, saying that he had been contracted by another
local planter to pick up a slave wench of his in Philadelphia. He
figured that at the very least they could have a bit of fun with her
on the return journey. She was heavy with a pup, he said, but he
kindly had an affection for women in that condition.

Morrison, walking a half-step behind him, heard this news with a trepidation he couldn't quite explain.

Ten

In the stillness approaching midnight William climbed the stairs of the cellar. He stood for a long time with his ear pressed to the door, listening, searching in the silence for any sound that might delay him. He found none and pushed the door open as quietly as he could. The room was a collage of lines and shadows, white walls and dark floorboards all in dimensions he was no longer used to. He took his bearings from the pathways the footfalls had made above him in the cellar. His feet, back once more in the remnants of his brogans, were louder than he would've liked. He fumbled for some time with the latches on the front door, but soon he was through them and out once more upon the streets of Philadelphia.

He didn't pause to take the scene in, but descended the steps and started walking. It was strange leaving the shelter of cellar, walking down the street that he had up to then experienced only through the grimy glass of the window. The buildings on either side of him seemed to lean in toward each other, blocking out all but a thin corridor of the sky above. He remembered the maze of his fevered mind and had to fight the fear that the buildings were conspiring against him. They were simply stationary objects, black and shadowy, yes, but made only of stone and brick and mortar. Sounds, though there were few, were loud and vivid in a way they had never been before.

The scuffing of his feet and tolling of a bell and a window slammed closed: all seemed to occur just beside his ear. They pierced into his brain unfiltered.

At the end of the first block he pulled the street map from within his shirt and studied it in the starlight. A few days before, Anne's youngest son had marked their house with a pen, and earlier that evening he had traced a route between that dot and the street that was his destination. William followed it as best he could, counting streets and turnings. He wove his way through miles of the city night, unsure the whole time just what he intended. He knew he should wait as Anne had suggested. The danger she spoke of was real. He might be putting everything at risk. But he just couldn't sit still.

He had almost an hour to think out a plan as he walked, but when he found the street he was looking for he had no clearer notion of what he would do. It was a wide avenue of close-set cobbled stones. Great trees lined the walkway like sentinels standing guard over the gloomy night, long-limbed and enduring. He moved forward, checking the houses for numbers or names, moving in fits and starts, through shadows and open stretches, hugging the tree trunks. His gait was half-casual, like a man strolling in the evening, and half-frantic, head snapping toward the slightest sound, hands tense and fingers stretched apart as if grown sensitive to each other's touch. But for all his fear he met no one on the street, and the houses that fronted upon it were uniformly dark. He moved on.

His heart thumped against his chest when he saw the house. Its number stood out clear and burning above the wide front door. There was no mistaking it. The structure was all so silent, so still and heavy it could've been carved of solid granite. It was, in its immobility, a great barrier to the world enclosed within its walls, each of those mundane features impenetrable, like those of a medieval fortress. At the end of the street he

halted and thought and surveyed the four corners of the inter-
section and looked back toward the house. It sat among the others with a shared façade, innocuous and yet so charged with
import.

The clap of a horse's hooves broke the silence. William
didn't wait to see the horseman. He darted away from the main
street, circled around and found a stony lane that ran behind
the houses. It was hemmed in on one side by a brick wall that
marked the properties' boundaries. On the other side an embankment supported a hillside thick with vines and bracken.
He stood a moment, listening to the clipped notes of hooves
on stone. Eventually, he stepped into the alley. He counted the
homes until he was sure he had found the house again. He stood
at the iron gate that marked the back entrance, not touching it,
but gazing between the black stencil of its metalwork. The
house was as still from the back as it had been from the front
and more forlorn yet. A white curtain swayed in one of the
open windows, bringing to his attention how slim the barrier
was between him and the inside of that house. Dover might be
no more than an open window's distance away. He could just
jump the gate and scale the wall and climb through. It seemed
like it would be so easy, and it took great effort to pull himself
away.

He moved farther down the lane, following the embankment as it turned away from the passageway. He settled on
a spot where the wall had partially collapsed. The area was
choked with shrubs. He wormed his way back into the ivy that
draped over the embankment. He turned and checked the view.
The house was a hundred yards away. Part of the alleyway was
obscured, but he could see both the house itself and the small,
dark square that marked the locked back gate. So situated, William rolled his neck upon his shoulders and tried to ease the
tension out of his limbs. He asked his heart to slow its beating

and wiped the sweat from the corners of his mouth. He began his vigil. He set no parameters on his mission. He just knew that his roaming was over. If Dover were employed in this household she would at some point pass through these back gates, as servants always do. He would spot her as she went to some errand, and, he believed, he would know what to do then.

GRADUALLY THE DAWN CAME. Features of the world stood in ever-clearer detail, monochromatic at first, but blooming into thin color. Shortly afterwards the foot traffic started. Throughout the morning there were occasional passersby through the lane; deliveries at the rear of houses, the coal wagon, workers trudging along with hats low on their heads and tools balanced at awkward angles from their shoulders or swinging at their sides. A man trudged by pulling a wagon, himself harnessed into it like a beast of burden. His feet found careful footing between the stones, muscles braced and tortured by the work. His load was covered over with a burlap sheet, but a smell escaped from it that stuck to the back of William's throat and brought to mind images of the dead.

As he expected, servants entered the expensive homes via their back gates. He watched them all, his eyes darting from person to person. At one point, three Negro women traversed the lane, talking amongst themselves. William studied them each in passing but noted no sign of Dover in their postures or movements or dress. Their voices came to him in fragments, but he knew from this also that she was not among them. Later in the afternoon a dog came bounding before its owner. It was drawn toward William by his scent, curious and loud, paws falling blindly on the earth. The canine was just a few feet away when its owner called it back. It went reluctantly, smelling but not seeing the man who huddled just before it, a hidden form entwined in vegetation like a tree spirit incarnate.

That evening he watched the world run backwards. The various maids emerged from their employers' back gates. Workers returned from their labors. Shadows stretched and the sun slipped once more out of view. His nose, sharpened by a day of fasting, scented the suppers being prepared in those grand homes. The three women left the Carrs' just after sunset, leaving in their wake the scent of roasted chicken in gravy so rich it was nourishing just to inhale it. His stomach rumbled so loudly he feared it might give him away. But the women walked on.

For the first few hours after dark, candles lit the upper rooms of the house he now doubted was the Carrs'. He half-decided to rise with the darkness and return to Anne's, but he didn't. He sat where he was, stiff and starved, waiting moment after moment, expecting to see himself stand and leave that place and yet not doing so. In his hunger and his fatigue he slept, and in his dreams he sat exactly where he was, across from the back gate of those large houses, waiting in the spirit world as he did in the physical one. When he awoke it was as if he had never slept and somehow this long period of immobility wearied him even more than his days in flight. It began to rain, a slow, gradual precipitation that fell unabated until dawn. The leaves around him dripped with moisture. Water splattered his shoulders and seeped into his hair and collected beneath him in a puddle that was at first lukewarm with his body heat but that soon grew cold.

As miserable as he was there, a memory came upon him sudden and vivid. It was an evening late in the summer of the previous year. He waited that night, as he did whenever he could, for Dover to leave her master's house. But this evening was different than the others, for when she came to him her smile flashed in the night. Her hands were anxious to touch him and soon her lips were soft against his. Her body pressed his with an urgency that shocked him. Her mouth opened and her tongue writhed within him, swirling around his in a sensuous dance. He remembered that she tasted of berries, of the sweet wine sipped from her master's unfinished glasses. They had made love outside that night, not far from the slave graveyard. That one night alone he didn't fear the spirits. He thought nothing of them or of the world of men or of his bondage. Entwined with her against the damp grass they had found moments shared only between them and belonging to no one else in the world. Afterward, he lay listening to her as she recounted things she had overheard that night, Northern talk against slavery, high ideals that, to her ears at least, her master had been powerless to reason against. It was this that had intoxicated her. Not the wine. Not William himself. But freedom. That was what mattered to her most. He knew then something that he had never put into words before. She was the stronger of them, the one with vision, with a determination that had never wavered. Wherever she was, she was free now in a way that he believed he never would be.

LATE THE SECOND DAY William crawled from his hiding place, stiff from his long vigil, sapped to the core. He hadn't actually conceded defeat, but he didn't need to name it as such. It was tide flowing into him, building each passing hour, unnamed but no less real. He wasn't even sure that he was going to return to Anne's. He wasn't planning that far ahead. He just needed to move. As he passed the back gate of the house, he paused and pushed his hands in through the iron grating. He wrapped his fingers around the ornate curls and leaves, feeling the cast metal's irregularities, the gritty texture where rust had begun to spread its decay. He set his forehead against it, pressing so hard and long that when he pulled back his skin was imprinted with its design. He walked away with his head lowered, seeing no further than a few feet in front of him: bricks and the space between them, leaves and twigs and horse dung and the unnameable rubbish that had been and always would be the material of any city street. It was only when he was back on the main avenue, having crossed it and standing on the other side, that his gaze lifted and studied the mansion. It was unchanged from before, except brighter now and more solid and that much more indifferent. He half lifted a hand, as if in farewell to another person, and then he spun to move away.

It was in this swirling motion that he saw her. She appeared on the opposite side of the street, trailing along at the heels of three white women. These three—two old and one young—walked in a leisurely fashion, hands folded before them, the youngest dangling a parasol at her side, all three talking at once, though William couldn't hear them because of the distance. His eyes pushed between them, catching brief glimpses of the Negro woman who followed them. He saw parts of her at first: half of her face and the hat above it, the length of her forearm, the low hem of her skirt. But it was enough. It was Dover.

She turned her head and met his eyes. Her step slowed, like a toy beginning to wind down; her eyes blinked and opened and blinked again; her gloved hand rose up and cupped before her mouth, as if she would catch her exhaled breath within her fingertips. She might have turned from the sidewalk and moved toward him, but the younger of the white women paused before the gate of the townhouse and called back for her. Dover hurried on, saying something to explain herself and fanning her face with her hand. She didn't look at William as she entered the gate, or as she closed it behind her and walked beside the woman to the front door. She turned and looked back as she passed through the house's threshold. It was a momentary glimpse, not enough to convey a message. Then the door closed.

William didn't move. He stared as if the door itself had done him harm and had something to answer for, awed that he had never for a moment imagined her entering the front door. The sky slid by overhead, bringing with it patches of shade and bursts of light. People passed him on either side, like water around a rock. He was aware of some pausing to study him and felt one man brush roughly past him. The minutes added one unto another, past the quarter hour and on toward the half. Still he stared, sure that it couldn't end so incompletely, but at a loss for what to do next.

But when she came it was from another direction. She must've exited through the back gate. She approached him from the alley he had himself emerged from. She slipped toward him so quietly that at first he didn't notice. It was only the fact that a being stopped near him that drew his attention from the door. He turned and beheld her as she was, no longer a creature of dreams, but flesh and blood there before him. She whispered his name. He nodded his acceptance of it. And that was all the voiced greeting that passed between them. They moved together, closing the gap of those many months and many miles in the space of two strides.

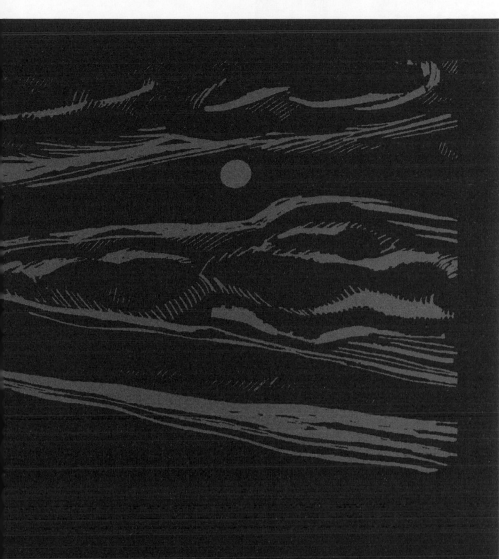

PART THREE

One

Dover whistled for William in the pitch-blackness that precedes
the rising of the moon. He stumbled forward, crouched low and
feeling his way with his hands. When he stepped out of the undergrowth and emerged beside her, she pulled him tight against
her. "Shh," she said. "Don't let nobody hear you talk." With that,
she set off, quick enough in her step to allow no dissent.

They had precious little time to speak upon their meeting.
Dover had done little more than verify through touch and a few
words that William was real, then she had ordered him back
into hiding until she could figure out what to do. It was too
brief a reunion, and it left William with a host of unanswered
questions. He waited as instructed, throughout the late afternoon and on into twilight and beyond, replaying those seconds,
searching each of her gestures and words for meanings hidden
below the surface. Though he was amazed by the sight of her,
something in their greeting left him uneasy.

They traveled on the side streets, the alleyways, behind

people's houses, stepping around the refuse that collected in such regions, the pungent mounds patrolled by rats wakening to their work. It was an intimate progress, this rear glimpse into people's homes. It became more so once out of that affluent neighborhood and into working class areas. The business at the backside of the city dwellers' lives was on display. The splash of liquids thrown from a back window, the piercing wail of a child left unattended, the glazed eyes of an old woman, alone on a porch, railing verbally against the rats she loathed. William started at the call of one Irishman to another, the two suddenly emerging from a fenced yard, dashing past them like school children, laughing as they went. Once their path brought them near a legless man. He shouted curses from the padded crate in which he sat, lashing out with his arms as if he could grapple with the world and so vent his anger. The couple circled him at length and moved on.

Their destination was a modest row house, a unit squashed between the larger structures. They approached it from the back alley, slipped in at a rickety wooden gate and fell into shadow, and emerged into the moonlight again as they climbed the stairs. The landing at the top was a narrow balcony of rough-cut lumber. It bowed beneath their weight. William wondered how Dover knew this route so well, but he didn't voice the question. She motioned him still and addressed herself to the door, a windowless portal whose lintel met William at eye level. She rapped against it with her knuckles. He noticed for the first time how hard she was breathing. Beads of sweat clung to her forehead. Noticing his gaze, she wiped them away with the flat of her hand.

The door cracked open. A man stepped forward, holding a candle close to his face, bathing his features in pools of light and shadow. His complexion was similar to William's, though his face had a muted quality very different than William's strong features. He wore wire-rimmed glasses that reflected the candlelight in gold. His glance first settled on William, quick and defensive, but it softened the moment he noticed Dover.

"Sorry to trouble you," she said. She leaned in toward the man, meeting his gaze and speaking as much with her eyes as with her mouth. "Have to apologize for coming by at this hour, but we need to talk."

William learned the other man's name was Redford Prince. His apartment was small but tidy, with a sparseness that at first disguised the careful selection of the room's decorations. Redford bade them enter and motioned them toward the sofa, an ornate furnishing with pale upholstery, with cabriole legs of a deep mahogany that concluded in claws clenched around the balls upon which the entire structure rested. Redford swept an assortment of books and papers from the coffee table and offered them tea. They both refused, but he stoked the tiny fire in his hearth with a few small sticks and set out saucers for them. He was largely silent through all of this, working with a quick dexterity, his fingers trembling while at rest.

William soon found himself seated on the soft cushion, a cup and saucer balanced on the rough contours of his knees. Dover held the same in one hand, somehow graceful with the porcelain in a way that made William uneasy. She explained the situation that had brought them there. A little of it, at least. But as she knew almost nothing of William's story it fell to him to tell his tale. He did so most reluctantly. Though he described terrors neither of his listeners could imagine, it was he who was most unnerved. He wasn't even sure why, but somehow, already, the glow was fading. Things were already different than he had imagined. Telling his tale only made him more aware of this.

Before long they began to talk of the couple's options, which proved to be painfully limited. They couldn't make a home for themselves here because William wasn't beyond the reach of the South. And Dover, despite her apparent freedom, was still the property of a man who could call her back at any time. They could flee farther north, or to the west, but to where, with whose help, to settle in what unknown territory, with what demons stalking behind them? At length, Redford began to speak of an escape to Canada.

"Canada?" William asked. He glanced at Dover, surprised that she did not share his shock. Yes, Canada bordered the States, but, as it was another country, it might as well have been Great Britain or Prussia or even Africa itself. "You expect us to go to Canada? I don't know nothing bout up there."

"It's the nearest truly free soil around. I know it's a difficult thing to consider, but you're already an exile from the place of your birth, William. Life there does have advantages, as I've already explained to Dover. I've a copy of the *Provincial Freeman* around here somewhere. It's a paper put out by a Negro woman about life in the provinces. She exaggerates the positive, I'm sure, but it's worth reading." Redford half-stood and cast his eyes about the room.

William's eyes darted between Redford and Dover, sharp on each. Everything about the free man's educated tone aggravated him: the brevity with which he shot down each proposal they made, the way the corner of his lips dipped before he spoke, the manner in which he explained the hard facts behind things as if to a young child. Even the way he held his teacup— the angle of his wrist and pauses in his speech during which he drank—seemed an insult. But what choice did he have but to sit and listen and try to learn enough to get some control back? He lowered his gaze and glared at the teacup.

"Anyway, I'll find it for you," Redford concluded. "This does pose problems of its own, not least the financing of such an adventure. We might be able to gain the support of some of the faithful, but you know how these things are—the fewer that know the better."

"You say we have to head to Canada," William said, his voice fighting for a composure he didn't feel, "and maybe you're right. You let us on think on it a bit. Meantime I'll work. I'll pay our own way."

The other two shook their heads in unison.

"That wouldn't be advisable, not unless it was work that I secured for you," Redford said.

Dover agreed. "It's best you just stay hid somewhere. No use bringing attention to yourself."

William lifted the teacup and deposited it untasted on the glass tabletop. Dover's words were simple and reasonable enough, but he felt a sting at the backside of them. Did he embarrass her? Was he so useless? Must he just hide and rely on the good will of others? The moment of connection he had experienced when they reunited was gone. It had only been a few hours, but the intimacy between them seemed to have faded completely. "Don't see why I can't just work. That's one thing I know how to do. If I could keep my wages it wouldn't be long fore . . ."

"Before you were chained and on your way back to massa." Redford said this with a touch of sarcasm, but, having spoken it, he changed his tone. He adjusted his glasses, looked from William to Dover and back again. "What I'm trying to say is that you're daily in danger. Perhaps I should explain to you the current laws of our land. You can't be expected to understand them. William, there are many good men and women in the North. I don't doubt that there are a few in the South as well, although they stay largely silent. The Christians of the North abhor slavery, and we are doing everything possible to see it overturned. But, the powers in Congress over the last few years have followed a policy of compromise. The Congress, and the President, want nothing so much as to keep this union of states together. As such, they've capitulated to the slaveholders, not so much because they share like minds, but because they see the denigration of the Negro as the lesser evil compared to dissolution. Do you understand?"

Dover said, as if translating, "They made a law that says the North gotta send slaves back south."

"Exactly," Redford continued, inching forward to resume center stage. "Anyone, anywhere in the United States is required by law to respect the property rights of slave owners, even here in the North. Law says that if you're a white man walking down the street one day and deputy yells for you to grab hold of the Negro standing beside you because he's a fugitive then you are required to lay your hands on the man. Before the new fugitive law an escaped slave wasn't exactly safe in the North, but he could live with some measure of security. He could live a decent life up here, marry and own property and get into business. Some even wrote of their histories and had them published. But the new law has emboldened the slave masters. They come up here and snatch men and women out of the lives they're creating for themselves and take them back into bondage. We abolitionists have fought this at each juncture, but each year the government bends further back upon itself. They capitulate, capitulate, capitulate. It's a dire situation. You can't trust anybody, and yet you're forced to trust somebody."

William stared at his teacup. Thoughts moved behind his eyes, thoughts different than those he spoke. "So you telling me that freedom's just a lie."

Redford cleared his throat and adjusted his posture. He reached for his tea. Holding the saucer just before his lips, he said, "No, it's not that simple. But, truth be known, we've married ourselves into a union with criminals. None of us are safe for it. We all live in constant fear. I've never been a slave, but I know there's no difference between you and I save the location of our birth. And even that's scant protection. Good brothers and sisters that were known to me personally have been kidnapped and taken into bondage. A man can labor all his life in the freedom of the North, but if a scoundrel takes hold of him he cannot utter a word in his own defense. That is why we must solicit the favor of honorable whites. It doesn't make one comfortable, but it is a necessity. And with Dover's condition . . ."

Noticing the downturned expressions on the couple's faces, he leaned forward and touched Dover on the knee. "But, listen, I will do everything in my power to help you. You have my word on that. Both of you." He promised to begin working on their behalf in the morning. For the time being, he proposed that William stay with him. He would see about securing a safer place for him to hide and would look into a way of getting them to true safety. It would not be easy, he said, and it would not be cheap, but all things were possible if one were willing to put actions in line with beliefs. That was what gave the champions of liberty strength, and, thank God, it was one weapon that the slavery interests could never truly raise against them.

DOVER PARTED FROM WILLIAM with a quick kiss. The sensation of her lips on his lingered long afterwards, not the touch of them, but the memory, the knowledge of their absence. He spent a sleepless night on the floor of Redford's sitting room, lying straight-backed on a quilt thrown over a woven rug. It was more luxurious bedding than he was used to, but slumber proved difficult. Nothing was as he had imagined it would be. He had found Dover, but instead of resolution he discovered a new host of hurdles thrown up against him. He tried to sort them out, to deal with each issue separately and thus move forward. But he couldn't approach a single question without an array of laws and politics flying in like a flock of crows, insatiable and raucous. And behind all of these machinations were more troubling doubts. Dover was as he remembered, and yet she was different also. She was as determined as before, but now she had the will to put her plans in motion. It was she who led him through the streets, who brought him to this place of shelter, who knew the city and the ways of the North. He felt like a child beside her, not like a husband, or a man soon to be a father. And what of Redford and his strained familiarity with Dover?

William was still awake when the new day lightened the room. Redford left him alone with instructions to rest himself, to keep the curtains drawn, to be as quiet as possible and to answer no caller save for Dover herself. He slipped outside briefly and returned with a bucket of water sprinkled with lye soap. William should feel free to wash himself. It wouldn't make for a proper bath, he knew, but he hoped it would suffice until he had the time to pump and heat enough water.

Alone, William rose, brushed and folded his bedding and set the quilt in a corner. He ate a breakfast of a hard, white cheese, sliced thin and topped with a preserve that Redford had set out for him. He had at first thought little of bathing, but alone with himself he became conscious of his body. His own odor floated heavy around him. The grime from his vigil coated him, leaving him feeling like he hadn't bathed since he began his journey. He stripped naked and stood in the tiny nook beside the stove, atop dry bits of kindling that stuck to the bottoms of his feet. He was pale beneath his clothes, a honeyed tone several shades lighter than his suntanned face. His skin seemed thinner than it had been before, stretched taut across muscle and bone. It was an awkward bath. He scooped up handfuls of the milky water and rubbed his flesh, trying all the time not to splash outside of the tiny wet circle beneath him. Eventually, he dipped his whole shirt in the bucket and used it as a wash cloth. He gave special attention to his back. He ran his fingers over his ridged scars, tracing the whip marks on his shoulders and upper arms, although unable to reach the layered welts that stretched down his lower back. He knelt and scrubbed his shirt within the bucket, then tossed in his trousers, which he washed carefully for fear that they would disintegrate. The water was no longer white when he finished. He hung the wet clothes over the wood stove and stood in the center of the room as if he planned to wait that way until they dried.

His eyes roamed over the writing desk on the far wall. It was so neatly arranged, quills and paper and letter opener all in their assigned places. It reminded him of a child's desk from long ago, a memory he had not recalled for some time. From there his gaze roamed over the titles of the bookshelf, words that his mind registered complete but without meaning, as if he was pronouncing the words of a language he didn't understand. He stepped forward and trailed a finger over the spines of the old volumes. Without noticing that he was doing so, he placed his fingertip atop one of the books and pulled it toward him. He turned and moved absently about the room, flipping through the book page by slow page, feeling the brittle paper against his fingertips, smelling the musty fragrance that, once again, conjured distant memories. He still didn't try to decipher the words, but simply let his eyes drift over them, drawn toward them with a pull he could neither reject nor acquiesce to. He marveled at how strangely right the book felt in his hands, like a tool long absent but never forgotten, a face remembered, an apple cradled in a palm.

He wasn't sure how long he stood staring at the ink and parchment, but he was startled when he caught sight of himself in the floor length mirror at the other end of the room. He stared at the man there—a naked creature with a book opened in his hands—with all the shock he would have shown if he had stumbled upon a stranger in that posture. He snapped the volume shut, feeling like he was intruding into another world, some sort of museum into which he had wandered uninvited.

Two

*A storm awaited the clipper at the mouth of the Bay. The ship
took the waves at an angle, cutting into the ramps of water so that
the lip of some crests spilled across the deck. Water surrounded
the craft like a boundless mass of moving flesh. Each time he
looked upon it Morrison discovered anew the great beast upon
whose surface they intruded. Salt was all about him, in the water
and in the air, in his clothing and dripping down from his hair,
that black-gray cap plastered to his skull. The captain urged him
into shelter, but Morrison remembered the damp internals of ships
all too well, the smells down there and creaking breath of it,
cramped beams bowed with the weight of the sea pressing against
them. No, he chose to face the beast with his eyes open. He stayed
on deck, sitting cross-legged near the midpoint of the ship, with
the hound close at his side.*

*Around him the crewmen shouted one to another, their words
whipped before the wind, portions of commands and entreaties,
calls only half completed and more urgent for it. He heard them
and felt all the elements at war around him and understood his
tenuous position within all this motion. But still he didn't abandon
the deck. Closing his eyes, he grabbed the dog about the collar
with one hand and twined his other within a coil of rope secured
to the deck. He let the spray wash his face and tried as best he
could to empty his head of all thought. He pushed away his memories of his first Atlantic voyage, of all the death he saw in the
hold of that decrepit ship. He beat those images back, but in their
place other memories materialized and would not be denied.
Visions played upon his eyelids like silhouettes cast by candlelight, and it was here that he saw the woman's face again, beautiful and dark as it had been all those years before.*

He had first met her in the spring of his twenty-seventh year.

She appeared on his younger brother's arm, his new love, his part-ner there for the entire world to see. He nodded to her, wished her well and pretended that he didn't truly see her. He tried not to notice the slow beauty of her eyes, black pebbles pressed home with an artist's fingers. They had touched on him so patiently, as if she were taking him in completely, looking to the back of him and turning him over and reading him. He tried not to give words to the images she conjured in him, like that her skin was the texture of the Bay's sandy beaches, down below the waterline, where the receding tide pulls the grains taut and smooth. He pretended that this was not the perfect hue for human flesh, the color God must have intended. He didn't let his eyes settle too long upon the fine bones of her neck. And having looked once, he tried to ignore the rich pucker of her lips, the moisture of her tongue, the flesh of ripe fruit. To him she was sin incarnate, and it shot him through with a host of emotions, not least of which was jealousy.

Alone with his younger brother Morrison berated him. What was he thinking? This woman was not for him. She was marked. She was property. She could never be his equal in the eyes of men or God, not in this nation or in any nation known to civilized man. Had his mother given birth to him for this? So that he might ven-ture from home and singe his blood with that of servants? Had he no shame? He spit the questions out with all the venom he could muster, and he half-believed them himself. He had taken on this country's prejudices and tried to make them his own as he would make the country itself his own. But for the first time Lewis did not heed his older brother. He listened to his questions and gazed at him and spoke little and cryptically when he did. Who are we to name God's accursed? he asked. Who are we?

Through the summer of that year Morrison watched Lewis build a home for the woman. This young one did not seem so timid anymore. He might still be a dreamer and poet, but he had the fortitude to create a life against all advice. He built their strange home with his own hands, with pilfered and salvaged lumber. He took parts regardless of their normal function and shaped them to suit him and created a mushroom of a house, part of a living tree, a thing so odd men laughed in looking upon it. Even Lewis found it humorous, but in a different way than the others. When he led the woman to it he gave it to her with all sincerity. He was like a servant to her, ever faithful, ever laboring, hearing and seeing little of the world except her. This too infuriated the elder brother, though at the time he had misunderstood just why.

Morrison opened his eyes upon the drenched creation that was the world. How had he and his brother turned out so differently? They were of the same blood, born of the same parents and shaped by the same land. They had been orphans together. Yet one of them had created a version of humanity unique to him. He had found a way to bless his life with love and had pushed all else aside, while the other had turned himself solely to death. If only that blessed life hadn't been so short, Morrison thought. If only he had no hand in destroying it. And if only he had recognized that the sin he saw upon that woman was the fault of his eyes, a sickness of his own heart and not a brand upon her at all. He looked down and ran his hand across the canine's wet back. The dog's tail thumped the deck in response. The man was grateful for it, more than she could ever know.

Three

Redford lay the chart across the floor and motioned the couple close. Dover slid from the couch to her knees, though William only inched forward a little, taking his view from a distance. Redford traced the lines of North America with the tip of his letter opener, drawing the Atlantic coastline, the shapes of the states, the border with Canada, and even describing what he knew of the Great Plains and the Rocky Mountains and the long coastline of California. Dover followed every motion with anxious eyes. She nodded as he spoke, her lips slightly parted, although it was hard to tell whether this was in thought or from the constant strain her body was now putting on her. In posture, William held himself aloof from the lecture, but his eyes were actually as keen as Dover's, his attention as rapt on the man's words. He was just determined not to show it.

"It really snow all the time up there?" Dover asked.

Redford chuckled. "The climate is harsh, but not as harsh as that. The summers are as mild as you could want. And the land's rich. This isn't a matter trying to pack the Negro off to Africa or Haiti or some such place where they're likely to die from fever or hunger. This is good land, good enough to attract shiploads of Europeans, English and Scots and French. They're all trying to find a better place, just like you are." He looked up and smiled at William, who returned the gesture coolly.

William's vision slipped past him, on to the map and then away from that to Dover's knees, her hands folded there, the fingers of one hand resting atop those of the other. "What about all them white folks?" he asked. "If all them white folks heading there they ain't gonna want us. How's that gonna be any different than the mess we got?"

Redford smiled. "Not all white men are devils incarnate. We both know that."

"They don't gotta all be devils. But you put enough of them together and times get thin—then it's the niggers who gonna lose out. Maybe you don't understand that like we do."

Redford heard this soberly; his smile faded. "I sometimes

forget the evil place that you've just come from, but I understand that it must have warped your faith in other men terribly."

"What?"

"Look, William," Redford said, a newly sprung tension trembled at one corner of his lips, "I may live in the North. I may be free, but I'm still a nigger in this country. Don't propose that I've never felt the burden of my race."

"You never been in chains, have you?"

William and the man were facing each other now, standing toe to toe. There was something in both of their postures that hinted at aggression: the tremor on Redford's face, the way William's shoulders bunched in toward his neck, as if the words he spoke were pushed up from the muscles of his back. Dover watched them, still seated, her hands held as before but her eyes moving from one man to the other as they spoke.

"No, I haven't," Redford said. "Perhaps that's why I know that the world is much larger than what you've been allowed to see."

"I've seen things."

"Okay, then I'm talking about myself, not you. It is not possible for me to be Negro and a free man and Christian in good faith if I ignore my brothers in bondage. Slavery binds us all, lowers us all and makes beasts of us. I fight for your freedom because I want to guarantee my own. If I offend you somehow it's not intentional, but I would happily offend a man to aid his freedom."

A knock on the door yanked all three of their heads up in unison. A moment passed in silence, only eyes moving, snapping from face to face around their triumvirate, darting away to the door and to the window and to the closet. Then the knock came again, three raps of the knuckles, calm, evenly spaced, with no clear message encoded in their rhythm. Redford flipped the map closed and handed it to Dover. He motioned for the couple to silently remove themselves to the bedroom. They did so, although the floor came alive beneath them, creaking and protesting their gentle steps.

The couple slipped into the bedroom and closed the door behind them. They stood facing each other, so close that Dover's round belly touched William's. Her gaze was hard to read. It was frank, as was her way, but whether that frankness hid reprimand or not was hard to say. William, for his part, set his lips and stared back, hardly blinking. They stayed that way, hearing nothing of note until the outside door closed, a motion that shook the house, like an exhaled breath strong enough to jiggle the bedroom door in its frame. William reached out and took hold of Dover's hand, an unconscious gesture that broke the spell between them.

The door sprung open. Redford stepped in and grasped William by the forearm. "It's okay. That was a messenger from Mr. Ferries. We've found you a safe haven."

THAT EVENING ALLOWED WILLIAM AND DOVER their first solitude since their reunion. Dover told her mistress that she was attending a prayer group. Redford was engaged till late in the night, meeting with the man who had offered William a hiding place. The couple was left alone in the tiny set of rooms, the air charged with an energy that might have been euphoric, but was tense and difficult instead. Their proximity created a tension neither knew how to quell. It showed in both their gestures. She was steady and calm in her actions but never fully opened herself. He was shy of her eyes, fretful and hungry for motion. He paced the room, looking at her only with passing glances. It wasn't meant to be like this, he thought. This wasn't what had pulled him from Kent Island and propelled him through each successive hardship. He should wrap her in his arms the way he had imagined. He should run his hands over her belly and push his fingers through the folds of her dress and touch her naked flesh. He should be swelling with the pent up desire that he had woken with on so many mornings. He should stand before her naked and complete and masculine, as she had asked him to do so often. And yet the thought of that was almost unimaginable now. He didn't know where to start, how to break down the barrier between them and set things right again. When he spoke he did so in a voice he barely recognized, with an anger he wasn't even sure he felt.

"I don't like this," he said. "Him out there talking to some white man. Don't know if I can abide it. How's that gonna do us any good? What white man ever did you a turn?"

"Your captain took care of you," Dover said. She sat on the sofa, studying the flame of the oil lamp on the table before her. A ripple in the glass shield cast a dark ribbon on her face. It bisected her features diagonally through cheek and eye, rendering her in a surreal composition, as if the two halves didn't quite fit together to make a whole. "Redford knows what he doing. He's a good man, and you'll just have to trust him."

William strode to the far corner of the room, turned and watched her from the safety of that short distance. He brought his feet close together and backed his shoulders up against the two diverging walls. "I gotta trust him?" he asked. "And what about you? You trust him?"

"Course I do."

"Course you do. How'd you meet him, anyhow? He ain't like no colored man I know."

Dover explained that she had met him at church. She had been more active religiously since coming north. A Negro church was one of the only places she felt at home. There she was surrounded by Negro voices and smells and sights, stuck shoulder to shoulder with people she almost felt at home with.

Redford had been born a free man, she said, the child of a minister father and an abolitionist mother, both of whom had come up from slavery by means she wasn't aware of. His father built a congregation within a thin-walled church. His mother urged him to set the sights of his holy wrath on the injustice suffered by those still enslaved. They did not forget where they came from or how tenuous their liberty was.

"Least that's what Redford told me. Said they the ones taught him all the important things he knows. That was a goodly time back, though. They dead now. Seem like since they passed Redford felt the calling that much more, calling to help people, I mean."

William was quiet for a moment, watching her, glad that she didn't turn toward him. He pressed his palms against the wall and felt the dry grain of the wallpaper. "Dover, tell me the truth, he been after you?"

The woman's eyes didn't lift from the lamp, but something in her expression soured. "As big as I am? Come on now, don't embarrass yourself."

"You saying he wasn't after you? Or you just not answering the question?"

Dover exhaled an exasperated breath and turned toward him. For a moment she seemed ready to chastise him, but in taking him in her expression softened. "Let's not talk about it. Whatever mighta happened didn't. You're here now. That's what matters."

"If something mighta been then it mighta been . . . And if that's the truth we got us something to talk about."

"William . . ." Dover shook her head, sighed and took her chin within her fingers. Some things were better left in silence, she said. Least it seemed that way to her now. She was a changed woman. Perhaps not the woman he used to know. Life could quiet even the loudest voices. Things pile one upon another and sometimes you look at yourself and wonder who you are and how you became so. She said this quietly and let it sit for some time. But as William stared at her and his questions yawned unanswered she finally took them up. The answer was yes. Redford had proposed that the two of them get together. He offered it in the manner of an honorable man, knowing that she was pregnant with another man's child. He said he would've raised the child as his own without a second thought about it. He would've helped her get free for good. Would've lived with her as man and wife.

"Yes, William, he did make that offer. That what you wanted to hear?"

"And how'd you answer him?" William asked quietly. He was afraid of the question but he asked it anyway because he had to. He needed to know how, or if, she had answered the man or whether his arrival had interrupted what she might have said. It occurred to him like a sudden inundation just how much his appearance had spun turmoil into her world.

"Gave him the only answer I could or would," she said. "Told him no. I answered him some weeks ago and that was that. You can't blame me for thinking on it. I didn't know I'd see you again. All I knew I was gonna be raising this chile on my own, with no family around. He gave me something to think on. You can't blame me for that."

"Didn't say I blamed you. Just wanted an answer." William peeled himself from the wall and stepped forward. He was silent for a moment. Without his being aware of it, the heat of anger had fled him completely. When he spoke his tone was resigned, so quiet that he might have been talking to himself. "All the time I been thinking bout how far I walked, the things I been through to get to you. Didn't hardly think about the confusion I'd be bringing to you. Running with the law behind me, bringing all that hate with me and closer to you. All I really did was put you in danger."

Dover's hands settled over her knees, which she cupped within her palms. She breathed a few slow breaths. "William, sit down. Sit down next to me." She waited as he did so, then slid an arm around his back and turned into him. "I ain't treated you right since you got here. I'm sorry for it. We're both of us in a mess. But don't think for a minute that I don't love you and want you here. I do. I just didn't expect it. Hadn't even let myself dream it. When I saw you, part of me filled to the top with joy. Other part of me sunk down with the fear of it all. Not just cause of the danger you talking bout, but cause I don't know if I can take losing you again. That's the thing, William. If I pull you in close to me I'll never be able to lose you again. That's a frightful thing. Slaves ain't supposed to think like that."

The two sat some time in silence. William wanted to speak but when he cleared his throat he felt the emotion contained there and was shamed even though he knew there was no shame in it. He would've told her that he understood her completely and felt the same. There was nothing for them to do but to put slavery behind them and be bound only by each other. The anger within him was only partially anger and the rest was fear, longing, desire. He would've told her this but he knew she understood it already, for this distance between them was no real barrier. It never had been. It was the tension of an evil world. Between them was something greater and she was right—it need not all be uttered aloud.

Dover took him by the wrist and placed his hand against her abdomen. His hand would've trembled if hers hadn't held it in place. He knew why she did this and put all of his attention in his palm. But still it was a shock when he felt the movement, one quick rumble, like a stomach growl amplified and made physical. It was so sudden, unexpected even though he had awaited it. It came again. And there was beneath his palm a moment of pressure that he understood as the crook of a limb rotating, as an elbow or a shoulder or the heel of a tiny foot. He whispered God into their presence, strange for the words came without his calling them. How great the burden of this; how large the promise. He thought then that he would do all and everything possible to see that little heel touch down on free earth and that it never wore an iron anklet.

"Feel that?" Dover asked. "Our baby's a tumbler. She's in there tumbling, getting ready for this world. Thing I can't figure out is if she's tumbling for joy or outta rage. I do feel she knows what's coming better than we do. Knows it, and she's getting ready one way or another."

William nodded. He still didn't try to speak. He put himself completely in his palm and tried to read the infant moving beneath. He didn't think to question her assertion of the child's gender. He just touched and waited, knowing that such moments come rarely. For once he paused to give it all of his attention.

THE CHOSEN PLACE was at the edge of a rambling estate beyond the city limits. Redford led William out there as the sun slanted the world into being. It was a Sunday morning, and they maneuvered through the greater part of the city unnoticed. By the time the faithful began to emerge from their homes, the two men were already out into the city's farthest fingers. William carried a satchel of food slung over his back; Redford a bedroll tucked under his arm. They were scant supplies, but they all hoped this wilderness exile would be brief. They strode along lanes that wound at their own leisurely pace through wood and rock, along streams, past country homes glimpsed only partially, set back as they were in the illusion of deepest nature.

For the greater part of the journey the two men didn't speak. Their feet kept up a dialogue of sorts, scuffing across the dirt, snapping twigs and crunching leaves. Occasionally, one of them kicked a stone dancing into the path ahead of them. The other was always careful to step over that stone in passing, as if something would be lost or stated or given away if they acknowledged where the other had trod. At the crest of a hill the two men stopped and looked back at the city. They shared the view in silence and then marched on as if it were nothing worth commenting on. William thought of Anne as he walked, ashamed that he hadn't sent word to her of the recent occurrences. He remembered the touch of her hip against his side, the click of her knitting needles, her chuckles as she told scandalous stories of her tenants. He had known her so briefly, but in that time she'd become a core part of his life. It was harder to leave her behind than he would have thought.

When they reached a certain bend in the road Redford indicated that they were almost there. Soon, they crested another rise and turned off the road, following an old lane up through the trees. It had been out of use for some time and was thick with a low level of undergrowth. Wagon ruts lay beneath the ferns and thorns like scar tissue beneath a new growth of hair. The trees that lined the lane gave it definition, but overall it was a work of man being reclaimed by nature. Off to one side a field stretched a good distance across the hillside, gently sloping, undulating terrain perfect for cow pasture, but grown tall with disuse.

A little further on, William caught his first glimpse of the carriage house. It seemed an unusually low structure for its purpose, though this may have been an illusion brought about by the tall grass and vines that crept up its walls. It was a dark structure of loose, moss-covered boards, canted to one side as if the hill had been slipping away beneath it over time. The dark mouth of the thing gaped open as they approached, and the two men stood at its threshold for a few moments before stepping in. They found a door at the far wall of the garage, which opened into yet a darker room. It had a moist dirt floor, cluttered with various pieces of lumber and bracken of no obvious function or design. The rafters above were ribboned by tiny shafts of light that pierced through numerous cracks and holes. A hornet's nest clung to the underside of the doorframe, and a bird hopped along a beam at the rear of the building, bobbing its head and warning them away with short, nervous calls. The whole place smelled of dirt and mildew and, faintly, of some animal's urine.

"Well, this is it," Redford said. He had worn a hat for the journey. He took it off now and fanned his face. "I know it's rough, but it's the best we could come up with on such short notice. The old house itself is just up the hill a ways, though I don't think you'll find anybody much comes out here."

William looked the building over. "I've abided in worse," he said.

"Yeah, I guessed that you might've." Redford set the hat back on his head and looked back the way they'd come. "You'd hardly know there was a whole city just the other side of those hills. Almost makes me wish I didn't have to go back to it. I sometimes fancy I'd be suited to a country life."

William turned and shared the man's view. It was true, one could see no sign of the city from where they stood, but he felt no inkling of the notions the other man referred to. As quiet and secluded as the spot was, he couldn't shake the illusion that the whole bulk of the city huddled just beyond those hills. He imagined that the entirety of it—the brick and iron and human life and human waste—had merged together into an ogre that lurked just out of sight. He didn't speak this thought aloud. He didn't share any other thought with the man who brought him here. Their solitude brought them into too intimate a proximity, and William stood with his eyes studying anything but the other man, anxious for him to go.

Before long he did. William watched him slide in and out of view among the trees of the lane. He emerged into the sunlight at the bottom of the field and stepped onto the road. He looked back at the last moment, raised a hand in farewell, then disappeared over the ridge and into the waiting mouth of that beast.

Four

Morrison first saw Humboldt's cohorts gathered on the dock in Philadelphia. They were unkempt men, hollow-eyed and stoop-shouldered. They smiled in Humboldt's general direction and seemed to view his arrival as a precursor to mirth. There was a tall man among them who had no front teeth whatsoever. He showed no embarrassment in this fact as he opened his caved interior to the sky. Another was so dark of skin that he must've carried within him native blood, or perhaps that of some warm-climed foreigner. There was a fat man who wore a badge and rested one hand on his holstered revolver, and there was a young man with bright red hair and fair skin that reminded Morrison of the land of his birth. Lastly, there was a boy, no older than his early teens, with black hair that hung to his shoulders and framed a face pockmarked by pimples. They all wore scars on the outside to indicate the damage they carried on the inside, pains that they each in their own way wished to inflict upon others and thereby find some solace. In a different time and place they would've been deemed criminals. They would've been pickpockets and cutthroats, rapists and murderers. They would've been the scourges of other nations, jailed, hung, and deported to distant lands. But in this country, in this time of slaves and masters, they were considered agents of God's laws of nature and man's laws of property. They carried badges and papers to this effect and could lawfully compel others into their service. They walked with the power of life and death, and as this was their only power they luxuriated in it.

There were other men among them also, but they came and went so readily that Morrison didn't distinguish them as individuals. He stood among them as all were introduced and he nodded his head in turn and met those eyes that would meet his. The hound took no comfort in this company and stood a few feet away, whining just loud enough to be heard, as if her protest was meant to be a secret for Morrison's ears only. But the tracker did not acknowledge her just then, a fact that confirmed the dog's suspicions that all was not well.

Humboldt called the informal meeting to order. He laid out the situation as he saw it. He explained their mission and the time frame he thought appropriate to its completion. He asked the men what they knew of this girl, the bitch fat with child. They knew plenty. They knew her whereabouts and customs and daily routines. One of them had a nickname for her and another said he had come so close in spying her that he could've patted her on that watermelon of hers.

She'll be easy to get, the fat man said, like picking fruit.

And my nigger? Humboldt asked.

Nobody answered.

Come on, boys, one of you must've heard something by now. What the hell am I paying you for?

None ventured an opinion on this. They admitted that they'd heard nothing of the fugitive. The red-haired one did offer a special piece of information, a secret beaten out of a poor sailor late one evening. Apparently, an Irish sea captain had agreed to transport a load of fugitive slaves to Canada. They were not sure of the exact details as to when and where the smuggling was to take place, but more could be learned, more could definitely be learned.

Let's do this then, Humboldt said. He told them that he had booked passage on a schooner heading back to Annapolis in a week, so they had seven days to accomplish their goals. He divided the men by their particular strengths and assigned them missions. Some would keep an eye on the bitch. Others would spread themselves through the city, dredging the scum of the place for their particular form of gold, socializing with the niggers if need be. Some would seek out information on this smuggling operation and others, including Morrison, would search the gaols for any niggers who couldn't prove they were freemen. Humboldt himself would contact the authorities and ingratiate himself to them and make it clear that their mission was of the highest order, one intended not just for their personal gain but also to rid the city of dangerous black fugitives.

They don't like niggers here anymore than we do, the planter said, though you'll rarely get them to admit it. If we do this here work right we'll be homeward bound with a boatload of niggers and each of you richer for it. This was met with a murmur of approval. That's right, he said. You mighta thought I just had it in for that one boy. And I do, but we might as well make this whole thing worth our while, right?

He asked the men what they thought of this and they thought plenty; all save Morrison, who had thoughts of his own. These he kept to himself for the time being.

Five

Sometimes, when the air was just right and the breeze blew toward him, William could smell the city. He was never sure which fragrances would reach him and was never confident of their authenticity, but they came to mark the passing of the days as surely as the sun's progression. In the mornings it was the dry flavor of smoke, a crisp scent, fleeting, washed clean by the evening's dew. As the heat of the day grew the city gave off a more noxious aroma. The reek of sewers floated out on a rising tide, a stench thick and heavy like a liquid. When he awoke from afternoon naps he many times believed himself still posted behind the Carrs' home, still sleeping in the city's hidden places, cloaked in that old hunger. And as day gave in to night, he would swear he could smell someone's supper, tendrils of scent that drifted up to him undiluted and taunting.

Though his provisions were modest, he was better prepared for his exile than he had ever been before. The sack he had carried out from the city contained bacon and salted whitefish. He had cornmeal biscuits from Anne's, a few loaves of flat bread and a jar of boysenberry jam, sickly sweet stuff that seemed to enter and exit him in roughly the same consistency. He portioned his food out frugally, as if measuring it for a stay much longer than Redford had projected. The bacon was precooked as Redford cautioned him against starting a fire. He ate it with mouthfuls of bread so hard that he moistened them before chancing his teeth against them. He filled his water jar at a stream a little distance behind the enclosure. This trip, made in the early morning and again after sunset, became his only routine of exercise.

His third morning in hiding, he awoke and recognized that summer was fading. The air was crisp in a way it had not been for months, the sky high-clouded and grand in its girth. A breeze stirred the trees and set a few, yellowish leaves to flight, thin golden shapes like palm prints twisting and flipping. For some reason they reminded him of fallen soldiers, but from whence this comparison came he was unsure. He spent the morning entranced by the natural world, watching dramas lived out in other forms than human. A tree of a type he didn't recognize dropped its hard fruit. Each time he saw the balls fall to the ground his heart leapt. Strange that he would find excitement in such a thing, and yet he was not alone. Squirrels were fast upon the fruit. They snatched it up in their forepaws and attacked it with a fervor that made William curious about its taste, though not enough to tempt him from his shelter.

He had seen no other people as yet, but when they came they did so in a gaggle. Picnickers appeared in the quiet hours of midmorning. He heard their carriages pull to a halt along the distant road, first one, then another and, eventually, four in all. From these they poured forth and swept up the hillside: men who folded their jackets and went about in vest tops, with sleeves rolled up on their pale arms; women in white dresses, parasols in one hand and hand fans in the other; children of every size and height, swarming between the older folks like puppies at play. They came with baskets of food, with lawn chairs and quilted blankets and the tools of gaming. In a matter of minutes they had transformed the field into a grand playground. The various individuals secluded themselves into the groups that fit them best. Thus the men of a certain age stood puffing on pipes, watching the younger men and boys at play, while the women saw to the food and kept the children near at hand. There was a contingent of the elderly who sat in the shade at the lower edge of the field, the women with the great folds of their dresses circling them, men with their bowler hats atop their heads, fixtures as permanent as any God-given accoutrements.

William watched them through the cracks in the wall, his face close to the boards. His heart thumped in his chest. He barely moved for fear that his tiny noises might somehow be overheard. And yet he was entranced, for he had never spied on the world of white people so. He watched them with a lopsided, squinting vigilance that shifted from one eye to the other. He could only hear them occasionally, some shout or exclamation, a head tilted in laughter or the pop of a bat against the ball. The sounds were muted, off-timed, so that the noise trailed behind the action that had created it. It was like spying upon the workings of an artificial world, images of bliss framed for the view of a single eye, sight and sound imperfect in its rendering.

The morning had passed into afternoon before he noticed the young couple strolling away from the others. The man carried his hat in hand. He was smartly dressed, sporting a jacket despite the heat, with prominent, if youthful, sideburns stretching down to his jaw line. The girl, who was taller than her companion, displayed a fan in the same position as the man held his hat. Her strides timed their motion, each step a gracious effort that kicked her skirt out and slid her forward behind it. They moved away from the rest of the group and climbed up the grassy lane that led to the carriage house.

William cast about him for someplace to hide. The floor was strewn with objects, boards and yellowed newspapers and miscellaneous pieces of debris. Tall grass sprouted along the edge of the walls, and shadows obscured the room's corners. But none of it seemed to provide adequate cover. When the couple was close enough that he could make out their voices, he opted for the only escape he saw. As in the pine forest a couple of months ago, he leapt upwards. He grabbed onto one of the exposed structural beams and swung himself up into the tangled mass of beams and shadows up there. He scrambled as the couple talked just outside the door. He froze when the door creaked open, stretched out along the length of a beam in the near corner, wrapped so entirely in cobwebs that he had to breathe gently to keep from sucking the threads in.

The couple entered, tenuous, shading their eyes and waiting for them to adjust to the light. They left the door open and situated themselves just inside it, taking some measure of shelter and solitude, but not daring to venture too far from propriety. The young man set down his coat for the girl to sit on. For himself he brushed clean a spot in the dirt, the very spot that William had been the moment before. The girl wondered if they would be missed, but the other said not to worry. They were just out for a walk. Nobody could fault them for that. They'd done everything honorably so far, he said, and soon none would be able to fault them for anything.

The girl's features from above had a porcelain quality both in shape and texture, beautiful, yes, but so frail as to put that beauty's value at question. William caught brief glimpses of her eyes, and from what he saw he concluded they were a watery blue. "Yes," she said, pouting as she did so, a thin pretension at reprimand. "Let's just see that we don't get ahead of ourselves."

The young man nudged her on the shoulder, more like one childish companion to another than like suitors, but it was clear that's what they were. They talked of the life they would have together. The young man spoke in the largest of gestures, of deeds that encompassed years of labor, of their beautiful home, of the work he would do to fund it, of the important man he would grow to be. The girl spoke far fewer words, but in her quiet affirmations were dreams just as large. She counted their children and gave them names. She designed their rooms and appointed their colleges and designed their careers. They would have a garden in the French style, she declared. They would not be so stuffy as to forbid the children from playing in it, and the girls and boys would be educated equally. He said they might have to see about that, but she asked just what was there to see about? Nothing, he said. He tried to explain, but the girl didn't let him. She struck a posture of indignation and talked of the equality of the sexes. Different in temperament, she said, but little different in substance, partners in God's plan, neither one nor the other of use alone. He did believe this, did he? He did acknowledge the progressive thinking newly at work in the land, didn't he?

The young man's head dipped to one side. His eyes fanned up and across the beams in which William roosted, but they never paused to pick him out from the background. "Yes, love," he said, in a tone of such patient resignation that it was obviously practiced, this whole discourse a joke between the two of them.

"Good," the girl said. "I wouldn't dare sell myself into bondage to a man without a liberal mind. Lord knows what would become of me if I did."

William held his perch long after the couple had departed. The picnickers gathered up their provisions and climbed back into their carriages and rolled away. But he still clung to his beam, motionless save for the quiet bellows of his breathing and progress of his tears, tracks burnt down his cheeks and staining the wood that supported him. He didn't know when he began to cry, when he lost his fear and found a great sadness instead. He felt a fool when he roused himself and climbed down from his roost. He wiped at his face, unsure why his eyes betrayed him, wondering at his weakness.

It wasn't until later that night that he dreamt again of that sadness and awoke with the realization of a suspicion long held. It was true; there were people on earth who lived an entirely different existence than he. The gap between them was unbridgeable, far greater than just that of master and slave. Even if he were granted all the freedoms of the nation he wouldn't fully understand how to use them. Though he be allowed to speak he would have no voice. He would never be able to debate the finer points of a French garden, or dream the colleges of unborn children, or be so confident as to imagine an entire lifetime shaped by his own inclinations. There would always be parts of himself that he hated. Those of privilege would never be able to understand him and neither would he know himself. If there was a creator, then he had shaped the world this way, with some men chosen above others as the most beloved. For some reason this reminded him of his mother and suddenly he missed her. He remembered all the days in between and in remembering he felt the pain of them condensed. He pulled that old pendant from his shirt pocket and fingered it, pressed it to the flesh below his Adam's apple and held it there. He wished himself a child again, with her again, so he could hear her speak, knowing that he would believe her now in a way he hadn't before. She had understood the world differently, and he wished for even a piece of that wisdom, a small sliver to see him forward.

WHEN WILLIAM WAS ELEVEN he had been hired out to a caulker on the outskirts of Annapolis. He was allowed to live at home that year and made the trip to work at the start and close of each day. He had, at this time of stirring adolescence, begun to place some walls between himself and his mother. There was a frustration growing within him, and, as he didn't know yet where to direct it, Nan received the brunt of it. But he was new to these feelings. The boundaries were unclear, both in location and in purpose, and his allegiances were still, at the core, those of a child in need of his mother.

One evening he met four slave boys a few years older than

he in an alley near the wharf. He knew the boys and they knew him and neither cared for the other. They were each of them blacker than he and though this made little difference to their mutual slavery it made a great difference within the unfocussed minds of youth. They blocked his path and one shoved his shoulder and another asked him if it was true that a gang of Irish sailors had raped his mother? William said that it was not. He tried to pass. They blocked him again, changing tack and suggesting other sources for his parentage, individuals known to them all and despised. The most lascivious of overseers. An old man in the latter stages of syphilis, who roamed the docks mumbling to himself, lice ridden and cadaverous. A harelipped youth famous for rubbing himself against the backsides of Negro girls. This latter would only have been a few years old at William's conception, but the point was clear enough. They were all white. They were all filthy, and so, they were saying, was his father. And, by extension, was his mother.

William swung for the boy nearest him with all the force he could muster. He hit him with a glancing blow across his temple. He kicked another boy hard on the kneecap. But this effort was not nearly enough. Boys becoming men can do damage to each other and these boys did that to William. He stumbled home with his eyes swollen and his sight unsure, one tooth loose, lip busted and dripping red down his shirt. He didn't want to go inside but instead scaled the house and climbed into the branches above it.

Nan found him there several hours later. He climbed down reluctantly, stiff and sore, eyes puffy and not just from outward damage. She rushed him inside and took his face in her hands and shot questions at him. He admitted that no, no white men had done this. Nor was it the work of devilish white boys. No master had whipped him on his own authority. No overseer had found fault with him.

"Nigger boys did this to you?"

William grunted and tried to twist his head from her grip. Nan held fast. "Why they do this?"

He wouldn't answer. He didn't have to. He wasn't a child, and it was her fault anyway. He wouldn't tell her a thing.

And yet within a few minutes he had spilled all. He told her everything, a child a little longer.

Nan knew better than to hold him to her. She didn't coddle him. She cleaned his wounds and made him sit and wait as she rummaged in the boxes stored beneath her cot. He had searched them before and couldn't imagine what she was looking for. But when she turned back to him she held something he hadn't seen before. It looked, at first, like a dull coin, pierced in the center and hung from leather twine. Nan held it before her and knelt down before her son.

"This here come from your daddy," she said. "It was his pendant, use to wear it round his neck. He got it from his daddy who got it from his daddy who got it him from his daddy afore that. Goes back a long way, this here. Your grandfather's father took it off the body of his dead father. This all he had to re-member him by cause he died in one of them wars they had, when white folks was fighting each other way off cross the ocean."

The pendant spun as she moved, never still for more than a second. The twine passed through one of the holes but there were four in all, spaced evenly near the center of it. Nan inched closer. William could feel her breath as she spoke.

"So that old grandfather seen his father die on a field fighting a war. That old boy loved his father like all of them did, but he had to leave him on the field or he woulda died himself. He was clutching on to him trying to wake him from death. Some others pulled him away and saved his life. All he took with him was this here. And that boy grew to a man and had his own chillrun and passed this on. And the next done the same and on like that. That's a lot of history in one pendant, and that history is part of you. Your daddy would've gave you this himself, but he ain't here to do it so I'm doing it for him. Here . . ."

She grasped the boy's hand and placed the object on his palm. It was warm from her touch, tiny against his palm and light as a seashell.

"Truth is, them boys beat on you cause they scared of what life planning for them. They scared of they own skin and they probably don't know they own daddy. Just cause they black don't mean they daddy loved they mommas. But you know yours did cause I'm here telling you bout him. This pendant yours now. Somebody ask you where it come from tell them your daddy gave it to you. Tell them they best watch out cause you come from a family of warriors."

William closed his fingers around the brass medallion. There was forgiveness in the touch between him and the metal. All else was forgotten and for a few moments he was sure of his mother and of his father and therefore of himself. But in the years to follow he began to doubt her story. Before long he disbelieved it, and finally he came to despise it. That pendant was just a piece of brass, hardly a design on it, old and worn and bent from its original shape. It was trinket with a great fiction attached. He hated himself for ever grasping for it and loathed his mother for spinning such lies. He thought many times that if she were still alive he would flick the piece of metal back in her face. He would let it fall where it would. If she tried to grab hold of him he would spring back and shout his own accusations in her face. He would make her admit that he hadn't come from any great love, no marriage between colored and white. He was born of lust just like anyone else. She could not wipe clean the sins done to her simply by telling tales to her simple-minded child. He would ask her who his father really was. Their master? An overseer? A drunken Irishman or a gang of sailors docked for only a day and a night? Just tell him the truth, so that he could put to rest the myth of a loving father. Had she been alive, he might have pressed her with all of this. With her death she denied him this satisfaction and this was another thing he held against her.

And yet he kept the pendant with him still. He couldn't wear it as a necklace, for it was sure to attract attention. Instead he had sewn it into each year's new shirt himself. In times of trouble his fingers sought it out and worked its smooth surface even smoother. Despite all his old anger, he pressed it to his chest in that decaying Pennsylvania carriage house. He didn't believe, but neither could he let go.

Six

Morrison was partnered with a boy from West Virginia. He was no older than his midteens but he had lived a hard life already. His left arm appeared to have been snapped midway up the forearm and set lazily if set at all. It bent at an angle of a few degrees at a point in which there was no joint. If this old injury weakened him he hid it well. At twelve he had left his mountainous state, chased out of it by his own murderous father. Before long he had wandered the width of Maryland and across to Delaware. He got work patrolling that state's northern border, one of the last brutal guardians of the Promised Land and good at his job. He knew only that type of work and had early found it suited him. To hear him tell it he had seen a dozen men killed.

*That's white men, he said. Niggers I seen dead it would take a
Jew to count.*

*As Morrison and this boy went out each morning, the hound
spent the days tied to a pylon near the ship. She didn't care for this
insult, but neither did she wish to explore this strange, jumbled
place. The city was wholly unnatural in its shape and function. It
was an olfactory confusion, scents crosshatched and chaotic and
nonsensical. It was too full of mankind and too cluttered by strange
machines and smelled too much of death. She had long ago decided that whoever it was they'd been searching for was beyond
them. She put that mission from her mind and wished the man
would do so as well. But he seemed intent to see it through.*

*In the course of a week Morrison looked full in the face of
misery. Though he had seen sorrowful conditions in the South and
respected the North somewhat more, they were investigating jails
and none of these were pleasant places. Damp, dark and chilled,
stinking holes or narrow cells, sweating iron bars and walls cut
from the rough bedrock of the city itself. The captives were not
Negroes alone, but presented a mosaic of the city's nationalities
in microcosm. Staring into those men's varying faces—black skin
and yellow eyes, a wide forehead tanned like cowhide, a Roman
nose crooked twice during its length, lips in every variety, as di-
verse as flower petals but in this case not nearly as sweet—
Morrison remembered the fascination, the awe and repulsion
of his first days in America. So different than his brother's reac-
tion... He tried to stop this train of thought before it took hold
of him.*

*He was surprised at how often the jailers seemed inclined to
offer the black men up for the right price: those imprisoned as va-
grants or drunkards or those without family and friends to vouch
for them. It was because of this that they picked up three Negroes,
soon to be heading south as returning fugitives, though in all
likelihood the unfortunates had been born and raised in the free*

North and probably in this very city. Could they have protested they would have, but they could not and the young West Virginian was happy to shut them up when they tried.

Perhaps the worst sight came at the conclusion of the week. In a cell deep below a park in the center of the city they saw five Negro men pressed together in a tiny space. One of them was dead, held upright by the pressure of the others against him, kept warm by their bodies but dead nonetheless. Fluids had escaped from the corpse and the smell was such that the West Virginian spit up chunks of his breakfast. He complained daylong about the whole experience, the taste it left in his mouth and the way his body felt tainted just for having been in the room.

But the young man had his own leanings toward brutality. One afternoon he spotted a fine-looking mulatto girl not more than twelve and this inspired him greatly. That evening he stumbled around drinking great quantities of a liquid he called "antifogmatic," though it must have been so named in irony because the effect was not at all one of clarity. He talked of what he would do to that girl if he owned her. No labor in the fields for her. None of that farmer shit. He'd screw her is all. Daylong with nary a break in the action just as long as his pecker would point. In the evenings he would prostitute her out and so finance the whole scheme.

The Scot sat silent the whole time, around them the other men adding their own stories, each worse than the one preceding it. Morrison had known men as coarse as these his entire life. He had conducted business, hunted and drank with them. He had slept back to back with such men at times for the warmth, each asking the other to forgive the proximity and to ignore it and think nothing of it, and yet each man needing it and not simply for the heat. He had spent months enclosed in the closest of quarters, trapped by snow and cold and isolation, pushed together with what humanity he could find. Yes, coarse men had been the prime companions of his life. He regretted this, but also in his regret he remembered that he was no different than they. He had lived no model life. These men's crimes were little removed from his own, no different in content than the wrong he did to his brother's beloved all those years ago. He would not have behaved as he had with her if not for the contrasts in their skin. Because of that he had named her race and believed that she deserved the brunt of his anger, and his desire. He knew that his hatred of these men began and ended within him.

Walking through an alley the next afternoon the boy expressed his wish to find the pregnant wench they were after. She would make the return trip better than the outward bound, he opined. Morrison felt hatred so sudden and complete it dizzied him. Low in his back the hunger burned and it was the hunger to voice his response in blood. His knuckles ached with the desire. He slowed his step and loosed his jaw and worked it right to left and tried to weigh his options.

But just then the red-haired boy appeared at the far end of the alley and called to them. We got that nigger-loving captain, he said. Ya'll shoulda seen it. Tried to act the man he did, till Humboldt put a rifle in his mouth. Fellah opened up like a London whore. Come on, got us work to do.

The red-haired boy spun and trotted away, the West Virginian close at his side asking questions, excited. Morrison watched them move away for a moment, wishing himself in the other direction but finding his feet not so inclined. Before he knew he had decided his course, he was jogging to catch the two youths. He would stay with them a little longer, friend of the devil and seeker of salvation both, if ever such a thing existed.

Seven

William and Redford shared a view from atop a sloping granite slab. The sky was a light, clear blue, ribbed with high clouds that seemed perpetually in the act of disappearing, though they never did so. They were different each time William looked up at them and yet the same as well, moving and yet motionless. Though they couldn't see Philadelphia, hidden behind trees and hills and distance, columns of smoke marked it clearly enough. A haze hung above the city and gave the uneasy impression of some great calamity just beyond their sight, as if the whole place had been put to the torch and left in smoldering ruins. Between the two men lay a tablecloth fashioned from Redford's handkerchief, spread with a small banquet of bread and anchovies and a handful of berries that he had picked on the long walk out. The free man had come up to the carriage house—flushed and out of breath from the walk—with news of new developments. He had met with a young Irish captain who had agreed to help them, and they'd as good as solidified the arrangements. The two men had shaken hands and concluded the business on the friendliest of terms, dates and times all arranged. All of this had put Redford in a fine mood, hence the picnic out in the open, a risk, perhaps, but not too great a one when weighed against the pleasures of the autumnal afternoon.

When William asked why this captain would risk helping them, Redford disgorged a long and detailed biography of the man. He had been born and raised in Ireland. Though he had come to America and considered himself an American, he had never looked kindly on slavery. He wasn't born into it, so he saw it with clearer eyes than most native-bred whites. As for the practical matters, he owned his own sloop and worked a route up and down the Atlantic coast. He had headed South several days ago, but would soon begin the northerly leg of his journey, which ended on the soil of Nova Scotia. It was as perfect a situation as they were likely to find. Redford mumbled that there was a financial motive as well. The Irishman, it appeared, expected payment for his efforts, but considering the gamble he was taking this could hardly be begrudged him.

William began to ask the details of this, but Redford lifted his vision above the trees and took in the vista, his mind somewhere else already. "Did you know that the first antislavery society was founded in Philadelphia?" he asked. "Many years ago, in the Revolutionary years or thereabouts. They were gradualists back then, fully in the belief that slavery would die out in due course, as man moved on to a higher spiritual plane. Even slaveholders themselves wrote such things. Jefferson did. Back in those days they didn't mind admitting that slavery was a faulty system and that the nation would be better off without it. They just didn't want to change it in their own lifetimes. That would be too hasty. We don't hold such notions anymore. If change is going to happen, it has to happen on somebody's watch, and history tells us the change is not likely to be painless."

An ermine appeared in the rocks a little ways below them. William watched it slip through the stones, his hunt a deadly serious matter but also somehow joyful, mischievous. He remembered, as a child, throwing stones at such a creature, an action that had been a joy then but made no sense anymore. "Ain't painless now, either."

"No. No, of course it isn't," Redford said. "It's a matter of sharing the pain, I guess. And then moving beyond it." He motioned with his hands, vaguely sketching the notion of this progress. But the gesture trailed away before it was fully formed, insufficient to the task and better left unfinished. "It's a shame that more Negroes can't use the words of white men against them. Or even the words of other learned Negroes. If every Southern slave could read for himself narratives such as Frederick Douglass's they'd rise up and overthrow the institution immediately. They're kept down because their will is broken. If they could taste freedom, hear from others the true meaning of the word, then the fight would be as good as won. I honestly believe that."

William licked fish oil from his fingers. "Slaves don't need nobody to tell them they slaves," he said.

"Well, no . . . I just mean that the words of fine men and women can spur others to action, put matters in a new perspective."

William cocked his head to the side, a noncommittal gesture. "Slaves think about being free all day every day. Each time a bird flies overhead he wonders how come that bird can come and go but not me? Each time a white child walk by going to school he wonders why my child was sold away from me? Why my body ain't my own? Why God says he just, but then make a world like this? How come my massa says I'm a beast no smarter than a horse when we both know that no horse ever worked a tobacco field or sung a hymn on Sunday or gave birth to that same massa's child? Slaves seen things that wouldn't none of them tell you bout. Things that they couldn't write down in a book cause such things never have been written down in all the time men been writing. Things that would make you look at them different. Crime been done to them, but you'd still look at them different. You think it takes a free man to tell a slave he ain't living right? To my mind, other way around makes more sense."

"You're saying that liberty is nature's true state," Redford said. He began in his usual tone, but midway through the sentence seemed to regret it. "Which I agree with fully. I do . . . We just have a different way of saying it."

"A nigger way and some other way, I guess."

Redford fingered the short hairs of his chin beard, tugged at them, let go and tugged again. "Don't think that white men are devoid of generous thought. They don't show it as often as they write of it, but there are many white abolitionists. And there are men like Captain O'Neil. It's just unfortunate that such noble work depends to a large degree on money. Financing, that's the thing. Captain O'Neil is a good man, but he still wants to see a profit out of this. A flat rate for ten of you. He's agreed to that and I'll be sure to deliver, but still it'll take some work."

"What?" William asked. "You say ten?"

"Yes, well, O'Neil is working with a number of others. That's how I first came to know him." You must know you're not alone in wanting freedom. I was asked to help some others and I've agreed, two who call themselves brothers and a complete family."

William rose and strode away a few steps. He snapped one of his hands into a fist and pulled it back as if he might punch the air before him, but was waiting for just the right provocation.

"There are two girls among the family, no higher than your waist. What else could I do?" William didn't answer and Redford went on, saying it wouldn't be cheap, but they could share the expense. True, ten penniless slaves were no richer than two penniless slaves were, but this way he could ask for help from others. It made the whole venture that much more legitimate. Having said this, he fell silent, his lips twitching as if they might talk on but unable to come to agreement. William hadn't changed position, still his back turned to Redford and not a word from him. "You would've done the same."

"Don't know that I would've," William said. "Can't just trust people like that, no matter how they look coming to you."

"True enough. All people come bearing secrets, don't they?" He let this question sit a moment, his voice betraying, for the first time, an anger of its own. He unfolded the newspaper that had thus far sat silent beside him, opened it to a certain page and smoothed over an article there. "Take a look at this. You're a famous man, of sorts."

William didn't look as requested. He swallowed and opened his eyes and set them on the distance.

"I noticed this some time ago," Redford said, "though I didn't make the connection immediately."

He read the article aloud. It told a tale that was not new to William: of the coffle heading south, of the revolt and shedding of white blood, of the escape, one and all, of the slaves from their bondage. Apparently that white boy had ridden all the way to Richmond and there told a story of a mass uprising. He made it seem that all the slaves had sprung free from their chains at once, all twenty empowered by the same murderous intent and he only escaping through tremendous effort. Fourteen of the twenty slaves were caught in the first three days, another two by the end of the week. Saxon and the little man had ridden south and made it as far as the Sea Islands of Georgia. Why they went there instead of toward freedom would remain a mystery. They were leapt upon by a band of no less than thirty men who had tracked them for some time. They were beaten beyond recognition, gutted and decapitated. Saxon's head was sent back to the Baltimore-based slavers, where it was posted upon a spike overlooking the holding pen. There it rotted in the sun: reminder, threat and promise all at once. The remaining two were still being hunted.

As William listened to this he thought of Dover and in thinking of her his eyes moved slowly toward Redford. At first, he had thought Redford's features were weak, washed out, like no one part of him had been formed with any character. But now he saw that there was something handsome in the sum of these parts. None of his features shouted to be noticed, but together his curving forehead and small nose and clipped chin made for a well-formed whole, for a beauty that was vaguely feminine. He was suddenly aware of why Dover might find him attractive, and it was this that he was thinking about. He felt distant from the incidents the man read about. They belonged to another lifetime, and though they burdened him they did so with the weight of ghosts.

"So, you were there, weren't you?" Redford asked.

William didn't answer, but in his silence there was somehow an affirmation. Both men recognized it.

"I see." Redford cleared his throat and folded the paper into a small, neat square. "And did you take part in it? I mean, did you . . . take part?"

"I didn't kill no one if that's what you asking."

Redford didn't say whether that was what he was asking. "But you were there?"

"Yes."

"Why didn't you tell me?"

"What difference it make?"

"Consider it. Here I am trying to help you, trying to win your freedom, drawing on the good faith of many people, while you're hiding things from me." He held up the paper and jabbed a finger into it. "Says here you're a killer, a white-man killer. You don't think that makes a difference? They think you killed one of their own. They'll hunt you down. They're hunting you right now. There's not even any guarantee that Canada will keep you, not if someone accuses you of the murder of three white men."

"I said I ain't killed no one."

"Yes, you said that. But they think you did. You're hot

property, William, and I should've known from the beginning. My life is on the line here too. Or did that not occur to you? Have you any other surprises for me? Anything else you haven't seen fit to tell me?"

"Naw."

"Dover know about this? I didn't want to ask her till I spoke to you."

William shook his head.

"Did you wish those men dead?"

"Don't know if I wished it or not. Might've. Even if I did wishing didn't make it so." He caught sight of the ermine again, slipping across the rocks, half-serpentine, a smaller rodent clamped in its jaws. "But I ain't shed no tears for them, and there ain't a thing bout what I saw that shames me."

Redford nodded curtly and looked away. His eyes sought out the weasel and watched it out of sight. He rose and said it was well past time for him to head back and that he should get going, but having said it he just stood taking in the view. William stood profiled next to him and the two men beheld the scene in silence. The sun had dipped below the trees behind them and cast the horizon to the east in shadow, dimming the world and doing nothing for that smoldering city's prospects. A lone tree near the crest of a nearby hill predicted the change of season ahead of the others. It had a blaze of red and orange running up one side, a flame set in rustling motion by a rising breath of air, slower in its consumption than fire but no less a harbinger of change.

"I told you before that you could trust me," Redford said, "and I'm telling you again now. You may think I'm a man of words alone and perhaps I am as yet, but like you I've taken my place in the world I was born into. I know you didn't kill those men. I guess I always knew it. Coming up here . . . I think I was hoping you had. I'd have shaken your hand and thanked you. There are many ways to do God's work. I don't doubt that some of them are bloody. I don't doubt it at all."

Back at the carriage house, before he took his leave, Redford instructed William exactly how to proceed. Two days from now, just after dark, he should make his way back to the city. As William swore that he remembered the way, Redford said he would meet him at his apartment. Redford planned to already have the other fugitives loaded on the ship. He and William would spend the night in his apartment, meet Dover early in the morning, and then join the others on the ship. God willing, they'd then be off to true freedom. He left telling William to prepare himself. The waiting was over and things were going to happen fast and furious from here on out.

THE NEXT MORNING WILLIAM AWOKE and could not remember having dreamed. This was strange for he always dreamed and usually vividly. He sat through the day watching the sun's slow progression. Never had that orb seemed such a stationary object. He watched it, sometimes staring into it so long it lingered in his vision afterward, imposed on everything he saw, a glaring spot both brilliant and black. But even this scrutiny couldn't shame the sun to move any faster and the day was an ordeal of waiting.

That night he slept short and lightly, waking in the deep hours when dusk was long gone and dawn nowhere in sight. He tried to recollect his dreams but he again realized he had none. That short sleep had been as barren as a desert at night and it was just that that had caused him to wake. It left him uneasy, a feeling that grew as the day progressed. One final day in stillness, and then everything would be decided. One last day, and yet it seemed unending.

Early in the afternoon of the next day a flock of black birds descended upon the field. William watched them, finding in their motions something primitive. Their calls seemed to him like those of humans, cursed and deprived of proper speech. Midday he rose and ran out into the field, waving his arms furiously. The birds rose up before him, wings beating the air, hovering above him loud and unrepentant. They moved on, but left in their wake a silence worse than their cacophony had been. He stood there some time in the field, exposed but unable to retreat too quickly.

He knew something was wrong.

Eight

Morrison stood in the lee of a warehouse for some time. He could hear Humboldt's men. They had gathered just around the corner in preparation for the evening's work. Their voices came to him in clipped breaths of clarity, mundane words spoken with mirth, jokes that gave little indication to the deeds they were planning. He could see them in his mind as clearly as if he were standing amongst them. He stood roiling with hatred like none he had felt before. He hated them for the deformities that marked them, for the tone of their voices and for the cold, thin souls within them. Why was he here? Why had the episodes of his life so ordered themselves that this moment was necessary? He didn't ask these questions in words as such, but he felt them through every inch of his body. A hunger for flight burned in his chest, but he couldn't give in to it. He had fled before and been brought back. He could not flee again.

He glanced at the hound. She stood near at hand, occasionally looking up at the man and then away, waiting, scenting the air and thus noting the passage of things the man had no inkling of. Though Morrison wished her by his side at that moment, he was thankful that she would not witness the things to come. He realized as he stood there that he feared the canine's judgment more than he did any living person's. He reached out, ran his palm across the coarse hairs of the hound's coat and pulled her tight against his thigh.

Come, he said. Let's get on with it.

A few of the men glanced up at his approach, but most of them barely noticed. Morrison saw first to the hound, tying a length of rope around her neck and securing her to a pylon. He glanced around to verify that the planter was not amongst them, then he turned his eyes down toward his gun. He listened as the others talked and so confirmed what he had already heard rumored. They had rounded up a total of five Negroes so far. Through a variety of means Humboldt had acquired the proper permissions to take them into slavery. He called them fugitives but in truth he could only verify that with two of them. The other three had probably never been outside of Philadelphia, but they were a bad sort for whom no white man would vouch. The authorities were willing enough to part with them. Some of their other men were away to gather up a sixth fugitive at that very moment. This would've been a good catch in its own right, but the true loot was still to come.

Humboldt strode in all motion and vigor. Awareness of his arrival passed through the men like a wave of electricity. He said he had come to prepare them with a frank statement of facts and they were these. The niggers may fight, he said, but they won't be armed. They'll be down in the hold of the ship. It'll be a nasty business prying them loose and getting them up top. There'll be some women among them, but don't trust them for a second cause they'll cut your prick off just as soon as look at. There'll be no crew to deal with. Just the captain, and we've settled up already. Took a little persuasion, but the captain got right sensible when I put the point to him.

Before they departed the boy from West Virginia jogged in with news that they'd grabbed the Negro girl as directed. Morrison moved closer and heard the boy say that it had gone smooth as cream. They'd jumped her right there in front of her lady's big house and carried her off. They did it quiet like. Nobody'd even know she had been nabbed. He asked Humboldt if he should take her to the ship but the man said no, not yet. He should pen her for now and send the others to join up with him. The more guns the merrier, he figured.

Morrison watched the West Virginian go off again, confirming his destination from the direction he turned, part of him a dart stuck in the boy's back.

See what I mean, boys? Humboldt turned to the gang of men. The good Lord himself's on our side. This next business'll be a walk on. Just keep your heads on and we'll be done in time for supper.

All told they were a group of eleven. As they moved out, Morrison fell in toward the rear of the line, lagging behind a half-step, eyes hard and slanted on the men before him. It was a misty evening. Bands of low-hung cloud crept in from the water, the light gray and otherworldly. It brought to mind a story he had heard in his youth, a biblical one he believed, a story in which death floated through the streets killing all those without the proper markings to identify them to God. He had never been a religious man. He wasn't even sure that his recollection of the story was correct. It was a child's remembrance, a child's fear and that was the problem. He felt like a child faced with a world beyond his control. He was not at all sure about the role he might play in the events to come. The players were moving toward each other with a rapidity that was a surprise to him even though he had watched it brew. He was waiting to see the way forward but he did not yet see it. Something would come to him, he thought. His internal gears whirled unhinged, spinning through ideas, waiting to catch. Something had damn sure better come to him.

The fog was thick across the docks but moved rapidly, the scenes behind fading in and out as if they were the incorporeal substance instead of the mist. They moved down alleys between warehouses, trod through puddles and around stacks of crates and reams of timber, past an enormous mound of something that looked and smelled like rotting coffee. The men chatted as they walked, nervous talk, spaced more and more frequently by uneasy gaps. Eventually, Humboldt ordered the men to silence with a raised hand. They walked on, each motion seeming louder now than normal: their boots across the stones, the wrinkle of fabric, the clink of iron against iron, a throat cleared of phlegm. All was white for a few moments, but with the next break in the low clouds came a view of the ship, clear and solid before them, masts thrusting toward the sky like the great trees they had once been, sailcloth bunched in folds, damp and heavy just to look at.

For Morrison the impact of seeing it could not have been greater if the mist had cleared upon a mountain. It was just there. There was motion on the deck, silent, but fast, a single person had seen them and sprung back from the near side of the ship. Humboldt leapt forward, caution gone in an instant. In a moment he was down the pier, the next he was climbing the gangplank, and then he was astride the ship.

The other men were fast on his heels, and Morrison close behind them. He was one of the last men to mount the deck, but once there he felt an urgency he had not a moment before. He pushed past a few men, ducked under the mainsail and leapt up onto a *thick coil of rope. From that vantage he saw that Humboldt had a black man pressed against the railing of the ship. Their faces were close together. Morrison couldn't see the white man's face, but the base of his neck quivered with anger. His arms moved as he spoke, his shoulders rolling in their joints as if they might pop loose. Morrison swung his rifle up into a two-handed grip, his finger on the trigger's crescent.*

This the one, then? Humboldt asked, motioning for the man beside him to grab hold of the Negro. This the one?

Another man, the Irish Captain, answered that it was. He stood behind Humboldt, his eyes skittering over the scene, his voice weak and distant.

Though he didn't lift his rifle to sight, Morrison let it swing in Humboldt's direction. He felt and heard the other men around him, but he couldn't think of them. He set his features immobile and knew that they would not see him at that moment. Their collective attention was all on Humboldt, all eyes except his. It was the Negro man he studied. He had a face of malleable features, full around the jowls even though he was not overheavy. His spectacles perched low on his nose and canted to one side. Behind them the man's eyes peered out with a singular intelligence, a knowing resignation that was sad to the core but not defeated. Morrison tried to find anything familiar in the man's features but for the life of him he wasn't sure if he did or not.

And are they all here? We get the whole load? Humboldt asked. He had to repeat the question several times before the captain answered.

Almost. There's one that didn't show.

This news captured the whole of the planter's attention. He spun on the captain. You're not gonna tell me that one is my nigger, are you?

I... I don't know. Who's your ...

William. For Christ Almighty's sake! Tell me we got him.

219

But the Irishman could not do that. They didn't have him.

Morrison lowered his rifle and let it dangle, glancing about him. There was little time to observe the other men, however. Humboldt urged them all to action. Morrison went with the others, propelled into the ship by the men all around him. They emerged a few moments later with the fugitives, bruised and battered, trembling and again in chains. This all fed Humboldt's anger further, for the one he most sought was not among them. He raged at the Irishman, at the bound Negroes and even at the men that drove them. But in the end he turned his attentions back to the bespectacled Negro. He asked him if he had ever been lashed like a common slave? He held the whip before his face and poked him with the butt of its handle. That's what he would get if he didn't open his mouth and say something useful. Why was William not here? Where was he? Where in this godforsaken Northern piss-hole? Humboldt's face pressed close to the man's, cocked to the side so that he received the man's answer directly into his ear.

Sir, the man said, I'll answer none of your questions. I'll simply speak to you in language you'll understand: fuck you and the sick bitch that squeezed you out.

Morrison was near enough to hear this. He was meant to be checking the manacles on the Negroes, but he didn't do so. He paused, watching the exchange. He noted the calm in the man's voice, his polite tone, the way the words twisted from the man's tongue. He wouldn't have thought such words would come from a man with such a face, but he seemed to pleasure in them.

Humboldt didn't take the statement lightly. He beat the black man with the full force of his body. The whip was little use from up close, but he used the knob of the grip to batter the man's face. When the Negro fell to his knees, Humboldt kicked him and kicked him and stepped back and drove the heel of his foot into his nose. He yanked him upright and spit the same questions in his face again. But still the black man stared straight ahead and chewed his thoughts and let the blood dribble from his lips like it didn't even belong to him. He met the man's gaze only when he imposed his eyes upon his direction of vision. He stared at him, past him, through him, as if each view was equally mundane.

Turn around, Humboldt said.

You can't hurt me, the black man said.

Turn around and we'll see. The black man didn't move so the planter spun him by the shoulder and pressed him up against the railing. You sure you don't have anything to tell us? he asked, his mouth close to the other man's ear.

Morrison took a step toward Humboldt. His finger twitched. He swung his rifle up into a two-handed grip, a reflex for no conscious thought spurred the action. He didn't know this man. He was just a black man. A stranger, not the one he was looking for.

Nothing you'd want to hear, the black man said, speaking through swollen lips. But tell me, who betrayed us?

God, when he saw you born a nigger. You gonna regret you didn't answered me rightly.

Morrison heard the tone of Humboldt's voice and knew what it meant. The man had already decided. That's where they were different. Humboldt had already decided; he, Morrison, had not. His finger was hot on the trigger of his rifle. His other hand clamped across the stock. It need only be a small motion, from where he stood he could aim one blast into the planter's kidneys. But then what? What with all these men around? He would be giving up his cause for a man he didn't know. Even if Humboldt's side exploded in blood it would change nothing of what had already been decided.

The black man spoke as if unaware of the shotgun barrel pressed against the center of his spine. He spoke looking out across the water, watching the progress of the mist. All I regret

*is that I wasn't more vigilant in my duties, he said. May they for-
give me. May they know my intent was true. But you, you can
give up your search this evening, for those other two are beyond
you. They're all beyond you, and your cause is lost. You are beyond redemption and already damned...*

*It's not two I'm looking for, Humboldt said. My men already
fetched the bitch. Nothing's beyond me. You'd know that if you
knew me. But the hell with it, I got things to do.*

*The black man's lips opened with a question, but his words
were clipped by the blast of shot that sprayed through his back,
splaying out around his spine and exiting his chest in a blast of
viscera. Morisson, from his profile, saw recognition on the man's
face, his own parts blown into the air before him and he still of a
mind to see and understand this. He tried to spin. His jaw worked
the air and one hand rose with a finger upraised as if he would
pause and make one last point. But his body gave way beneath
him. His legs buckled and he tumbled. The deck smacked hard
against his head, crushing his spectacles, a lens of which popped
from the rims and skittered across the deck. As soon as his weight
settled against the boards the man went still, slack and staring,
eyes suddenly filmed and empty.*

*Humboldt spat over his corpse and into the water beyond the
railing. He turned and, without comment on the dead man, gave
orders pertaining to the slaves huddled on the deck and to the one
still at large. He stepped into action, swearing that he was not yet
quit of this night's work, swearing that he was not yet to be beat
by any nigger. He turned his attention to the captain, for there
were still things he could tell him about where the dead man had
lived and where this missing one might be.*

*Morrison wished his eyes to rise from the dead man's face.
He didn't want to look into it and yet could not easily look away.
It took an enormous effort to tilt his head and push his chin up to-
ward the sky and close his eyes. Shame washed over him, not just*

shame at this moment, at the fact that he had watched this man die while knowing he did not deserve such a death. The shame went further back than that. There before him was an image to be twinned with his brother's tale of the Negro from years ago, dead and pressed into the mud. In thinking of that man he thought of his brother, of how Lewis had cried for the man's death, how he had wept for all those earlier dead, the ones beloved to them but now gone forever. At the time he had pitied his brother his heart, but now he knew better. A caring heart is not soft.

Twenty minutes later Morrison disembarked the ship at the end of the line of chained Negroes. He walked behind them a little ways but did not follow them all the way to the other ship, into which they were to be secured. Instead, he chose his moment and slipped into an alley and away. He had someone else to attend to. Shame is of no use unless one is prepared to learn from it.

Nine

A little after dark, William decided he had waited long enough. The hours and days, weeks and months that preceded this moment all assailed him. He was more full of doubts and questions and fears than he had ever been, even more so than on that night some months ago when he had first stolen away from his hut and fled Humboldt and Kent Island. He sat counting the minutes, knowing that he was not ready for this, but knowing also that one never could be ready for such moments. He could only step forward into it. If he was strong and God was willing, he might step through it and might one day be able to live the life of a normal man.

He slung the sack that contained his few belongings over his shoulder, cast his eyes about the dark lair that he had come to know each corner of by heart, and then he cracked the door open and slipped out. The night expanded around him with a great rush, as if the sky and the stars and trees and all the animals and insects in them had been huddled just outside the door to the carriage house and had jumped back when he emerged. The whole world hung about him in this façade of distance and indifference, a great charade to trick him into believing that he went unwatched, to convince him that this night was not about him and him alone. He crouched just outside the door for a moment, listening to the chaos of chirps and whines and buzzing, trying to search through it all for some other noise, a voice, a snapped twig, the crackle of weight pressing down upon dry leaves. But there was nothing, nothing save a million insects shouting out their existence.

He moved forward, tentatively at first, crouched over and sly, using the shadows beneath the trees, swishing through the tall grass at the very edge of the field. But the further he moved from his hideout, the bolder he became. He found that he did not really fear his own detection by some slave catcher. He could deal with that. He would run or yell out or fight as he had to. He would grapple with the man and strangle the life out of him, bash his head in on a rock, or stab his fingers into his eyes, drive them so hard and deep those orbs would pop beneath his thumbs. There were so many things he would do if confronted, and he almost hungered for the chance to have it out, to unleash these pent-up emotions in a barrage of physical acts. Perhaps something in the purgatory of the past months had nurtured in him a desire for bloodshed. At least in this he was equal to any man. At least his own hands were not ruled by a nation's laws, by histories he had never been taught and grand notions he had never seen realized. Yes, he thought as he jogged forward, let there be blood, freedom or bloody death, but never again that life in between.

He followed the winding road at times, cut forward through the trees at others. Before long he began to pass those great houses. And shortly after that he found himself on paved streets, smelt the coal and wood fires, heard the shouts of men and the clatter of hooves and carriages. He walked forward, amazed that he could so easily return into this cramped world of humanity. The first people he saw seemed like phantoms, apparitions that moved in the shadows, under hoods and hats, with eyes that never looked directly at him, but which always seemed to be following him. He tried to keep his head lowered, but he couldn't help searching out each passerby, wanting to recognize friend or foe before they recognized him. A person coming out of an alleyway nearly collided with him. The man looked up, his white face startled at first, then scornful a second later. He showed William the length of his cane in threat, and then walked away muttering curses against all things black.

It was not easy retracing the route he and Redford had taken up to the hideout. The man had quizzed him during their last discussion together, asking him to describe the route he would take and the landmarks he would pass, trying to ensure that William could find his way regardless of the weather or time of day or any other factor. He did his best to recall the landmarks: certain shapes in the roads and signs, a round chapel and an enormous house garishly painted. He took the back streets as far as he could, walking fast over the rough stones, through dimly lit alleys, trying to hold his course while still secreting himself away, as if he were stalking his route instead of following it. At one point he dropped down into a trench that moved him forward at a level just beneath the city, as if he were under its skin. He slopped forward through muck that he didn't dare look upon, that he knew only by its texture under his feet and the smell of it in his nose. He stumbled through it and soiled his hands and found himself trembling and tried to take deep breaths but then rejected the air for its foulness and moved on.

When he emerged from the trench he recognized nothing. The road he had been following had diverged some time ago. He was in an area of thoroughfares that thronged with people, with carriages and horses and railway cars. He pulled up facing a main street and clung to the shadows away from the gaslights. A block away the sky opened above a park of some sort, and in that park was a brass band playing a tune he vaguely recognized. Behind him, in the opposite direction, came some other form of music, the tinny sounds of cheap bells and the rhythmic clapping of hands. And added to this was the murmur of all those voices and the clopping of hooves and the grinding progress of iron over stone and a sound that was a chorus of laughter brought about by some street act that he could not see. This was not right. This was not the right area at all. He had never heard such a commotion before. Almost without thinking it out, he slipped back down into that trench and followed the winding course it led him on.

He climbed out of it some time later, in a much quieter area. He began to roam without direction, taking turnings at random, on hunches but with no clear vision anymore. He felt like he had those first few days in the city, a tiny being lost in a maze of inhuman proportions. That creeping fear plagued him again, like on the first night as he ran from the hovel and crossed the Bay. It appeared behind him, dodging and hiding, just out of sight, but somewhere behind him, keeping time with him, laughing as he grew more and more disoriented. It was like a living thing, like some carnivorous animal. He heard its breathing, felt its warm tongue licking at his back, waiting for him to stumble and fall and give in. It was this, above all else now, that kept him moving forward.

He didn't recognize the alley until he was already half way down it. The realization sent a wave of exhilaration through him. He paused and placed a hand against the wall just next to him. He asked his heart to slow, to calm and return to him and not race away as it was doing. He walked forward, little stealth left in his posture, and finally he saw Redford's apartment. There was no window on the back, and for a moment he thought of going around to the front to see if the lamp was on. But he didn't.

He approached the house slowly, one hand trailing along the rough stone and mortar of the opposite side of the alley. There were pedestrians at either end of the alley, but they moved by without so much as a sideways glance, framed for a second in attitudes of motion, then gone. The alley itself was dark and deserted, quiet enough that William could hear the rats scrounging through the garbage. He eased forward, reached out toward the gate of the tiny courtyard behind the apartment. It swung open before his fingers, and he carried the motion forward, easing to the staircase and up.

His knuckles rapped on the door. He waited a few seconds, and then knocked again, a little more firmly this time. Still nothing. He placed his ear against the door and tried to listen through the dead wood, but there was nothing save the pressure of his head against the door and the great noise that made. He pulled back and knocked again. In the silence that followed he realized two things. First, that he had forgotten about the fear the moment he realized where he was, and, second, that the fear was returning. He felt it tracking him through the alley and he knew it could smell him again. It had lost him for a second, but here it came again. And this time, there was nowhere to run to.

A noise behind him drew his attention. He turned to see a man emerging from the bushes on the other side of the alley.

He walked forward with something in his hand, kicked open the gate to Redford's back garden, and strode on toward the steps. Behind him, William heard noises from inside. He looked over the far edge of the balcony and thought he could jump from there into the neighbor's yard. He took a step that way, but then heard the door open. He turned to yell an alarm.

But it was not Redford who stepped through the portal, nor Dover, nor any person of color. It was a thin-shouldered white man. He had his shirt opened down to his navel and his arms were bare to the shoulder. He looked wholly inbred, pale and ill figured, with an expression of joyful rage on his face. And he came armed. He stepped onto the porch swinging an ax handle. The first blow caught William at the base of the neck. The next landed on his back as he spun. The third cracked atop the center of his skull. William saw the railing elude his grasp, saw it rising toward him and felt it bouncing off his chest. He tried to grab it, to steady himself and spring over it, but his body no longer heeded him. He slipped sideways and felt the ax handle dig into his side and felt something shove him. For a moment he saw nothing but the sky above him, as if he were floating into it. But then the world came back into view, flew past him, over his head and under and over him, battering him all the time. He hit the bottom of the steps flat on his back, looked up and saw the two shadows descending toward him.

PART FOUR

One

The West Virginian leaned against the doorjamb, hat raked forward to shade his face from the mist, a guard, but an inattentive one for he concentrated mostly on the mug of coffee he cupped before his face. Morrison stepped out of the night so near at hand that the boy started and spilled his coffee. Goddamn, he said, you a spooky son-a-bitch. But he forgot his fear in a second, asking how it went at the ship, cursing his luck for being left to guard the Negress, though she was chained anyway and he didn't see the use. Ya'll get them sons-a-bitches?

Morrison ignored his questions and asked the boy how things had really proceeded with the woman, the true story and not that shit he had dribbled out for Humboldt. Acknowledging no insult in the tone of the question, the boy told him how they snatched the pregnant woman from the sidewalk across from her mistress' house and dragged her through the streets. She screamed and spat and fought and called out to passersby, who watched her with shocked faces and did no more. They put her in chains in the cellar just below them, stretched her arms wide and fastened her to the wall. One of the men pulled her backside around toward him and pressed his groin against her and told her all that he would do to her, the manner of torture he would choose and the pleasure he would take from it. He whispered these things close to her ear, like some lecherous lover to his mate.

It was a sight to see, the boy said.

But the woman would have none of it. She spit in their faces and belittled their manhood and made oaths of blood she couldn't possible actualize. For this response she got a good beating. They whipped her with a razor strap across the arms and legs and...

Morrison interrupted him. You beat her?

The boy said he hadn't beaten her himself, but that several of the others had. He said they might have taken it all further except that Humboldt was a peculiar son-a-bitch and they hadn't wanted to stir his ire.

I see. Morrison considered this for a moment, then told the boy to wait on where he was. He began to push past him but the boy asked him where the hell did he think he was going? Morrison just said for him to wait where he was.

What you gonna do to her? You do something to her I ain't taking the blame for it. Humboldt'll be on your ass. Don't say I didn't warn you.

Morrison found the woman in a cell at the rear of the old gaol. She was bound by each of her limbs. The chains were long enough for her to sit up, with her back against the wall, her legs straight out before her. He was struck by the heaviness of her pregnancy. He didn't know much of such things but it was obvious she was nearing the end of her term. She cradled her belly in her arms and hummed a lullaby that died on her lips when the white man appeared. She sensed him, but did not look up. Her clothes were tattered, torn at the shoulders and ripped across the bodice and stained by what fluids Morrison was not sure. He knelt down a little distance from her. Her nose ran with a mixture of blood and mucus, and her jaw hung open slightly, as if that was the only position that didn't cause her pain. It was obvious that her captors had used more than a razor strap.

Morrison left the room and returned a moment later with a tin cup of water. He knelt and offered it to the woman. At first she seemed not to notice. The man inched forward, the cup held in both hands. He drew close enough that it almost seemed he would put the cup to her lips, but then the woman moved. With one gesture—a sweep of her hand so quick he didn't see it coming—she knocked the cup from his hands and sent it clattering into the far corner of the room. He sprang back. The woman returned her arm to her belly and all was as before.

The man was silent for some time, and the two just sat: an aging white man, a hunter of animals and humans, and a slave woman almost nine months pregnant with a child. Morrison thought he could hear her crying. It was a faint sound, far away, as if it came from outside the room, a low whimpering that seemed to him that much sadder for the lengths she went to hide it. But when he gazed at her he wasn't sure. She was motionless. He couldn't see her face, as it was downturned and hidden behind her hand and her hair. Perhaps she was not crying. Perhaps his ears were playing tricks on him, for the sound went on, so faint and constant it might have come up from within the floor of the cell, from the earth itself. He didn't know what to make of it, but he knew that they could not stay this way, at least not if they were to have any say in the future careening toward them. When he opened his mouth to speak he was not at all sure of what he was going to say.

I don't for the life of me know where to start. I could try to apologize for the things those men have done to you, but I doubt

*that apology would mean much to either of us. Wouldn't be com-
ing from them, anyway. They're vile men, right enough, and
they've no remorse to speak of.*

The woman didn't acknowledge him.

*I do have some things to apologize for myself, he said. And I
will do. I will do. But first I need to tell you a tale. Then you and I
can figure out just how we're going to sort this all out. And we don't
have much time, either. You mind if I talk a wee bit?*

She raised her head and spat at him.

*Morrison wiped the spittle from his chin with his fingertips.
He looked at the moisture and then cleaned his fingers on his
britches. She had given him an answer, but he had to tell his story
anyway. I can't ask anything of you, he said, but I'm going to
make you hear me out. This story starts way off in another country, a fair many years ago. It's about me, aye, but in a way it's
about you as well. Just hear me out.*

*Morrison introduced himself slowly, starting all those years
back, across the ocean, in the land he had first called home. He
told of the hardships his family faced under the Laird, of their
poverty and displacement, of their slow deaths. He spoke of his
brother and of the voyage those two made together, of the dying
time that was his introduction to America, and of their first years
living along the Bay. He recalled the early work they took, as
slaughterers of horses, as chimneysweeps and hewers of wood,
and then as haulers of manure and, finally, as diggers of graves.
He told her all of this in his somber cadence, not rushing it, but
moving steadily forward through the years. As far as he could tell,
she listened to him.*

*His tone changed, however, when he entered a new area
of his story. He spoke more hesitantly of the young woman his
brother loved, as if he were learning his way through the events
even as he gave them voice. He had spoken so many words against
her, he admitted, but what he really wanted was for her to be with*

him. He wanted the strength to draw her to him, and then to stand with her against the world. He wanted to take the world of men by the neck and throttle it, to beat sense into it, to reorder the universe and make it right. This was a strength he didn't have. Not even by half. But his brother did. That frail poet, that dreamer of a brother, he who cried tears freely and without shame. He had a strength Morrison did not. And this became a wedge between them. He felt the fabric of his brotherly bond stretched to breaking, and one evening, fired by the warm liquor inside of him, he went to the cabin and found the woman alone. He spoke easy to her, and then he spoke hard to her, and then he shouted at her the things that troubled him. She laughed at him. He said things to her that he did not mean, things meant to hurt her, but still she laughed at him. He struck her with the flat of his hand, and she struck him back with a clenched fist. And then he grasped her in his arms and breathed her in and that consuming hunger came upon him again. He lifted her in the air and ran his hands over her body and told her she was a whore, a slut, a nigger. She said she might have been all of these, but that his brother was a better man to judge than he was. His brother might have been younger, frailer, his emotions might dwell just behind his eyes: but he was still more of a man than he was. For this he slapped her, open-handed, but with all the force he could muster.

Morrison had been looking at the floor beneath him, but now he looked up and studied the woman. Nothing in her posture had changed. Her face was still hidden. He tried to read the lines of her body for some message, but there was nothing other than the mute refutation that she had shown him thus far. He wanted to explain himself in some way that went beyond the words he was speaking. He wished he could get to the other side of them, so that she would understand him from the inside and know that he knew how wrong he had been. He wanted her to hear how much he cursed himself for uttering those words against her. And mostly, he wanted her to understand that he would give his life never to have touched her that way. It was unforgivable, and yet in speaking it aloud to this woman, this black woman, he was not only telling. He was also asking. He wanted to be understood and punished, chastised and damned and forgiven all at once.

The woman didn't respond.

There was a noise in the hallway. Morrison pulled his hands from his face. His gaze shot over to the closed door. He waited and listened and let one hand come to rest on his rifle. There followed a rattle of chains and the sound of something heavy being dragged across the floor. Men's voices came through the wood and Morrison recognized a few of them. But whatever it was they were attending to had their full attention. They passed the door without opening it and their sounds faded down the hallway.

My brother and I had an awful fight soon after, Morrison said, continuing his tale. Only brothers can fight like that. As close to him as I was he was part of me, but he was a part of me that I'd just as soon see dead. He must've felt the same. It was an awful brawl. Morrison studied the floor below him and let something pass unsaid. I ran away after that. Just ran and spent years out west, hunting, trying to forget. But you cannot forget such things. You can only relive them, again and again. Relive them till you've lead the same sorry life a thousand times, and watched yourself make the same sorry mistakes a thousand times. That's been my punishment, and I doubt God could've thought of any better one.

The tracker uncrossed his legs and stretched them out and then crossed them again. He took his head in his hands and dug his fingertips into the rough skin of his face. He thought, for a second, that he might reach into his eyes and tear them out. He would tear them out and squirm forward and offer them, the bloody orbs, to the woman who sat before him. Perhaps then she would look at him and see him. And if she didn't, then at least he wouldn't see her indifference. But then he shook off this thought too, for it was

no less self-indulgent than all the sadness he carried in himself.
He was embarrassed by it, and he wasn't yet finished saying the
things he must.

Last year I got a letter, he said.

It was from that woman, his brother's woman. It took a year
to find him, hand delivered by a man he barely knew and only
met by chance. She wrote that she was about to die, and she had
some things to say before she went. After his brother's death she
had a child. She had loved him from the day she first felt him
inside of her, and on the day of his birth she had gone crazy, she
slipped into a mad love that had never dimmed since. She had seen
her son grow into a good man. She said that every day of his life
she had watched over him. She had prayed for him and cast spells
for him and been at his side even when he was far away from her.
She had helped him on, for she believed she owed him that much
for bringing him into the world. She had thrown the weight of
love over his shoulders, and, despite the distance she saw growing
between them, she knew she had created a good man. She said she
had done the best job she could and that she would die proud of
that much. She had told the boy of his father many times, so that
he would understand that he came from two trees.

Well, she wrote some of that, Morrison said. Parts of it at
least. Other parts might be my own thinking. Anyway, it was that
note that brought me back. His words trailed off. He mumbled
something under his breath, something in that strange, other
tongue of his, and then he composed himself for the moment
to come.

That woman's name was Nan, he said. Don't know if you
ever met her but you know of her. She was William's mother.
Her . . . Her husband was my brother, Lewis. My younger brother.
I haven't been tracking a runaway. Don't you think that. I've been
hunting my kin.

The black woman finally raised her head.

Two

The men knew their work and addressed it with relish. They beat William to the edge of consciousness, focusing their blows on muscle, beating any strength out of him. He tried to fight them but from the first blow it had been too late. They chained his hands and legs and dragged him through the streets, stones wearing his knees ragged and bloody, a spectacle for the evening's pedestrians to gawk at. He had a notion that they were taking him to be lynched, but this was not what they had in mind.

They paused before a decrepit building, an old gaol perhaps, but one that no longer had an official function. They spoke briefly to the boy on guard there, then opened the door using William's head as a battering ram. They tossed him down a flight of stone steps, kicked him along a hallway and into a cell where they rearranged his bonds for a new purpose. His wrists and ankles were bound with iron cuffs, fastened so tight they pinched his circulation and left his extremities numb. Each cuff was attached to the wall by a short chain, and he hung supported partially by his own outstretched arms and partially by his legs. Around his neck they fastened another oval of iron. This was attached to a rope which ran up through a staple in a ceiling beam and down into the hand of a tall, toothless man who grinned when William's eyes touched on him. He nodded a greeting and then hung his body weight on the rope. It went taut up through the staple and pulled William erect, the iron cutting his breath short and pinching his arteries and stretching the muscles of his neck. The man hung there so long that William grew lightheaded. His vision clouded with moving spots. He felt the vertebrae in his neck groaning against the pressure and thought that he might die this way and suddenly realized that he could accept that. Death would end this, and, above all else at that moment, he wanted this ended. He knew he was leaving Dover, but how much could a man do? How hard must he try before he was allowed to give in? The notion of death seemed so complete that he stopped straining against the chains. He was weak. He could take no more. He asked the living to forgive him. He would meet them on the other side . . .

CONSCIOUS AGAIN, he still hung in his biblical posture, breathing heavily and looking at a black world and slowly realizing that his eyes were closed and that the blackness was in his mind as much as in the world. He realized he had not yet passed away and remembered his wish to do so, although that wish seemed far away now. He had no idea how much time had passed, but it felt like a great deal had. He opened his eyes and took in the room for the first complete time.

It was a jail cell, dank and windowless, carved entirely out of the living bedrock. The walls were made of the earth's stone itself and gave him the impression that he was far below the surface of the world. A row of bars ran across the far end. The gate was ajar, as was the door to the hallway beyond, although he knew these portals were not open to him. Two torches protruded from supports along either wall. They cast a somber, fluttering light and blackened the ceiling with smoke that escaped through cracks in the ceiling.

If the lighting was medieval in design, the men who occupied the room were no different. A fat man leaned against the opposite wall, twirling his fingers through the hair of his chest and studying William with a proprietary interest. There was a dark-skinned man that William at first thought to be a Negro, but soon realized was not. Though his skin was dark, his mannerisms and deportment were not at all like a black man's. And there was one other, a teenager who stood toward the far end of the cell, naked to the waist and as bony as an alley dog. The tall man still grinned. He held the rope in one hand, tugging on it occasionally as if he were testing a fishing line.

The fat one was the first to speak. He stepped close to the captive and spoke low and secretive. "We got your woman in the other cell," he said. "Didn't know that, did you? Caught her just as easy as we caught you. Had a good time with her too. Felt up every last part of her. Put my hand on that belly of hers and felt that little one kick. Can you believe that? Little nit tried to give me cause."

William didn't respond.

"Answer when you're spoken to," the dark man said. He popped William on the jaw with a clenched fist. William's head stayed rigid against the blow, and the man pulled his fist back. He twisted away, cursing and holding his wrist clenched within his other hand. "Goddamn the hardheaded son-a-bitch."

"Damn near busted your hand," the tall one said. "Him with intent, too. I wouldn't stand for it."

"Should break his jaw, is what you should do," said the teenager, in a voice that was both high-pitched and syrupy.

"Could do that," the fat one said, "or we could leave him hang and go in the other room and work his woman over some more. Could bring her in here and let him watch."

This idea met with a chorus of approval from the tall man and the teenager, but the dark man ignored it. He still rubbed his wrist, but he moved back close to William. "He ain't got no idea the kinda things I could do to him." The other men agreed to that, and the dark man went on to describe just the type of tortures he had been known to use in the past.

William tried to block out his words. He tried to think past them, to rise above them. But it was hard. The man spoke with such relish. He spoke of faces mutilated and tongues cut out and limbs amputated by ax blade. He said a man wouldn't ever be any good at his work if he didn't take pleasure in it. And, the dark man said, he was damn good at his work and found within it an ecstasy rarely duplicated in any other legal amusement.

"You hear me now, boy? Scared yet? You got a right to be. That's the only right you do got, the right to be shit scared. You know what I got a mind to do?"

"What?" the teenager said, a tremble in his voice as if he were the one being questioned.

"Geld him."

"You can't do that," the fat one said. "Humboldt'd tar your hide if you ruined him."

"Humboldt?" William muttered, the single word enough to clear his head.

The dark one cocked his arm back to punch, then thought better of it. "I ain't gonna ruin him, except as a stud. I won't even draw that much blood. Just a couple quick cuts is all it takes. I'll give his nut sacks to Humboldt for a tobacco pouch."

But the other men would not agree to this. No broken bones, the fat man said. No open wounds, nothing that could kill the bastard or leave him lame. They argued among themselves, devising competing tortures for William, comparing past experiences and theories of the pain. William heard the words in the background and knew they were speaking of him, but he was detached from them. They weren't nearly as important at that moment as the realization that this was all Humboldt's doing. That man had reached his hand out across the water, across state borders, across the time that separated them. It was all for nothing. Dover was in his hands. The complete import of it all was too much. It hit him like mighty fist and left him reeling, breathless.

The dark one finally acquiesced. "Tell you what we'll

do . . . You want to pain him without damaging his value then you gotta be creative. First give him a pull, Walt."

He nodded at the tall man, who jumped on the rope, lifting William's rigid body taut and fighting, muscles striated with rage, arteries like worms burrowing through his skin. But this could not last for long. He passed out. When he woke seconds later, he felt the man's hands on his body. They unhitched him from the wall and spread him face down across the floor and found new eyebolts to fix his chains to. The dark man sent the teenager away with instructions. While he was gone they placed wooden blocks beneath William's shins, propping his legs up so that his bare feet angled toward the ceiling. He tried to fight them, but the men just laughed at his efforts. His body was weaker now than ever, bruised deep like tenderized beef, clipped here and pinched there and pressed flat against a floor of amazing cold, damp that seeped up from it and into him.

The teen returned with a dowel, about an inch around and five or six feet long. William saw him walk in with it held loose in his fingers, a dandy with a walking stick, satisfied with himself.

"Okay," the dark man said, "that'll do nicely. Let's have some fun."

Three

The woman stared at Morrison. Her gaze, now that she gave it to him, was more than he could bear. Eyes of a caged cougar, a creature who should not know him but one that seems to. He took off his crumpled hat and held it in his lap, awkward. He sat trying to think what to say next, feeling he had not fully explained himself, knowing he had not told the entire tale, afraid of the unspoken portion for it changed everything, cast everything that he was or claimed to be in doubt. And doubt was not what any of them needed just then. He looked back at her, as earnest as he could muster, but she seemed to see through it. She suspected him of greater crimes than he had confessed. He was holding back and she knew and her eyes were hooks pulling more from him. He looked down, his hat rumpled within his own fists, his hands large and monstrous. He put it back on again and forced himself to meet her gaze.

They really get all of them? she asked.

Not the question he feared but still one that made him cut his eyes. She's strong, he thought, but then a black woman would have to be. He told her what had happened, the fugitives all caught, the freeman aiding them dead. Only William had escaped them, though they were doubtless hunting him as they spoke.

The woman listened to all of this and was quiet for some time, her face a mask to Morrison. He couldn't read her emotions, though her silence now was different than before. It wasn't directed at him. It was no longer a weapon but was something sadder. Where is he? she asked.

Was hoping you might tell me.

But she wasn't sure. He might've gone to Redford's, she said, but she couldn't know for sure. That had been the plan but plans were a thing of the past. This news came into Morrison and sat at his center, a weight, though he didn't tell the woman. He needed to move delicately, aware that her confidence was a gift he might lose at any moment, each word she had spoken a jewel he hadn't expected. But they had so much to do.

Well, he said, Let me see about those chains. If you don't

mind we should start by getting you out of here. He moved a little closer, easing the woman with his palm, as one might approach an unknown dog, hand outstretched for her to scent or bite either one.

The woman didn't acknowledge his gesture. She lowered her eyes and said, They won't let you take me.

I didn't aim to ask permission.

They'll kill you for trying.

They wouldn't be the first to try. He was close to her now, near enough to touch her, to smell her at the back of his throat, her blood congealed but not yet fully dry. He lifted her wrist chains and turned them over, studied how they were strung to-gether and weighed the lock in his hand. I'd say there's nothing for it but I get the key from that boy out there. He said this matter of factly, a statement of the obvious, something clearly within reason.

But he never got to hear the woman's response. A noise dis-tracted them both, indecipherable for a long moment, then gone, faded to silence. Then it came again, clear and complete, the sound mixed with the rush of blood to Morrison's head. A scream, and a scream again. The yells were muffled by distance and man-gled by its passage through corridors and through the cracks in the door and all the more horrible for it. They came in gaps, spaced unevenly. Each silence worse than the scream itself for Morrison knew it was coming, knew that whatever action caused the scream was occurring or about to occur, knew that for all his horror in the hearing there was somebody out there feeling that horror and shouting to the world.

The woman's eyes drifted toward the wall, not as if she might see through it, for they glazed unfocused, but as if she had forgotten ocular sight and saw instead with her ears. That's him, she said.

Morrison didn't ask her whom she meant. He was up in one motion, legs spinning beneath him, single arm sweeping out and coming up with his rifle, strides flowing one to the next and he was at the door. He put his ear against it and listened a moment and then cracked it open. Air rushed in dank on his face and tainted. The corridor was empty and sounds of pain came clearer now. He spoke from the corner of his mouth, telling the woman he would be back directly. It would be all right, he said. He would see to it. She should just wait here and he would be back and they'd be on their way. He paused there as if waiting for her to respond. But she didn't, and that was that. He stepped into the hall, pulled the door shut behind him and began to prime the rifle.

Four

Each time the dowel smashed into the base of William's feet it was as if long needles had been driven into them, up through the flesh and bone of him, through his thighs and groin and into his torso. The pain was incredible, blinding, complete, driven home to the center of him, where it beat slowly, dissipating breath by breath until the next blow. And then the whole thing over again. And again. This torture like no other in that it didn't dim with the passage of time, each blow was like the first and again, despite himself, he wanted to die and be free of it. He tried not to cry out. He didn't cry, not voluntarily. Pain shot through him and wrenched open his mouth and spewed out. He had been beaten before but this was impossible.

Each man got only so many blows. He heard them arguing over turns, each one keen to give it a shot. He had long ago closed his eyes, but he opened them again when a hand grasped his hair and pulled his head back. The dark man, his face close, moisture dotting his nose, black hairs on his chin, each strand not curly but bent, twisted. He asked him something but William could not make sense of it. Part of him knew he should listen but the greater part was beyond that, was thinking, what could he do to get them to kill him? What words would enrage them so much they'd release him? But he could think of nothing and the man's face spoke on, mouth moving, words unheard.

Then his face pulled away and William saw past him to the door. A man stepped in and stood for a moment framed within it. He was a gaunt man, graying in his beard and in the coarse hair that stood out from the side of his head, beneath a beat up, mangled excuse for a hat. His face was severe, eyes quick in their business, which was to take in the room as if doing inventory, counting each man in turn, measuring the size of the cell and coming to rest, after this quick survey, upon William himself. He held a rifle in one hand, pointed at the ground.

"What's going on here?" he asked, and with his words William could hear again. His voice was deep. He moved words about his mouth like they were stones, but at the same time there was something melodic in his pronunciation.

The dark man leaned in close to William. He didn't answer the old man's question but expressed great mirth at his arrival. He said the old fellah had just had himself a ride. He asked the man to confirm this. The old man did not, but the dark one didn't notice.

"What are you doing?" the old one asked. He stepped in from the door and slid a little to one side, measuring the room, his voice calm, tinged slightly with something else, an aggression that didn't go unnoticed.

William closed his eyes, thinking it strange that with all the pain in his body a few moments of breathing eased him so.

The fat one said that they were just dealing with their

prisoner, if it's any of his business. They had it under control and he could shut up and watch or else move on. What had he been doing with the girl, anyway? the teenager asked. The old man ignored him. When he spoke again he was on the other side of the room. He asked where Humboldt was and the dark man said he didn't give a damn. He spoke on, his words suddenly laced with profanities that William didn't catch. He felt the man moving again, heard him ask for the dowel and say something that the others found funny.

"Hold on a minute," the old one said. "You just want to wait on that."

The smooth grain of the wood brushed the heels of his feet, a soft touch, just a kiss. William knew that when that kiss ended the wood would pull back and then it would start again. This time he wouldn't yell. He would hold it in no matter what. He had to be stronger than he had been.

"You don't know what you're doing."

But the dark man believed he did and said he would demonstrate just what he was doing. The baton lifted on the upswing. William opened his eyes. They came to focus on the old man and, as if spurred by the touch of his eyes, he acted. The old man raised his rifle with the power of a single arm and brought it to sight with the help of the other, steady and motionless, the barrel so long it seemed almost to reach out and touch him. William thought that the man was acting out some plan the slavers had concocted while he was unconscious and was preparing to shoot him. But the aim was slightly off, and when he pulled the trigger the slug didn't enter William. Neither did he see clearly all that happened but he saw pieces of it and this is how it fit together.

The blast was deafening. The first shot ripped through the soft spot in the tall man's neck, severing the artery there, blood bursting from the wound in a sudden rain. But the lead was not

247

spent. The angle was such that it slammed with undiminished force into the dark man's skull, entering through his ear and existing through the entire far side of his face. William snapped his head around but on seeing the dark man poised behind him he could make no sense of it because what had been his face was now nothing that he could recognize.

The old man spun. He jabbed the muzzle of the rifle into the fat man's face with enough force to crush the bridge of his nose and gouge deeply into one of his eyes. The man spun again, moved forward and swung the butt end of the rifle around and caught the boy in his stupefied face and snapped his jaw. This pain spurred the boy to motion and that motion was flight. He kept spinning with the force of the blow, his legs slick on the stones, pawing for purchase but finding none. The old man tripped him. The boy landed on his chin and the force of it made the break complete. The lower portion of his face was a shapeless mess when he rolled over. He was trying to scream but he could not and instead he grasped at his face with his hands and tried to set things right and realized he could not and tried to scream again.

The old man looked around the room at each of the men, calm in the way of some men during scenes of amazing violence, as if in the act he had found a truth and though it wasn't a pleasant truth it was one deserving of thought. Only the dark one was completely dead. The tall man leaned against the wall trying to stay the squirts of blood pulsing through his fingers where they were clamped to his neck. The fat one lay squirming on the ground. He tried to pull his revolver but couldn't get a grip on it and began to curse it in a voice that cracked higher and lower with each alternating word. The old man dispatched each of the three in turn with the butt end of the rifle. Then he turned toward the prisoner.

William felt a moment of fear. But only a moment. Then

the emotion changed to hope. Perhaps this man would kill him quickly. But the old man did not. He tossed the rifle down and touched him gently and wiped away the blood on his face and felt over his body as if checking for wounds. The man was so close that William could smell him and hear his breathing and feel the tremble in his hands. When the man was satisfied he pulled back a little, just far enough to meet William face to face.

"Sorry you had to see me like that," he said. "I'd ask you to forget it if I thought you could, but I know you never will. Your first memory of me is always gonna be the sight of me killing four men. That's a damnable bad showing but there was nothing for it."

William heard him but he didn't comprehend even the smallest part of it. He lay there dumb as the man rummaged through one of the dead men's pockets, came up with the keys and unshackled him and helped him stand. But when his feet touched the ground splinters of pure white agony screamed up his legs. He heard the man speak to him but he couldn't sort out the words. They had stopped making sense almost from the moment the man began speaking and now each new word just piled onto the ones preceding it and added to the confusion.

The old man seemed to understand this. He grasped William by the shoulders and looked at him squarely and didn't speak at all, just looked and in that look tried to say something. No, not to say something, but to stop saying anything and create a silence between them, to find a calm and to anchor them to it and to share the moment.

"Come," he said. He bent and grasped William about the legs and lifted him to his back. William felt himself hoisted up, felt himself come to rest across the man's shoulders, and felt the man push himself erect. The room spun with the man's motions, and in the spinning William again lost consciousness.

HE AWOKE IN AGONY. His legs were aflame, crawling with fiery ants, pierced by shards of colored glass. Just the flexing of his muscles as he pulled himself upright sent splinters of pain shooting through his entire body, sucking the wind out of him and leaving him panting. He realized that he was in a different room than before. In the corner of his vision he saw a shape rise and move toward him, but even as he turned to look he fell back to a prone position. The effort of the motion was too great and at that moment nothing was as real as pain.

The body moving toward him spoke. "William."

It was Dover's voice. It was her face looking down on him. "We're safe now," she said. "Understand? We got out of that place."

Staring up at her he realized he did understand. They had left that dungeon. He had been carried out on that man's shoulder, he that had somehow wreaked a world of violence on those others. He had killed them one and all in the flutter of an eyelid. Everything had changed and then he had spoken, lifted him and carried him out into the streets. This pain was not new. He had lived with it as the man carried him. He remembered wondering where they were going and not caring, and then realizing that Dover was with them and suddenly caring again. He had tried to lift his face up to her but his head never moved as commanded. He saw bits of her in passing, her walking along beside him, hip rocking, one hand as it moved through his field of vision.

Now they were in a room which for some reason he recognized, a single cubicle with an opening behind Dover, a dark space into which he couldn't see. There was a lamp on the table at the far end, its glow warm on the yellowed walls. And then his eyes were back on Dover's. He reached up to touch her, moving slowly for exertion of any part of his body stirred pain in distant regions. He needed to feel her. The motion was only half completed before she understood it and leaned down close to him. Her cheek touched his and she whispered that it was all right. They were safe now. Her voice spread warmth over him, in the hollow of his neck, against his ear. The scent of her skin was more acrid than he remembered. But it was her nonetheless, and he tried to hear her words and take them in and hold them. He wanted to believe her, and for a moment he did, that closeness to her was enough. But as soon as she pulled back and air rushed to fill the space between he remembered there was more to it than that.

"Where's he?" he asked.

Dover hesitated, eyes studying him as if to gauge his capability to receive the answer. "He's up talking with Miss Anne," she said.

So simply said but conjuring a world of questions. He realized why the room was familiar. It was his cell below Anne's house. He remembered being carried down the steps and set down on the cot. He had caught a glimpse of Anne's round face, saddened and serious, but he had already filed that image away as a part of a dream. How was that possible? Though he had some fractured recollection of his journey here, it only made sense in glimpses, as segments but never as a complete whole. Dover explained that they'd had to get someplace safe and nearby. She remembered what he had told her about Anne and, together with the old man, they'd found her. Anne had taken them in with only the briefest of explanations.

"A wonderful woman," Dover said. "Few like her in the world."

William listened to all of this, still staring, his face unchanging, still full of questions. "Who is that man?" he asked.

Dover glanced over her shoulder as if the man in question might be listening. Without answering, she rose and moved away to the washbasin. Her motions were slow and pained also, her belly supported in the crook of one arm. She picked up the basin and returned, sat with the chipped porcelain in her lap, a piece once valuable but now ancient with neglect. She said he was just a man who'd helped them. He would have to explain anything else himself.

"He the man Redford talked bout, the captain?"

Dover spit out a scornful breath. "Not hardly. That man had sold us out, each and every one of them, even Redford hisself."

He heard the derision in her voice. He rolled the words around inside of him, thinking, trying to put them before the aches of his body. It was some time before he spoke again, but when he did it was as if there had been no pause. He steeled himself and asked, "Redford? What happened to him?"

Dover shook her head and stirred the cloth in the bowl with her finger, swirling it with such attention that she seemed to have forgotten William. But she had not. "He's dead," she said. She raised her finger up out of the water, watching the cloth revolve slowly in the current.

William asked her how and she told what she knew, which wasn't much. Her story was fragmented and incomplete in all details save two: Redford was dead and the other fugitives were now in Humboldt's hands. The whole thing was a failure. At that moment, only the two of them still held on to some semblance of freedom. She pulled a dripping cloth from the basin and wrung it out. She wiped William's face with it, starting with his forehead and moving down.

"He's dead?" William asked, not looking for an answer but saying the words out loud to help digest them within. The shock of it was complete. Of all the tragedies he had imagined he only envisioned himself or Dover as victims. Of all the ways things could go wrong, he had never really believed Redford was at risk. It wasn't his fight. He was not a slave. He was a free man. He couldn't have died for a cause not his own. It didn't make sense.

William suddenly wanted very badly to leave that room. They weren't safe. They had to flee before somebody came for them. What were they doing sitting in a room, her dabbing his forehead with a cloth? He almost said as much, but he knew it was impossible. He couldn't even sit, much less rise and take charge and lead Dover to safety. He was helpless, and the full realization of it was different than any fear he had thus far felt. It was a quieter panic. The room seemed to revolve around him, as if he was at the pole of the world and all else rotated. It seemed this motion had always been there and yet he had just now recognized it, just now realized how helpless he was. He closed his eyes against the feeling of motion.

"What bout them others?" he asked.

"Told you. Humboldt got them."

"I'll kill him," William said. He knew the words sounded foolish but he was unable to stop them. He wanted that man's death so badly that he had to speak it out loud. "Shoulda killed him already. Shoulda broke his neck." His arms rose up as he spoke. His hands clenched the air, fingers trembling, so tense they seemed to strain against a solid object. But only for a second. He dropped them in exhaustion and lay panting.

"You ain't gonna strangle anybody anytime soon," Dover said, her voice that of a mother, knowing better, speaking reason to a child. "That's all right, though. He ain't got us, does he? We breathing free air right now."

William turned away from her and shut his eyes, thinking that sentiment an absurd one. Air had always been free. That was no change. This was not freedom, not when his body was so raw and pained. Them in this room that wasn't theirs, brought here by a murderous stranger. How could she find any peace in that? He heard her speaking, talking about his legs. She said that nothing had been broken. That was the trick of it. Nothing broken but a whole lot of damage done. He felt the tips of her fingers touching his thigh, moving down over his shins, which he realized were exposed. Her touch was meant to be gentle, but it pained him. His body was useless. Didn't that make it broken? Wasn't he just as crippled as if his legs had been snapped at the midpoint? He opened his eyes and stared at her again.

"Don't look at me like that," she said. Her face was composed, resigned somehow, hopeful somehow. "All we been through and you look at me like to strangle me instead of Humboldt."

He stared on, his mouth opening, lips starting to form words he couldn't fully put together. Didn't she see the situation they were in? Didn't she care about Redford and the others? He wanted to hear her voice quaver with fear, to see her eyes full of tears, face full of sorrow. He wanted to know that she felt something, but in the end all he managed to say was something that he had feared for a long time. He questioned whether she had any heart in her. "What's inside you, woman?"

Dover moved as if to rise, her lips a tight line, eyes flying up from him in exasperation. She half-turned, but that was as far as she got. She turned back and gazed at him. Her eyes wide, pupils so large they nearly filled the circle of her irises. "You don't mean that. Sugar, you know what's in me. You. You are. Always have been." She said this so gently that William forgot himself in staring at her, awash with emotion and yet confused by it. How can love come so fast upon anger?

"I don't understand anything," he said.

"I know," Dover said, touching her fingertips to his forehead and tracing his hairline. "I know it. It's not much longer now and you will. We're coming through this. May not feel like it to you, but we're walking through it. You trust me on that? Cause you're gonna have to. Tonight more than any night yet. You ain't done being tested. So trust me, and we'll walk through it all."

William held her gaze, unsure what she meant but hoping that trust was all they needed.

THE OLD MAN DESCENDED the steps ahead of Anne. He cleared his throat as he stepped into the room, as if he feared catching the couple during an intimate moment. He was bareheaded and in the dim light the gray streaks in his hair stood out with more prominence than their black counterparts. His beard was thick, tending even more toward white, a frame around his lower face that served to soften his otherwise sharp features. His eyes were somehow prominent beyond the norm, melancholy in their movements, lids slow in blinking, making of the downward curve a solemn act, a thing not done lightly but with fore-thought. His gaze touched on William and then Dover and then William again, not flighty in its motions but nervous beneath his deliberate calm. He cleared his throat and might have spoken, but then he remembered something. He looked down and checked the back side of his hand, the palm and then the back side. On his face there was no clear indication as to whether he found what he sought.

Anne was the first to speak. She asked how William was. As the question seemed more directed at Dover than at him, William held his thoughts. Dover answered for him. He couldn't take his eyes off of the old man and yet he kept trying to, looking from him to Anne and then back, up at the ceiling and then back, to the tiny window and then back. He thought at first that it was just the incomprehensibility of this man helping them that drew his eyes. Or perhaps it was that he had seen him moving with such violent precision. Or the suspicion that he must yet have some evil intent. It might have been all of these things but it wasn't. What drew him was the feeling that the man—this older, white man, savior to him and murderer of others—was afraid to look him in the face and meet his eyes. He still knew nothing about him, and yet from the hesitation in the man's eyes he learned something, enough to quiet him and calm those other questions.

While he pondered this, the conversation went on, both men mute while the two women spoke for all of them. Anne was much as William remembered, speaking easily with Dover, asking questions of the immediate, as to whether Dover needed anything else. There was water warming upstairs for her to wash his wounds further with, although she should seat herself and let her take care of them both. There was a nervous pitch to her voice, a quaver at the tail end of some of her words. She disguised it with small movements of her hands, with laughter placed at the end of sentences that wouldn't otherwise have been humorous. But this could not go on forever. The silence of the two men was too strong a force. It was heavy with all the import of the world outside that room.

"Well," Dover said, having taken a seat at Anne's insistence, "you two was up there talking. Whatchu done decided?"

He cleared his throat. When he spoke William was startled to recognize his voice. Of course, he had spoken before, in the gaol, but the easy cadence of the man's words surprised him still. His voice did not match his sharp features. It didn't suit his violent actions or the lanky strength of his body. If it balanced any part of him it was his eyes. His tones had something of the same deliberate nature, each word clearly formed and executed. No sentence was rushed. Instead it was placed before them complete, irrefutable and pre-reasoned.

He had spoken with Anne and her boys and together they had come up with a plan. This was no mean feat for their circumstances were peculiar, what with a crippled man and child-heavy woman and an old man, all three of them fugitives from the law. He said it was fortunate for them all that Anne was such a reasonable woman. She had sorted him out when he went astray and this is what they came up with. He would book them on a carriage heading north in the morning, passenger perhaps, but cargo more likely, anything to get them out of the city and moving north. They'd travel to New York, where he would cash in the bonds he held to a Chicago bank. With the money he would book the two of them yet another passage, on a ship, one that would take them out of this country.

"Out of the country?" Dover asked.

Aye, the man answered. It was no small thing, he knew, but they hadn't chosen their circumstances. They just had to deal with what they had. "That sound all right?" he asked.

William didn't answer. That plan was incomprehensible. Impossible. Carriages and cities and ships. Money drawn from banks. Sailing to another country, forever leaving behind the things they knew. Strange as it felt even to himself, he wanted to back out of it. He would just say that no, that didn't sound all right. There had to be another way. Let the old man go on if he wanted to, but they could never do all of that. They were Chesapeake slaves without a penny between them. Though their lives depended upon it, he couldn't imagine accepting all that the man had just offered. But Dover spoke before he got a chance to.

"How we gonna get to that carriage?"

Anne was seeing to that. She had sent one of her boys to fetch the coal man, he that had so long wanted her for a wife. He would pick up William and Dover in the early hours, hide them in the coal wagon and transport them to the carriage.

Anne was sure he would do as she asked. She might have to marry the man in payment, but that wouldn't be too high a price to pay. She was fond enough of him, anyway. "Just been holding out a little," she said.

Dover thought this over. "That sounds fine," she said.

"Good," the man said. He glanced at William, waiting for a moment to see if he would agree, his face unsure if such agreement was necessary to continue. "All right, then," he said. "I'll go now. We've no time to spare." Having stated his intention the old man stood as if he had not. His eyes rested for a moment on the folds of the blankets covering William's legs. "Are you all right, lad?" he asked.

The other three all froze, the question trailing off into a silence weighted beyond reasonable proportion. The old man seemed to recognize this or find something at fault in his question. He shook his head as if he would retract the words and start again. "Well, I ken you're far from all right. It's not that I mean. What I wanted to say was . . . I just want to know that you'll be all right, that it's not too late. I mean, I didn't get to you too late, did I?"

The man's gaze met William's full on. The effort of the act was palpable on the man's features, tension written in lines that seemed to etch themselves deeper with each passing second. It was on this drama that William concentrated. He heard the man's question and part of him struggled to find the words to answer it. The slave in him felt he must respond and promptly, but that part of him had been newly altered and no longer made up the whole of him. The better part of him just studied the man, unsure how to answer because he was unsure of the answer. His hand slid down his torso, seeking the button. His fingers rubbed the edge of the circlet through the fabric, one rim around and back to itself. No, he thought, it was the question itself that he was unsure of.

"It's not too late," Dover said.

"Course it's not," Anne said, her hand nervous at her lips and then pausing, surprised that she had spoken.

The old man was not satisfied with this but he nodded as if he was. He lifted his hat and put it on. The crumpled mass somehow sat with dignity on his head and with it on his face was again composed. "I'll be going, then."

Five

In the foyer of the row house the tracker considered his needs and gathered his supplies accordingly. He was alone, but he knew the house was full of boarders, quiet beings unnerved by him and the danger he had brought into their home. They were detectable not by the sounds they made but by their hush, their palpable presence on the other side of the thin walls. Knowing that they would not break from cover, he knelt and opened his large bag. He had to fish through it for some time before he came up with what he sought, a leather pouch, palm-sized and heavy with coins. He weighed it on his upheld hand and found it suitable. He set it aside and slipped his hand in a side pocket of the bag, pulled out a folded piece of paper, which he didn't look at but simply stuffed in his jacket pocket. He kept his hands moving and tried to fix his mind on the events to come so that none of them would come as a surprise. This was a quiet moment in the eye of a storm. He had felt it many times and knew the tranquility to be deceptive.

But below these focussed thoughts his mind wheeled on a more chaotic axle. He replayed the conversation in the cellar. He heard it differently each time, and of those recollections not one of them pleased him. He had spoken calmly and reasonably but only about the details, not about the heart of the matter. He had looked around the room, eyes anxious for something to focus on, the whole time seeing only that colored man lying prone in the bed, feeling the touch of his eyes, sensing every portion of his battered body as it lay sliding forward toward him. Though he tried he couldn't help but envision him as he had first laid eyes upon him, bound and trussed like a beast, soiled, bloodied, a vent for the lowest of men's pleasures, a slave. A Negro. The world of difference between them had choked his speech. And yet he could not ignore this man. He could not deny that he saw the man's mother in his face and saw too the features that made him a Morrison. Both Nan and Lewis had been there in the room with him and it was partially to them that he had spoken. It was this that troubled him for never had he seen clearer proof that one cannot escape a past unquenched. He had thought this before but had always tried to dismiss it as the fancy of his own deranged mind. He would not do so anymore.

He had just closed the bag again when he heard someone ascending the stairs from the cellar. He stood and waited. The young woman appeared. She stood framed in the tiny doorway, listening for a moment. She walked toward him. For the first time he noted the awkward progress of her pregnant gait.

We should know your name, she said.

Of course, he said, surprised that such formalities had yet to be addressed. It seemed absurd considering the intimacies they'd shared in the last few hours. Andrew Morrison. And they call you Dover?

The woman nodded. She didn't look concerned that he knew her name, but she did take his in carefully. She seemed to sound it out before accepting it. Well, Andrew Morrison, you really gonna do all that for us?

Aye.

And you gonna put us on that boat? When he nodded, she added, Alone?

Thought that'd be best.

The woman agreed that it might be best, but she also shared the fear that the notion put in her. Where was that boat going to take them? No place in this world that she knew, that was for sure. Away from all that they'd ever known, that also was a definite.

Morrison was quiet for a moment and then answered, *I know that feeling. I felt it years ago and haven't ever stopped. Truth be known. Still, it'd be for the best. This country's got a great evil in it.* He looked uncomfortable about using those words and added, *Man told me that. "A great evil,"* he said, and he knew what he was talking about.

That's true as spoken. We going, don't think I'm doubting that. I been scared before and I won't shy away from it. And I do want a world of things for this child that I ain't yet seen this country to offer. That's what it is, but what I'm wondering about is yourself. You putting us on that boat, but what you doing with yourself?

I'm no good as a traveling companion. Been inclined toward solitude for some time now.

And you like it that way? She let this question sit just long enough to get an answer from his silence. *If you wanna get on that boat too I won't argue the point,* she said.

Morrison's eyes drifted over toward the open cellar door.

The woman read his question and said that her man wouldn't dispute it either.

Morrison had his doubts about this, but he felt already that this woman was not easily argued with. He didn't know what to say and was surprised at himself by what came out because he hadn't yet known he thought it.

Feels like I should've talked to him more, he said.

Well, the things you got to say ain't the type a news you give on the brief.

You don't resent me the things I told you?

The black woman thought this over and answered that that wasn't her place. Those things were between him and Nan and William.

I didn't tell you all of it.

And you don't need to, the woman said. You got guilt around your neck like a stone. Looks to me like it's a load you can barely carry but you walking with, been walking with it for some time. Figure you punishing yourself and that's rare in a white man. Mostly they find someone else to punish for they crimes. Look here, I don't know just what you done or just what kinda man you are, but I do know you came back. Nobody living in the world to accuse you but you came back. And you brought that there cannon with you. She motioned at his rifle. A smile flared on her face and was gone just as quickly. And unless I'm mistaken you ain't done yet, are you?

Morrison answered indirectly, saying that there was no excuse for the things those men had done. People like that should pay with their lives. At least that's my way of thinking at the moment, he said.

The woman studied on this. That's been my way of thinking too, she said. For some time I thought just that way. Use to wish I was a man. Figured I could do more damage that way. And I would have, too. But if I had I'd be dead now. I wouldn't have this baby in me. I woulda lived and died without ever understanding why we're doing it all. That's a crime I believe men are guilty of more often than women, but they wouldn't be if they paid more attention to they children.

Morrison looked down. His eyes landed on her belly but moved on as if that was not what they'd intended. He stared for a moment at the satchel in his hand, then hoisted it up to his shoulder. Maybe you ought tell him. The things I told you, I mean.

Well, she said. We'll see.

Something about those last two words had a note of finality to it. Morrison hesitated for a moment, wondering if there was more to say. Of course there was, but if he said all there was to say he would never stop speaking. And anyway, it was ultimately not this woman he had to confess to. He was grateful to her for allowing him these moments for without her he would be at a complete loss. He thought he should perhaps convey this to her, but as he stooped to scoop up his rifle he saw the expression on her face and knew that he did not have to. These people understand the things not said, he thought. And with that he nodded, hooked his finger around the door latch and pulled it. The house inhaled the evening air. He paused in the doorway, feeling the breath on his face like passing fingers. Without thinking it through and with no foreknowledge of his own impending action, Morrison dipped for the note in his pocket. He extended it behind him until he felt the woman grasp it. He said, If need be let him read this. Or have it read to him. He opened his fingers, felt the note move away from him and stepped through the door.

Outside, the hound rose from the stoop and greeted him, her head moving side to side, tail still, a message in this though she doubted the man would recognize it. Morrison pulled the length of rope from his jacket pocket and shook it out. The hound, seeing this, whined her displeasure. She stepped back and lowered her head and raised a forepaw in disapproval. But when the man stepped toward her she leapt to the side, turned and contemplated him.

Come here, the man said. Don't be a devil just now. He stepped forward and the hound again backed out of his reach. He straightened his posture and pitched his voice louder, as if the dog's hearing was in question. Come here.

The hound did not.

If you knew the trouble you're causing me... Morrison

chased her in a circle, bent over and, for a few seconds, frantic in pursuit. The hound ducked and shifted from him, head low to the ground, paws wide and sure on the paving stones. Her tail pricked up behind her, not wagging, but raised in an indication that she found something mirthful in this exchange.

The tracker pulled upright. Damn it. You're a vile bugger. He studied her for a moment longer, scowling. The rope dangled from his hand as if he might make a weapon of it. Instead, he tossed it away and said, Do what you like, then.

The man turned, scooped up his rifle and satchel and started off, his pace fast and determined. The hound watched him a moment, skeptical. As the man neared the end of the block the canine set out after him. She fell in step beside him, glad that little discrepancy was behind them.

Six

William heard the door shut, not the normal slam but enough of a familiar disturbance in the air for him to recognize it. A few moments later, Dover descended the stairs and stepped into the room, her eyes on him as if she had been there with him the whole time, intent and knowing and somehow unnerving. He had meant to question her straight away, but mumbled instead and indicated that he wished he could sit up. Dover nodded and disappeared again. She returned a few moments later with a mass of cotton bedding in her arms. She kneaded it, folded it over on itself and patted it into a shape little changed for her efforts. Helping him up with one arm, she stuffed the linen beneath him, whispering to comfort him, working fast. She stood erect and studied him. He was more upright, but awkwardly so. One shoulder jutted higher than the other did; arms limp on either side of him; head canted forward so that his chin touched his chest. Dover spent a few more moments trying to set him right.

"You're too heavy to be waiting on me," he said.

"Too heavy? You got complaints about my care?"

"That's not how I meant it. You shouldn't have to wait on me."

"William," she said, just his name but stated in a way that stopped him.

He looked around the room as if his new vantage might give him some different impression of it. It did not. All was the same as before and the same questions pressed him. He felt choked from asking them though they were simple questions that any man would have asked. But they sat in the back of his throat like goiters growing within him. "I need time to think," he said.

Dover—too quick for his mindset, too obliging—offered to leave him alone for a time. She would go on upstairs so that he could get a little rest.

"Naw, I don't want to sleep. Couldn't sleep if I tried."

She said he might be surprised. She would just leave him be a little and see if Anne needed help.

"Quit walking them stairs, woman. You'll lose the baby you keep that up."

Dover paused and thought this over and responded guardedly, saying she knew something about her own body and the baby inside it.

William interrupted her. "What was you talking to that man about?"

"Just bout the plans. Gotta make sure this goes off right."

"I asked you before," William said, his voice trembling though he spoke with more calm than he felt. "Now I'm asking you again—who is that man? Don't tell me he's just helping us. Tell me the truth. He somebody you know someways?"

If Dover heard accusation in the question she didn't acknowledge it. "Never laid eyes on him fore today."

"That don't make sense."

"Well . . ."

"Why won't you tell me?"

She snapped her eyes at him, up and sharp and then down again. William thought he saw anger flare on her face but knew the next second that he was mistaken. Her voice was kind when she said, "Cause I don't know how you'll take it. Thought maybe we could just get through this next bit a trouble . . ."

"Look here, Dover, don't act like I'm a child. I don't know a single thing about that man. He doing things for us and I don't know why and something ain't right about it. He's a white man. And you say you don't know him, but you sitting there acting like all and everything's all right. That don't match up. So whatchu ain't telling me? Whatchu know that I don't?"

The cot creaked as she sat down beside him. She faced him and looked at him directly, though not into the eyes. She seemed to lose herself in the study of his features. "They say blood is thicker than water," she said. "I ain't never seen that to account for much, but maybe it's true. Sometimes. Maybe it's rue to them that believe it."

William, despite himself, despite knowing that she was testing her way forward, wriggled as if he meant to get up. He scowled, at her or at the pain or both. But she ignored all this, only pressed her palm against his chest. With her other hand she slipped a square of paper from her bodice. She turned it over in her fingers, one yellowed side and then the other.

William watched it. The lamplight was warm behind it, illuminating the marks enclosed there, hieroglyphs betrayed by the thin skin.

And then Dover began to tell what she had come to believe, saying that his father had a brother. That was enough to still the man. And from that statement she went on, note held in her hand, forefinger running over the edge of it as if she were testing the hone of a blade.

Seven

Morrison spent the better part of the night trying to find a coach bound for the North. He had come to know the city somewhat during his stay and used that knowledge as best he could. He thought of the places he had seen coaches: the depots for interstate travel, the street corners, lining the parks. For the most part he found each of these as pitch black and quiet as the night. He banged on doors when he thought he could get away with it, threw rocks at windows and shouted loudly enough to set the hound to baying. Most places answered with silence, a few with curses, one with night pan flung toward him with groggy aim. A burly man came at him with an iron bar from one carriage house, woken from a drunken sleep and intent on damage. Morrison shifted as the man came forward, clipped his legs with a blow from his rifle and left him scrabbling on the paving stones like a frantic crab. The hound darted in and nipped him on the shoulder just to have some part in the action. After this encounter Morrison considered looking into rail travel, but he knew that a train wouldn't do. They needed privacy. They needed closed doors and shuttered windows.

Most of all they needed for nobody to ask questions, no fellow passengers, no porters, nobody who might find curious a battered mulatto and a heavily pregnant Negro and an old white man.

In the end he found his answer from a different source altogether. He happened upon a young man unloading freight from a cargo wagon, alone in the gaping mouth of a warehouse. The lad was nervous with him at first and close-lipped, until they'd exchanged enough words to mark them both as Scots. It turned out the lad was new to the country and spoke English interspersed with Gaelic words. He had come in from an estate north of the city and would be returning that way around sunset. It was far from perfect, but with twenty miles between them and Philadelphia Morrison figured they could catch a proper coach at less risk and so carry on. He propped a leg up on the wagon and produced a flask and shared it, coming at his plan directly for time was short. The young man agreed to carry him out of the city, and then agreed even more heartily when Morrison placed a gold coin in his hand and showed him the others that would be his upon completion of the task. The lad's eyes were full of questions but he kept them to himself, seeming to feed upon the suspense of the proposal. Morrison left him with the details of the time and place for the rendezvous, telling him there would be two others, two other good people in need of help. He explained that one was a pregnant woman, and that the other was an injured man. But he gave no details beyond this. He left praying that the boy would be true, uneasy at having to rely on a stranger but seeing no way around it. Having made the arrangement, he put it behind him. He had one more thing to do and it would require all of him.

It was still the dead of night when he reached the warehouse. He approached cautiously, laying his soles flat upon the stones, setting them down and pulling them up, kicking no debris and stirring no pebbles. He shot a hand back to caution the hound but this was not necessary. The dog read the man's body language and followed suit. The night had cleared of mist but was still heavy and darker for it. They somehow found shadows of still greater black and it was through these that they moved. Morrison knew this territory for he had walked it just the day before. Now, as then, he pulled up in the lee of the warehouse, in an alleyway choked with crates, rubbish and discarded bits of machinery, prehistoric in their angulations and just as silent as those deceased creatures. He stretched out a hand that the hound came to and set her head beneath. He rolled the rough barbs of the beast's hair in his fingers and listened to silence to discover if it were real. He believed it was.

A row of windows ran under the eaves of the warehouse. They folded outward for ventilation and to provide some scant natural lighting inside. He expected to find these open but few were, and the ones most easily reached were black with soot. He climbed up on a crate to get a better view. He had to duck beneath the eaves and lean his head into the shadows there. The hound below studied the perch. She bent at the knees and considered leaping up, but as the man did not turn and motion to her she stayed as she was.

Morrison brushed the glass with his fingertips. The filth was resilient. He spat and tried the flat of his hand and then the cuff of his shirt. He gave up on the effort and just peered through the grime, breath still lest it fog the glass. Two lamps burned on the table, casting a liquid light that flowed across the bodies of the men strewn around the floor on bedrolls, two on cots, from the ends of which their feet dangled. They slept in disarray unusual even for these men and it was clear they had only recently bedded down after the evening's turmoil. Humboldt was nowhere to be seen. Morrison climbed down and sat beside the crate, hidden from the front entrance to the alley. He set the rifle down and slipped the sack from his shoulder.

The hound stepped toward him, head low, eyes looking off to the side and then back, off and then back. She thought they might rejoin the others. Though she had mixed feelings about this she might at least get some food out of it. Those men seemed never to tire of dangling food above her, tossing pieces of meat into awkward places and shouting and hooting until she managed to get to it. She nudged the man's foot, stepped back and whined, but the man showed no sign of rising. Eventually, she checked the ground beneath her, circled over it, looked to the man and circled the ground again and then sat down. This life was made up of so much waiting, bursts of action and then more waiting. So be it. She crossed her forelimbs and set her head on them and inhaled.

For his part Morrison's thoughts were someplace else entirely. He knew why he was here in the alley and what he would do when the opportunity came and he knew he just had to wait for that time. He sat thinking of William, trying hard to remember him by that name and not by description alone. What was he thinking now? Had he learned the content of that letter and if so how did it effect him? Rage or joy or fragments of both, the past ripped apart and only this tattered reality left to explain it. And he was not sure that he would ever be able to explain it. Words tended to make excuses, and that was something he couldn't do. There were no excuses. There were just things done long ago, so far back they couldn't be remedied, or explained away, so much a part of them that they would never be forgotten. But how could he ever explain it? He had not lied when he spoke to Dover but neither had he given the whole truth. He had argued with Nan just as he told her. He had questioned her race and her intentions and denied her right to a place in his family. And when she insulted him he pulled back his hand and hurled it at her. All of this was as he told the maid. But it hadn't ended there. Nan took his blow. It knocked her back and left her on the floor. She looked up at him, her hair suddenly loosed from the band that had contained it, wild around her. She asked him why he was here, and it was only then that he knew. Lust follows fast on violence and that night the two converged within him. In a moment without thought he had lifted her from the floor and thrown her across the room and came at her on the bed. She had fought but that was no deterrent. That was part of it all and somehow he reasoned that he was simply fighting her. He was ripping off her clothes but he was just arguing with her. He was prying his way between her legs but he was just teaching her a lesson. His hand was over her mouth and he was stifling her screams but that was because he had heard enough from her and now it was time for her to hear from him.

A sound jolted him back to the alley. For a moment it seemed loud out of all reason. Then the noise was gone and he knew it had just been a rat knocking over a can. He reached for his rifle and held it as if unsure of what to do with it. He heard the rodent scurry away and felt the hound shift as she scented it. He whispered to still her. He ran his hand over the rifle stock, hefted it and measured its weight. It was an unadorned weapon, no brass strapwork or silver adornments. He brought the old percussion lock close to his nose, inhaled the fulminate of the cap and studied it a moment. It was a simple mechanism but one that he had relied upon many times before this. It was powerful enough to take down a bear. A cannon the woman had called it, one that he carried on his shoulder. He trusted it, but he knew also that the muzzle held only one shot of lead, powerful, but singular. There were no second chances, at least not for what he intended. He tilted the weapon as if he might reload it. But he stopped himself. What's done is done, he thought. Leave it be. And yet he had never managed to do that.

There was no pleasure in his memory of that night with Nan. There was no sex even. He didn't remember pushing himself inside her though he knew that was at the center of it all. And the hardest thing of all was that in his remembering he knew what he hadn't known at the time. He was not ashamed of his brother's love for her. He was jealous of it. Lewis was all he had and this woman had taken a piece of him away. Though he hated her for it he coveted her also and had not the strength to answer these emotions as he should have. When she said Lewis was the better man he had known it to be true. His younger brother had a more honest heart and no blot on his conscience. He saw her without seeing only her skin. He knew her for who she was and this rewarded him with a great love and for this Morrison had wished to punish him. It was first a brother who betrayed his brother. Morrison was no better than that first son of man.

Lewis came for him the next day. They did battle silently, needing no words to incite them. The younger brother had a rage in him too and it drove him forward with wild swings. He came on teeth and fists and knees and elbows. His fingers talons aimed for this brother's eyes. But Morrison was best in moments of violence and his younger brother was no match. He boxed him about the face and drove his fist up into his abdomen and slammed the flat of his palm down upon the base of Lewis' neck. He popped him with short jabs that made a mockery of the younger man's anger. And then, as if all that were not enough, he hooked an arm across his chest, under his shoulders, lifted him up and spun and tossed him down with the full force of both their bodies. He meant the injury to hurt, to hurt like hell, to knock the wind out of him and end the fight. He didn't mean to slam him down on a barb of rusted metal. The nail split his brother's flesh to the bone. He didn't mean for the injury to be fatal, but that's just what it was.

In the following weeks the sickness set in. Lewis's fingers went rigid. The muscles in his neck stood out like taut ropes. His jaw locked shut. His fury and anger and love were all contained within him. When he died he did so crying, crying and speaking his first language through his clenched teeth, words the woman could not understand. The words cut right to the older brother's soul and allowed him no peace, forever after. The younger brother cursed him in the language of their birth, swore his love in the language of their birth. His love for the woman, that is. He allowed no love for his brother any longer. Only in death was Lewis calm and only then had Morrison reached out and touched him. He whispered his sorrow and cried and understood how empty the world now was and just how great his crimes. He had pulled from his pocket the memento that his father had given to him as the eldest son, a button handed down several generations already, the sole trinket carried from a bloody battlefield wherein clans fought clans in a fool war that rewarded other men entirely. He pressed this against his brother's chest, left it there and moved away.

From that day on life was a punishment. Of all his people he was alone in the world and this by his own doing. In dreams he relived that fight countless times. In waking he asked God to change that moment so that it was he who fell upon the nail and not Lewis. But God was silent. In battle he wished for his own death and it was this that had led to the death of so many other things. It had felt to him at times—lonely moments at the edge of the plains, frozen mornings when his toes went numb and his hands were two mallets, nights spent staring across campfires shared with silent ghost people, any moment in which he defied mortality by killing that which would have killed him—that God was not allowing his death. He had thought life an affliction all those twenty-some years. Until he got the note. He had read the words and heard again the voice that spoke them and saw that beautiful face as it had been. Then he thought, maybe, just maybe, he was being allowed one more chance.

Morrison stirred, realizing that there had been a change in the light. Just slightly. There were the hints of forms where before there had been only blackness. There was a shadow cast by the warehouse and on the far wall the faintest indication of the patterns in the masonry. Dawn was still far off, but night had acknowledged its coming. The old man lifted the rifle and smelled *the cap again. It was almost time. Perhaps it was foolish, this mission of his, but he would never get this chance again, not quite like this. One more chance, and one more death to go with it.*

Eight

"What are you telling me?" William asked. He had been listening to her. He had heard her reaching back into his past and uttering names of the dead and moving events around as if she would revise the story of his world. He heard her, but he couldn't form a new whole of her words. Fear crept over him like ice forming on the skin of a lake. "Just what are you saying?"

"I'm saying that man's kin to you."

"What kind of kin?"

"What's your daddy's name?"

William looked away from her, suddenly gone shy. In all their time together he had never shared this simple fact of family history. He knew the name. It was instantly in his head, but when had he ever uttered it? When had anyone other than his mother asked him of such things? It hadn't mattered. He was dead. He was white. William was as content to be fatherless as any of the millions who shared his skin tones were. He looked back at Dover, no guile in her face, no mirth, no judgment. Just the question. "Lewis," he said. "Lewis Morrison."

The woman closed her eyes and let out a breath. Her lips trembled and then went calm. She held up the square of paper and opened her eyes. "He gave you this."

William, confused for a moment, stared at the note as if it had been delivered of a ghost.

"Gave it to me fore he left. Said you should read it."

Still staring, his hand rose up and took the note, both their fingers firm on it for a second. Then hers opened and the document was his. "Did you read it?" he asked.

Dover shook her head. "That's for you to do. Don't tell me you don't read. I know you learned. Know they tried to shame the learning out of you, but you've still got it. I've seen it in your eyes sometimes, you looking at words and them meaning something to you. You never could put on a dumb face. Not to fool me, at least."

William held the note between his fingers. He didn't want to read it. He didn't want to, but he knew that not wanting whatever it was the letter would tell him had little to do with it. He lifted it and held it trembling, folded it open, turned it over and placed his eyes upon the unsteady loops and curves of the script. He felt Dover's hand on his thigh and was thankful for it. He read.

Andrew Morrison,

You going to be surprised to get this and maybe not all that happy either. Seen Mr. Moser out here and he said he seen you in Saint Lewis. Said he might well see you again and if he did he would deliver of you this message. So I writing this down. That probably surprise you but this old negress can write it took my whole life to learn it. Just hope you old Scot can read. I gonna pass on soon to the next world but had to say my peace afore then. You know how I am. So here it is.

After you left out of here and Lewis went in the ground I did have a chile. A boy massa named William. I brought this boy up and told him bout his daddy, Lewis, and about the country he come from and tried to make him proud a something. Don't no if I seeded in that. Other thing is that that was a lie. Lewis not his daddy but you are. I no that cause I

*felt you in me and dont ask me to explain it. He your son. I
no this to be true though I cant explain why. But youll feel its
true when you read this. It will ring inside you and that all
the proof either one of us needs. Aint it?*

*Now, I got two things to ask of you and if your a Scots man
youll do them both to honor your brother and the family what
come before you. First you need to come on out here and take
William from here and see him to freedom. Your own son a
slave and now you no it. So take him out of here. Tell him the
truth as you no it to be. You his daddy, but that boy come out of
the love between Lewis and I and that is a greater truth even
than blood. Between you and I was something but it was not
love. Let the boy come from love. Teach him bout his daddy.
Make a truth out of the crime you done to Lewis and me.*

Thats all now please see to it.

Annabelle.

Having read it, William let his head fall back against
the bedding. His gaze drifted across the ceiling for a moment,
and then he closed his eyes. He heard Dover move beside him.
She cleared her throat. He knew this was a sign to him but he
still did not answer. It was too much. He needed a few moments. A few moments to restructure everything he believed
of his life. He had a father. He had seen his face.

Nine

*The sky grew light in the pre-dawn. There were no signs of the
sun itself, no crimson hues stirring fire into the firmament. There*

weren't even any colors in the dank alley, only blacks and grays and the shades in between. But the day was stirring. Morrison sensed it, and so did the men sleeping in the warehouse at his back. Somebody awoke with a string of sneezes. Some heavy metal object clattered down against the stone floor. A chorus of groggy voices called out in protest. The calls faded into a silence which tried to be as it had been before but which was not. It was quiet for some time, but the night was broken. Soon the men seemed to grudgingly acknowledge this fact. They stirred and cleared their throats of phlegm and greeted each other in grunts that slowly evolved into true dialogue. Morrison rose and flexed his fingers, trying to ease the stiffness out of his old joints. He climbed atop the crate and peered through the sooty glass. The hound lifted her head and watched.

The men inside had kindled a fire on the stone floor of the warehouse itself. They now huddled around it, waiting for the kettle that had been set precariously atop the boards that served as fuel. Morrison's eyes floated over them, taking inventory, touching on each man. While he cared little for these weak-willed men it was not them that he was after. Satisfied of this, the old man climbed down and resumed his wait.

He sat recalling that in an earlier time he might have stridden right into the warehouse, rifle leveled. He would have taken out whoever moved first and kept going, swinging the rifle itself as a blunt weapon and then tossing it away and using his hands. He would have spun among them and understood exactly the distances between them and known instinctively each man's speed and intentions. He would have seen the fragments of their bodies at which to strike as if a light had been pinpointed on them: that nose to be shoved upwards under the eyes by the base of his palm, a larynx to be crushed against the fat of his hand, the knee joint to be taken from the side by his heel. He would have asked for death and therefore it would've escaped him. This was what he was good at, his violent gift. No matter how much time passed between these savage episodes he knew that gift was still his.

Though there was a part of him that hungered for this abandon at that moment, he knew things had changed. He wouldn't ask for death anymore. He no longer wanted to die. He couldn't imagine quite what the future might hold, but for the first time in twenty-some years he wanted to see the morrow, and the day after that, and on. He wanted to sit with that young man and see what they could learn of each other: Morrison with his translucent pale skin and William with his stained, umber tones. The two of them talking, searching each other, finding meaning in what the other could add to their lives, and to the lives of those no longer with them. It was a strange notion, yes, one his father would never have imagined, but his father was dead and long decayed in another country entirely. That old man had lived and died as a poor peasant in an ancient place. He had never known the world beyond Scottish shores. What could he ever have known of his son's life? This country was a strange one. It pushed men in directions formerly inconceivable. It made a mockery of traditions held sacred. But—Morrison was just coming to believe—this nation also allowed the creation of new meanings, of new symbols, of new definitions of race and creed and blood. There was something rare in this. Humanity had yet to fully understand it. Strange that it took him twenty years to realize this. Strange that he only now felt his mind clearing.

Humboldt's voice snapped his attention back. It broke into the murmurs of the others, rose above them and pressed them down to a hush. He must have arrived from the other side of the warehouse. As usual, he entered full of purpose, loud and bold. Morrison scrambled up to a crouch, eyes up toward the eaves, on the thin sheen of darkness that was the window. He could hear the men rouse themselves more completely. He imagined them shaking the sleep from their heads and digging at their eyes and slurping their coffee. The hound rose, disconcerted by the man's strange posture, but Morrison hushed her with a clicking tongue. He placed the rifle flat before him and climbed onto the crate.

Inside, the men had gathered loosely around Humboldt. He was a clear target at the center of them: the massive expanse of his chest, his teeth and eyes catching sparks from the fire, arms gesturing with an energy no other man displayed. He spoke loudly, though his words seemed ill timed to the movements of his lips, disjointed like those of a puppet in unskilled hands. He was bare-headed and some quality of the light exaggerated the effect. His balding scalp glimmered unnaturally, red and yellow and orange as he moved, a devil's halo.

Morrison set his feet at shoulder width, bent and lifted the weapon. It seemed heavier than before. For a moment he thought something was hung up on it but this was not the case. He was simply tired, fatigued and stiff and ready for this all to be over. He felt vaguely the irritation that some men would think him a coward for his plan. But this was simple practicality. It was strategy, a voice of reason newly risen in him. They didn't all need to die, even if they deserved it. He didn't have to risk everything, nor did he have to comport himself to other men's notions of manhood. What use was manly decorum to rabble such as those gathered in the warehouse? Would he duel with Humboldt? Could he gain satisfaction through the ceremonies of antiquity? He could not, for those men didn't abide by such outdated notions. And, anyway, Humboldt had long ago given up the right to a proud death. He had whipped a man better than he, with older, nobler blood. Despite his poverty, Morrison thought, his own father would never have let such an offense go unpunished. And neither would he.

The hound let out a faint whine.

Morrison ignored her. He lifted the rifle and placed the muzzle near to the glass. He drew the hammer back and felt it click into the first notch. The hound voiced her complaint again, but Morrison shushed her, his attention focussed on the weight of the weapon. The muscles in his shoulders ached already. One of his biceps twitched; a pain radiated from the back of his other hand as if a pin had pierced the flesh of his knuckle. He had to see through these things, he thought. Past them. His damn body would not betray him now, not now that he cared. He brushed his nose with the backside of his hand. It was this motion that allowed him a glimpse of what the hound was trying to communicate to him. Morrison froze.

The hound rose.

A man appeared in the mouth of the alley, some forty yards away. He stepped out of the shadows and into the pale gray light. For a second Morrison thought the man had spotted him and in that second he imagined the entirety of his goal to be lost. He couldn't see if the man was armed, but he knew what he would do whether he was or not. His rifle was no longer a weight in his hands. It was as light as dry driftwood. His body was burned clean of fatigue and if it was the last thing he would ever do he would not fail at this. His finger caressed the trigger, pulled back just enough to feel it catch, that familiar pressure point just this side of chaos. He held it there, knowing all he had to do was turn his eyes back toward Humboldt and complete things. But he didn't yet take his eyes from the man in the alley, and because of this hesitation the moment passed.

The man walked on muddled feet, clearing his throat, one hand grabbing his crotch in a wad and scratching. Morrison recognized him, not a man he had spoken to, but one who had joined Humboldt just before the assault on the ship. They'd gone into the hull of the ship together. This one had been nervous in his work, silent and somewhat tremulous. He had been following orders then, but now seemed purposeless. He walked in a tight circle, pausing to stretch and then standing mute, taking in the *ground before him like an idiot. The man finally found his desire. He lent one arm against the warehouse wall. His other hand fumbled with his trouser buttons, at it some time before he loosed himself and began urinating. The liquid splashed upon the stones, loud in that chambered corridor.*

The hound stepped forward and paused, one paw in the air, nose uplifted, eyes tight on the man, back hairs curling. Her ears pulled back over the crown of her head, flat and taut. She glanced up at Morrison but the man gave no guidance. She knew the man was aware of her, and so she held back, waiting for a sign, a call to action. She set her eyes back on the newcomer, annoyed at the man's presumption, angered that he should choose this alley to mark and to mark so exhaustively. A growl started low in her throat and rose into her jaw.

Whether the man heard the hound or whether some other sense finally stirred within him Morrison was not sure. The man looked up. His gaze settled on Morrison, on the shape that must have been barely visible in the shadows. He stared and then cocked his head to the side and then pulled his hand from the wall and wiped at his eyes. Only after that did he give way to frenzy. He cursed under his breath. He pinched the flow of his urine and tried to shove himself back inside his trousers and began to shout. His words made no sense in his excitement, but they were enough that they needed to be dealt with.

Get! Morrison said. The hound jumped at the command. Morrison turned away and attended to his goal. He yanked the hammer back to full cock, aimed and fired straight through the glass. The whole wide pane went white and then to dust and then fell away. For a second Morrison could see nothing but a sparkling brilliance. He feared his eyesight had betrayed him. But then the scene came into view, and with it Humboldt. The man was staring at him, one hand pressed against his chest, surprise etched on his face. The other men ducked and bolted, stumbling into each other, coffees thrown down, chairs kicked out of the way. Humboldt alone stood still, one hand covering the hole that had just been torn into him, the entry point of a lead ball that had shattered his ribs and torn through his heart and lodged snug against the vertebrae of his spine. His face still held the same twist of surprise as he stumbled over something on the floor and began to fall. His mouth opened and he seemed at pains to say one last thing. Before he could gravity yanked him down by the shoulders and he was gone. Morrison stared a moment longer but the man had fallen out of sight and there was nothing more he could do. It was done. He ducked out of the window and leapt to the ground and stumbled into a run toward the mouth of the alley. There he received yet another shock.

The hound and the man had been engaged at close quarters, but they were still now, the two of them a jumble on the stones. And then there was movement, but it came not from the hound but from the man. He rose from the paving stones, stunned, arms dangling like two ropes, one of them ending in the silver silver of a knife. His penis hung from the opening in his trousers, limp and fatigued as if it too had some part in this work. He stared down at the hound. For a few seconds she writhed on the ground in an attempt to stand, but she quickly gave up this effort and lay still. The man was so fascinated by what he saw below him that he didn't notice Morrison's approach until it was too late.

The tracker smashed his nose with the stock of his rifle, sending slivers of bone up into his skull. Before the man even hit the ground, Morrison was on his knees. He scooped up the hound. Her body was limp against him, and he knew that the wetness on her was her own blood. He turned with her pressed to his chest and strode back down the alley into the shadows, chased by the shouts of the men and clatter of their feet on the stones and pistol shots sent after him. But he didn't stop to answer them. He had no more fight to give. He just ran, burden in his arms.

Ten

William lay still as Dover took her turn silently reading the note. He stared up at the ceiling, his eyes once more engaged by the water-stained circles on the wooden beams. No matter how long he stared they seemed always in the process of expansion, each ring echoing outward, a moment captured in stillness, hiding motion even as his eyes imagined it. He lost himself in the contemplation of it, watching the ceiling, thinking of a pond, the undulations of a smooth surface disturbed by a rock, a stone that was in his own hand. He saw himself winding his arm back and tossing the stone, followed its arc through the air and down into the center of the ripples that had somehow formed in anticipation of its fall. It was a memory of sorts, though whether from reality or dream he was unsure.

Dover's reading was no better than his was. Doubtless she did not comprehend the letter in complete detail, but when she lowered the note to her lap and met William's gaze her face indicated that she had grasped the greater portion of it. There was no surprise on her features, no sign of anxiousness, no questions. Her façade was composed, held firm by a resolve William wasn't sure how to read.

"Now you're the one looking strange at me," he said, not speaking his mind but needing to say something.

Dover shook her head. It was a simple movement, but one that shamed his inconsequential gripes to silence. With it she hushed all the nonsense he might wish to speak. "Let's not waste words," she said. She didn't hold up the note, but nodded her head in a way that made it the subject of her speech. "This is your momma talking to you. She put herself down on this paper and now she's talking to you from the grave. She's doing from that side what she never could in this one. She's just brought your father to you."

William had seemed almost lulled by her words, but at the mention of his father he awoke. "I don't know anything bout that man. I don't care what that note says. My mother told a lot of lies in her life. Could be that's just another one." He tried for some sort of firmness, but he couldn't muster it. His words faded toward the end of the last sentence, his lips doubting them even as he spoke them.

Dover heard this and answered gently. "You never did your mother justice. Ever since I've known you you had things to say against her. You tried to forget bout her, wanted me in to fill her place in your heart. Don't deny it. Think bout it. Live with that for a while and see if I'm not right. But don't fight this, William. Don't pretend it ain't real. You don't have to take this all on at once. Let's us just do what we have to tonight and let tomorrow come in its own time. Let next week come and the week after that. You got all the time you need to get to know him."

William glanced at her and away. He began to speak but then bit his lower lip between his teeth and pressed down till it pained him. "She shoulda told me," he said. "She was all the time talking about him . . . about my father. About the other one, I mean." He lost the train of his words and met the woman's eyes again. None of it was clear. His head was a muddle of thoughts and emotions, memories and the melancholy they always pulled in their wake. Putting it into words just made it worse. "She shoulda told me," he repeated.

"She did," Dover said. "That's what she done. Just took her time about it. Just made it so that the message came with the messenger and not before."

They both heard the knock upstairs on the front door, the footsteps moving to answer it, the quiet tones of conversation, and then the more solid tread of a man's boots.

"That'll be the coal man," Dover said. "Guess it's time."

"I need time to think," William said, his eyes up on the ceiling, following the footsteps, watching the dust knocked free beneath the footfalls.

"But you don't have time," Dover said. "This night could set us free. You know that, don't you? That man, Andrew Morrison, he's the one sent to help us. He's the one. I don't know what sort of things he's done in his life, don't know who he is or just why he's come. But he has. I don't need to know everything bout him. I can see what I need to in his eyes, and in his actions."

The young woman scooted closer. She leaned over William as best she could and blocked his vision. "You're beautiful, William, and you're strong. Thing is you don't always know just what and how to use that strength. I used to think I knew best. Wanted you to rage at the world. Wanted to use your anger as a weapon." She held one hand out before her mouth, her fingers trying to draw the words out of her and present them just right. "But that's not the only way. This ain't about forgiving him, not tonight, at least. Remember who wrote this note. Nan wrote it, and whatever was done between them she believed that he deserved the chance to set it right. Now I'm asking you a big thing, a harder thing than rage. But I need you to have the heart to trust her. To believe that something impossible might be possible. Ain't that what this note's telling you? Ain't that what Redford was trying to teach us?"

William had closed his eyes as she talked. He opened them now. They were red and full of moisture, unsteady and flickering. When he spoke he didn't answer her question but addressed something else altogether. "I didn't believe her," he said. "All them years I thought she was lying. Thought she was just like any nigger woman and I was just a bastard who didn't have no father."

"Well, that ain't the first time you been wrong," Dover said. She smiled. "And it won't be the last."

The door to the cellar opened. Voices slipped down to them. The stairs creaked.

"You gotta decide now," Dover said. She reached out with one hand and wiped the tears from the corners of his eyes, delicate with the moisture, taking it from him and lifting it to her lips. "Your momma's come back to school you. You gonna honor her this time?"

Eleven

Morrison's lungs burned in his chest. His legs were each a pedestal of torture and his lower back became the center of him, pain radiating from it as if a great spider was clasped there, sucking the life from him. But he didn't slacken his pace. He moved through the alleyways as if he knew them by heart, trusting his legs, stumbling at times, once falling hard upon his kneecaps, once knicked across the forehead by some protrusion he hadn't seen. Initially, the other men were close behind him, but he took a circuitous route, around warehouses and through back lanes, under a gated fence and through a market just awakened. He ran past the startled merchants—an old man in a frenzy, limp canine in his arms, wild eyed with grief or anger or resignation. Before long the gunfire faded. The only sounds were those of his feet and voice, his breathing and the slow rasp of the hound.

He talked through choked breaths as he ran, whispering courage into the hound, telling her the things they would do together in the future, the great hunts, the wide open spaces, the freedom. She had strength in her yet, he said. She would pull through yet. He cajoled her to stay this side of death. He ordered her to do so. And then, in his fatigue and pain and grief, his voice choked with sobs. He paused in an open, wooded area at the edge of an avenue. He would not have chosen the spot, but emotion grabbed at him in gasps. It took all of him to fight them down. He lowered the hound to ground and studied her wounds with more care. She had been slashed in one long stroke from under her ear down her shoulder. The gash was thick with blood, deep enough to have cut through muscle and cartilage, the lower end flashing glimpses of ivory. It was a horrid wound, but it was not the one that threatened her. There was another mark, barely an inch wide, the only small sign of a stab wound. The knife must have punctured a lung for the hound's breathing came both from her mouth and in a strange rasp out of her chest cavity itself.

Morrison flung off his jacket. He held the material in his hands as if he might shred it, but then tossed it down and tore off his own shirt. He ripped the garment down the back, making two halves of it. He knelt down with them, testing them against the wounds, trying to measure the hound and best bandage her. And then he realized he didn't know how to bind such wounds. They didn't fit together neatly. He needed help. He bent and, still shirtless, heaved her into his arms again. She groaned as she came to rest against his skin. Her eyes opened and rolled up at him. She growled and seemed not to recognize him. She kicked her hind legs, but as they found no purchase in the air she gave up. The man ran on, talking again, explaining that he was taking her to help. This was too much for him. He had gotten her in over her head and he was sorry for it. He would still see her to safety, he promised. He would carry her all the way. She could trust him still. He would run with her, but not from her. He wasn't that type of man anymore.

He was upon the meeting area before he knew it. He strode into the corner of the square and paused, casting about him. The sky was an opal blue now, lit to the east with a pink hue, smooth and delicate like the inside of some seashell. But it was too quiet in the square, too normal. The façades of the homes stared out, each a face of window-eyes and door-mouths. At first glance there was no movement save that of pigeons sweeping down from the roofs and stirring bits of rubbish as they landed. For a moment, Morrison was taken over by the ringing fear that this was it. It had all come to this. To nothing. He was alone in the world, even more so now that he had killed she who had been so faithful and since those to whom he had tried to make amends had spurned him.

Then he saw them.

The covered wagon was there at the far edge of the square, some fifty yards away. The coal sled was drawn up near it, and the young immigrant was helping Dover into the back of the wagon. Morrison could not see William, but he knew immediately that he was there, resting beneath the cloth covering. They were all there. He began to stumble toward them across the square, under and through the great oaks that shaded it. Midway across the others saw him. Dover's face peered out of the wagon and a moment later William peeked out as well. Their two dark faces watched his progress. The old Scot trudged toward them, tired like he had never been before, with the limp body of the hound cradled in his arms, thinking that here before him was all the family he had in the world.

Epilogue

From the hull of the ship cries are heard. The crew looks one to another and, like superstitious men, they say nothing. The cries are crazed howls at the edge of life and death. At times they are moans so deep they seem to be protests from the tortured spine of the ship itself. Other times they are sharp-edged and raw and cut through the sea noise like talons through flesh. But all of these sounds come from a single woman. They are the cries of a life-giver, and the emotion behind them silences all the crew with newfound humility. The boat rocks through it all, for the motion of the world and its seas do not pause to mark the arrival of any one creature.

The woman in the berth below has a rhythm of her own and it comes to her in defiance of all else. She feels herself splitting, feels a great, great pressure, as if her body contains all of creation within it and she can hold it back no longer. She pains but in her own way that pain is pleasure, for she believes that this baby will be born into a world without masters. Nobody within miles and miles and miles will lay their hands upon this child in ownership. She pushes, not for the first time, but this time, for a moment at least, the boat's rhythm is one with the woman's. She pushes, and the boat leans to aid her. She grits her teeth, and the boat holds its breath upon the back side of a wave. The woman hisses a curse at life, and the boat begins its downward slide. Before it ends, the child slips forth into its father's arms. The newborn is slippery and moist, flesh soft and gray. Air hits the child's face like a shock and all is silence.

The boat creaks as it begins to ride the next swell. The men on the deck are battered by the wind and they hear nothing save the roar of air and water. And deep within the silence lingers long, long, long. The father stands trembling with the joy and fright. He doesn't know what to do and stands awed until the white man speaks in his ear and instructs him with knowledge that comes from he knows not where. This old man who never thought of himself as a father—who took life often but never knowingly gave it—seems as adept as any midwife. He checks the babe's mouth and nose. Deeming them clear, he pushes the father's hands, and therefore the baby, toward the mother's breast. In these moments the Scotsman feels something he has not felt before and that is the grand bliss of life. And also beneath it is a sadness that he doesn't wish to address at that moment. The mother takes the child in her arms, the cord between them still pulsing. The moisture on the babe is a great bloody filth and yet it is her filth. She would happily lick the child clean, no different in this devotion than the hound who watches the scene from the edge of the cabin.

The baby wakes from her brief stupor and plays her part in this drama as she knows she must. She lifts her head and opens her mouth and cries the trauma of birth. She cries for the wonder she has just awakened to and for the wonders yet to be found. She cries with the voice of all those who came before her and who live on within her. She cries, as do they all, each of them in that small chamber, overcome. They cry another baby into this world.

As do we all.

Acknowledgments

Not only is *Walk Through Darkness* dedicated to my mother,
Joan Scurlock, but I must also acknowledge how indebted I
am to her for its very conception. This novel sprang from the
research that she was doing into our own family's history. She
opened my eyes to the diversity of the American experience and
challenged me to uncover and explore rarely acknowledged as-
pects of our troubled past. Thank you, Mom. Your work goes on.

My heartfelt appreciation also goes out to Marita Golden.
Thank you for creating the Zora Neale Hurston/Richard
Wright Foundation over a decade ago and for being a source
of guidance and inspiration ever since. If anyone hasn't heard
of the Hurston/Wright Foundation, please do check out their
website. This organization supports, encourages, and challenges
aspiring African American writers, thereby helping to positively
influence the future of American literature.

I'd like to thank my editor, Debbie Cowell; my agent, Sloan
Harris; and also Bill Thomas, Steve Rubin, and everyone else at

Doubleday. I appreciate not only the support they've shown for my first two books, but also for their willingness to dream of a future with me. Thanks to Jeffrey Lent and family for providing me with the necessary long conversations about novels, children, horses, and about generally staying sane while trying to make this writing life work. Also, my heartfelt thanks and love go out to everyone whom I call family. We've been through tough times this last year, and I will never forget the strength and wisdom you all showed. And, of course, I'd be nowhere without my wife, Gudrun, and kids, Maya and Sage. It's also in them that my mother's work goes on, now and forever.

While this work was inspired by real, rigorous historical research, the novel itself is a creation of my imagination. All the characters and events are completely fictional and the settings, such as Annapolis and Philadelphia, are used with the utmost respect. While I've done my best to ensure the accuracy of all historical details, I also accept the full responsibility for any errors. I won't catalog all the titles that I consulted while writing this novel, but I will admit that as a fiction writer I steal unabashedly from the works of more disciplined scholars including James Hunter's *A Dance Called America*. One title, more than any other, inspired key moments and plot points within this fiction: *Runaway Slaves*, by John Hope Franklin and Loren Schweninger.